VALLEY OF DYING STARS

Cannibal Country Book 3

TONY URBAN

DREW STRICKLAND

PACKANACK
publishing

Copyright © 2021 by Tony Urban & Drew Strickland

Published by Packanack Publishing

All rights reserved.

No part of this book may be reproduced in any form or by any electronic or mechanical means, including information storage and retrieval systems, without written permission from the author, except for the use of brief quotations in a book review.

Visit Drew online - http://drewstricklandbooks.com

Visit Tony online - http://tonyurbanauthor.com

"Therefore the fathers shall eat their sons in the midst of thee, and the sons shall eat their fathers; and I will execute judgments in thee, and the whole remnant of thee I will scatter into all the winds."

— EZEKIEL 5:10

1

No matter how firmly Wyatt squeezed, his mother's hot blood escaped through his fingers.

She's dying, he realized, and he tried to press harder, to mentally propel the flow to reverse itself so that his mother's blood went back into her body rather gushing out, spilling over him, raining into the dirt.

The dirt didn't need that blood. Barbara did.

He could smell the iron in the air.

She was slipping away.

Even in the dark, he could see that.

Why couldn't he save her?

They were still sheltered by the rusted cars at their backs. Stray bullets ricocheted off the metal, confirming it. That was one less thing for Wyatt to worry about as his mother bled out. But the carnage from behind the wall still went on.

Gunshots.

Screams.

Cries of pain, anger, and what Wyatt could only think of as punishment.

People were dying all around him.

Then, like it never even happened, the land turned silent.

There were no more screams. No more cries. No more gunshots.

Wyatt thought he heard a pained groan, but it was carried away by the wind into the silent night as if it was never there.

They had all wiped each other out. The cannibals and the casino dwellers.

But none of it mattered to Wyatt.

Not even the thought of Franklin meeting his end in a dirt ditch could pull Wyatt from the task at hand.

His mother was dying in his arms.

"Seth, I— I can't—"

Wyatt looked up to his brother who still sat in his wheelchair, staring out past the severed heads on pikes. The figures were there, closing the gap at a steady pace. A faceless mass of people drifting toward them in the darkness.

Supper growled from the relative safety of Seth's lap as the dog caught the scent of those approaching in the night. With one hand Seth caressed the dog's neck to calm him. With his other, he reached to the ground and snatched Barbara's gun.

Seth leveled it at the new threat heading their way. Ready to fire.

"Wyatt, I can't see how many are out there. I don't know how many bullets are in this gun but--"

"Put it down, boy" a woman's dry, sandpaper voice called out from the darkness.

Seth glanced over, met Wyatt's eyes. The two of them shook their heads. Wyatt didn't want to go down without a fight. There was no way these new, south of the wall cannibals would talk them into easy deaths.

The woman continued, "You fire that gun, boy, you're all dead. You must know that. If you prefer to live and give that woman bleeding out a chance too, then let us help. Drop the firearm. Now."

Seth still clutched the gin, his hands trembling as he aimed in into the dark. The figures remained just beyond discernable view, lurking in the shadows. There could be five or five hundred. A few in front turned into a few more behind, and then it all blended into the featureless desert.

"It's time to call it," the woman said. "Are you going to live or are you going to die?"

Wyatt felt like a heel making his brother choose their fates. He knew he should speak up, rise to the occasion, be the big bro. But his words had been stolen from him. The sight of their mother fading away in his arms had turned him mute.

The woman had said they could help her. But how was that true? Were the Morrill brothers supposed to believe there was a hospital out here, in this barren, hardscrabble landscape of nothingness?

Wyatt expected Seth to shoot. To go out gun blazing. It was a Seth thing to do, after all.

Instead, his hand fell and opened. The pistol clattered to the ground at his feet.

And just like that, the crowd charged.

2

Wyatt strained to see them, to see the coming death. They were filthy, clothed in rags. Thin, haggard, most old - or old to an 18-year-old boy, that is. In their hands, Wyatt saw what he most worried about. Hand made weapons. Knives, hammers, spears, and worst of all, the same axes hewn from bone that he had seen do so much damage to people he was supposed to help protect.

"Cannibals," Wyatt said.

But it was too late. All he could do was watch them charge.

In some ways, death would be a relief.

Wyatt clutched Barbara tight against his chest. His fight was gone. He was ready for the end.

"I love you, mom," he whispered. And, to his amazement, her eyelids fluttered, then opened.

She peered around, confused, frantic, pained. Her skin glowed white in the night, from blood loss. "Wyatt? What's happ--"

Before Wyatt could respond to her, or rise to fight off the attackers, the cannibals were on them.

The smell hit him first. It was sweat and piss. A waft of body odor filled his nose, mixing with the rest of it and made him gag. As if their clothes and weapons weren't confirmation enough, their aroma sealed the deal. These people were feral.

Wyatt had seen enough death at the hands of people like this to know how it would go down. They would swarm, full force, relentless. They'd stab and bash and chop. Bones would break. Organs would be punctured. Limbs would be severed. Heads would be crushed.

It would be painful, exquisite agony. But it would be quick. That was the lone mercy their coming feet brought with. It would all be over very soon.

He'd be with Allie again. Trooper. Seth would be reunited with Rosario. Maybe they'd even see their father on the other side and find out why he'd never made it home from that business trip in Boston.

They'd be somewhere that they didn't need to be afraid anymore. Afraid of starving. Of cannibals. Of megalomaniacs. They'd be the land of milk and honey, at least, Wyatt thought that's what the Bible promised. He wished he'd have taken the time to read it. Hopefully, his ignorance wouldn't be held against him.

Closer now. Yards.

Death was only a few more breaths away.

Only, it wasn't.

Instead, they stopped within arm's reach. No weapons were raised, but they all held them at the ready. These too were people who had lived through the horrid violence that consumed this dying, merciless world where no one could be trusted.

The woman who'd been speaking to them led the group. She was unarmed. And she was… smiling?

No, that couldn't be right. There was no reason to smile these days.

She held out her arms. "Give her to me," she said. She was in her forties with a lion's mane of dusty hair.

"No," Wyatt said.

With that, the woman raised a fist and four men stormed them. They pried Barbara free of Wyatt's grip. He tried to fight them off, caught one of them with a solid right, but four against one was no match.

Barbara moaned, either from fear or pain, maybe both. "Wya--"

The men had her, hauled her into the crowd, passing her amongst them like she was crowd surfing at a rock concert.

Wyatt jumped to his feet, ready to carry on the pointless fight. "Give her back!" he screamed.

In seconds she was out of sight, lost in the sea of wild men and women. Gone.

What were they doing? Eating her? Raping her?

Wyatt lunged for the gun Seth had dropped in the dirt, his fingers closing over the grip. He turned, ready to shoot.

And caught a foot in the jaw.

The woman, the seeming leader, had struck out with a heavy boot. The impact left him dazed and the black sky was suddenly ablaze with stars.

"You gonna stay down now, boy?" she asked.

Wyatt answered by opening his mouth and letting blood run free.

"Good. Now calm yourself. We're taking that woman for help, but from the looks of her it might be beyond our control."

She bent at the waist, extended her hand toward Wyatt. He flinched, thinking she was going to strike him. Instead, she helped him to his feet.

"I'm Roo," she said. "What's your name?"

Instead of answering her question, Wyatt came back with his own. "Where are you taking her?" he demanded.

"To a place where we can help her. Maybe."

He looked to Seth who held Supper with both arms, the dog's bared teeth a sign of what would come if he broke free. The woman followed his eyes.

"I ain't seen a dog in years," she said. "Thought they all got et."
Roo looked at Seth. "How about the dog? He got a name?"

"Supper," Seth said, the word coming out in a whisper.

"Ah," Roo said. "That why you keep him around? Back up should times get real tough?"

It was Seth's turn to snarl. "I'd kill myself before I ate my dog."

Roo nodded. "Got a good heart. Maybe a small brain, but a good heart. Could be worse afflictions."

The woman reached over, holding a steady hand in front of the dog. Supper looked from her outstretched appendage to her face. Then he stopped growling. Instead of biting, he licked her fingers.

If Supper showed this woman kindness, then that was good enough for Wyatt. "The woman is our mother," he said. "Take us to her. Please.".

Roo nodded and motioned to follow her. She turned away from them and her sea of followers parted to allow her passing. They remained that way, waiting. Wyatt swallowed hard, grabbed the handles of Seth's wheelchair, and began to push.

"Wyatt, we don't know these people at all," Seth said. "For all we know we're marching to our deaths. Maybe they've got a roaring assed campfire in the valley and are going to roast us like hogs."

"Doesn't matter, Seth. Mom's going to die if we don't let them help. She might still. But I'll be damned if I watch another person I love die without trying anything I can."

Seth didn't say another word.

Roo led them through the open dirt field and onto a small, shale road upon which they walked in silence for hours before coming to what passed for a town, or settlement, or maybe a hobo encampment.

Roo continued to lead them down the road until they reached one of the more substantial of the buildings, a squat, concrete block structure upon which *Pharmacia* had been stenciled.

"She'll be in here," Roo said. "I had my quickest men bring her as time is short."

There was no door on the building, just a curtain. Roo pushed it aside and waved for the boys to enter.

They did.

A dim, oil-fueled lantern felt like a flood and it took Wyatt's eyes a full minute to adjust. When they did, he saw a makeshift medical station where an old hospital gurney sat in the center of the room. Shelves of long-expired medicines lined the walls.

A man who looked ancient hovered over Barbara who was on the table, naked from the waist up. A rag covered her breasts. The man worked on her gunshot wound, digging deep inside with medical instruments, the sort of which Wyatt knew no names.

The elderly man threw a glance at them as they entered. "She with you?" he asked.

"Our mother," Seth answered for the both of them.

"Aw, shit," he muttered.

Wyatt pushed Seth's chair closer, so they were at Barbara's side. Her eyes were open but vacant. Her skin, almost transparent.

"Mom, Seth and I are right here. These people are going to save you, you understand?"

Barbara didn't react.

"Did you give her something?" Wyatt asked the man who he took to be a doctor.

"Some morphine for the pain."

"Is that why she's not talking?"

"No, son. That's not because of the medicine. That's because she's near expired."

The cold, clinical way he said it startled Wyatt who'd already known his mother was likely to die but hearing it put that way, like she was a carton of milk approaching its sell-by date, flipped a switch inside him.

Before he even knew what he was doing, Wyatt grabbed the old man by the shoulder. He was so frail he could feel all the bones and tendons and thought, if he squeezed hard enough, the man might break.

"Do something for her!" Wyatt screamed at him.

"I have," he said. "The bullet severed an artery. I tied it off best I could but she'd lost two-thirds, maybe three-fourths of her blood before she even arrived."

"Can't you do a transfusion?" Seth asked, already rolling up the sleeve of his shirt.

That sounded like a damn good plan to Wyatt who did the same. "Yeah," he said. " Take as much as you need."

The old man examined the both of them, then let his gaze fall to the floor. "You're good sons. But she's passed the point of no return. If you have anything left to say to her, I suggest you not dawdle."

He shuffled past them, toward the exit. Wyatt heard the curtain flutter as he passed into the night.

Seth latched on to Barbara's left hand, so Wyatt moved to her right side. She already felt cool to the touch.

"Mom? Can you hear me?" Wyatt asked. He brought his free hand to her face, traced her jawline with his fingertips. "Seth and I, we're both here with you. Supper too. We won't leave you."

Her hand spasmed, her grip tightened. Did that mean she heard him or was it nothing more than a reflex?

"I never said this enough," Seth said, "but you're a great mom. I know I was a real shit a lot of the time, but I always knew you had my back, no matter what." He began to cry.

Wyatt wanted to do the same, needed to, but he also felt like he had to hold it together, to be the strong one. To be the man of the family even when he felt like a five-year-old boy who only wanted to feel his mother hug him one more - one last - time.

Barbara didn't say anything. Wyatt didn't know if the act of speaking was even possible for her anymore. But, to his shock, her eyelids fluttered.

Her gaze was weak and unfocused like she was looking miles beyond them. And maybe she was. But then her pupils contracted and, Wyatt thought, she looked at them.

She didn't have to say anything. Her eyes said it all.

Keep each other safe.

Then her hands slipped from theirs, her arm falling limply, lifelessly, to the side. It swayed to and fro, to and fro, for a few rotations, then stopped altogether.

His own waterworks erupted.

Their mother was dead.

3

Seth struggled to comprehend it. First Papa, then Rosario, and now his mother. All within the past few hours.

Was this his punishment? Was this all because of his betrayal?

It didn't seem real. It was like he was floating in some dream world.

His heart pounded. He felt on the verge of passing out. All he wanted was to close his eyes and end this nightmare. But he knew that wasn't going to happen.

He watched his brother cry. Tears mixed with the snot that hung from his nose. He sobbed harder than Seth thought he had ever heard or seen his brother do before.

Wyatt was the sensitive one.

But it was more than that.

Wyatt had a much closer bond with their mother than Seth ever did. Maybe it was because they were more alike. Or maybe it was because Seth had bonded so much more with their father, that he didn't get a chance to form that same deep connection with his mother.

In a way, Seth losing his father years earlier made this loss easier to accept. He still felt sick and still wished he could rewind the night's events in the most epic of all do-overs. But he managed to hold himself together, for the most part, while Wyatt dissolved.

Barbara was Wyatt's compass. Their father was Seth's. And now he was going to have to help Wyatt through this, just like Wyatt had done the same for him.

Wyatt reached over, rubbed Seth's shoulder, and mumbled, "It'll be okay. As long as we have each other."

Seth reached up, grabbed Wyatt's fingers, and gave them a reassuring squeeze. "I know, brother. I know."

Then, Wyatt pulled away. A hitching sob broke loose and he ran from the building. Seth wanted to go after, but he knew Wyatt needed to let out all the sorrow and pain. He'd give him that time, but when they needed to move on, he'd see to it that they did.

After what Seth allowed to happen to Allie, and now what happened to their mother, the last face Wyatt needed to see was his. Even if they were brothers, and even if Wyatt had said they were okay, Seth knew better deep down where it counted. They had a lot of healing to do.

The only sound was the crying of Wyatt outside. It came and went in waves, a morbid lullaby and as Seth stared at his dead mother, it nearly lulled him to sleep.

Then, Roo cleared her throat. He's missed her entering, stepping behind him. His instincts, which he'd worked so hard to hone, had dulled. He'd need to work on that too.

"What's your name, boy?" she asked.

"Seth."

"And your brother?"

"He's Wyatt."

She nodded. "Good names." Roo moved to the opposite side of the gurney and stared down at the dead woman.

"She was Barbara," Seth said.

Roo placed her hand on Barbara's forehead and closed her eyes.

Her lips moved but no words came out. It took a moment and then Seth realized she was praying. He wondered if he should bow his head or close his eyes, but before he could decide, she was finished.

"Sorry we couldn't save your mom," Roo said.

Seth nodded. "I know."

"I'll get the men to digging. She'll need buried tonight," she said.

Seth nodded. "Thank you," he said. He noticed that she was apologetic and kind with her facial expressions, but she also seemed on edge, on guard. Flinching at every sound, eyes darting at imagined movement. He wondered if she was half-crazy.

He followed her out of the pharmacia. Dozens of men and women waited and watched like this was the most exciting thing to witness in eons. Seth was able to get a good look at them for the first time, but there was nothing good about them.

They looked like a defeated army. A tribe of lost souls. The rags that passed for clothes were shredded and stained with dirt, blood, and God knew what else. Their eyes were wild and fearful. Those of prey animals, always on alert for a coming predator.

"Where are we?" Seth finally asked.

He watched some of the men separate from the group. He knew what their job was and he was relieved he didn't have to partake in that part. There was guilt too, but he was far too exhausted to feel too bad. This had been the longest and worst day of his life and it still wasn't over.

"It's part of our territory," Roo said.

"*This* is your territory?" Seth asked, hoping the skepticism he felt didn't carry through in his voice.

"We're nomads," Roo said. "We wander about, stay some places longer than others, but never one place too long. Comfort in this world is the same as death. Staying alive means staying on the move, staying on your toes."

Seth couldn't imagine anyone cobbling together a life in this hellscape. "How do you live?"

"Forage mostly. Somethings we pick from the cannibals."

"So that's not you? The pikes with the heads out there?"

She smiled. "Those are ours. Like I said, picked up a few things from the cannibals."

"The heads are..." Seth couldn't finish the sentence for fear of what his imagination would come up with. He glanced back at the pharmacia, wondering what would happen to his mother.

"They belonged to people who wronged us and paid the price. Don't got to go into more detail than that. But let's say, it's a fine deterrent."

"Does it work?" Seth asked.

Roo grinned. "Mostly. But not always. Seems there's an unending stream of folks who think they need to prove they're meaner and badder. They're usually wrong."

She turned her head, looking to her people, and Seth noticed a ragged scar that ran from her cheek to her forehead. It disappeared in her hair but left a bald streak in its wake.

Maybe that's why she seemed off. Brain damage. Or maybe that's just what happened to you when you roamed the desert long enough. Either way, these people had helped them. Or tried, anyway. Seth and Wyatt were both alive, heads intact. He figured, for all that, he should be grateful.

"After we bury your mother, we're going walkabout. Now that the wall's blasted open who knows what will slip through. We prefer to be far away for a while."

Roo looked to the east, the directions from which Wyatt's sobs still emanated.

"You're welcome to join us. Can't promise we're good company, but there's always safety in numbers."

Seth smiled as he surveyed them. Here was another group of people wanting them to join their flock. The last time hadn't worked out so well and he wasn't quite sure what to say.

It turned out, he didn't have to answer.

Wyatt stepped into the scene, wiping tears from his bloodshot eyes. "We appreciate you trying to save our mother, but we won't stay with you," Wyatt said. "I don't intend to be rude, but we've been sidetracked too often already. We have a plan. Our mother's plan. And we're going to see it to the end," he said. "We're going south."

4

Wyatt was up early, already getting a start on the day. The group of people that had tried to help them was cooking something that smelled delicious, but he kept to himself. He didn't want to get to know them because, if he did, he might want to stay. To find a new family.

Seth, however, was different. He sat in a large group of them, the conversation boisterous. Wyatt wondered how his brother could have the energy, or desire, to talk right now. With their mother fresh in the ground.

As usual, there was no sunrise, just a lessening of the darkness. Although, and it might have been his imagination, it seemed lighter here. Not much, no sunny day with clear skies, but it seemed as if the sky was less leaden.

About twenty people sat around the fire, around Seth. Wyatt thought there'd been more the night prior but didn't care enough to ask questions. Four men stood further out, on guard. A smart idea.

Roo approached Wyatt, a small mug in her hands. Her face was smeared with dirt and possibly old blood.

"You should eat before you leave."

Wyatt looked into the mug. Steam drifted from the concoction, but he couldn't place the exact contents. Nevertheless, his stomach betrayed him by growling loud enough to make Roo grin.

"What is it?"

She handed it to him. "A bit of gravy and some makeshift biscuits. Not much, but something easy enough to whip up on calm mornings like this."

He wasn't sure where they got flour or grease for the gravy, but he was hungry enough to not care.

"Thank you," he said between the three gulps it took to down it.

"Why south?" she said.

"I'm sorry?" Wyatt asked.

"You said you were going south. Why?"

"To escape nuclear winter." Saying it aloud made it sound like bullshit though. Like some crazy dream not grounded in reality

"The south isn't what it used to be," Roo said.

"You've been there?" Wyatt was so shocked he almost dropped the mug. Not that there was much to spill. He poured the remaining tablespoon of goo onto the ground for Supper to lap up, which he did greedily.

Roo nodded. "A few years ago."

"What's it like? Why didn't you stay?"

"It didn't get hit by the bombs like up north, but they have their own problems. Too many people went down there. The governments didn't last long. First, the armies took over. Then the rebels. Then the warlords. It's survival of the fittest."

"You saw this with your own eyes?" Wyatt asked, already feeling sick enough to lose his breakfast. Had all this loss and misery really been for naught?

"Not mine eyes," Roos said. "Mine ears. I was in southern Mexico for a spell. Crossed into Guatemala. I heard from plenty of people who lived through it. People who came north to escape it."

Wyatt shook his head. "Sounds like rumors to me."

"What?"

"What people said. You don't know they were being honest, do you? You said yourself, you've never been there. You only heard second and third-hand accounts."

She nodded. "I suppose that's true. Rumors don't mean truth. And if that's where you want to go, we'll send you on your way with full bellies. But, the offer still stands. You can stick with us. We've made it okay out here."

Wyatt watched a man from their group do a poor job of eavesdropping. He was in his fifties, the hair at his sideburns gone gray, but it was black up top. He saw Wyatt looking and averted his eyes.

"I appreciate the full bellies, but it's still a no," Wyatt said.

Before Roo could respond, the man found the courage to speak up. "A boat."

Roo turned, pulling her blade up at the sound of his voice. It seemed that they were all easily startled.

When she saw him, she returned the knife to her rope belt. "Ernesto, you know better than to sneak up on me," she said.

He ignored her. "You should take a boat. You'd sail past it all. Southern Mexico and Latin America wouldn't be a problem that way. Sail past the equator, all the way to the Falklands if you so desire."

The suggestion made Wyatt laugh. "A boat? On the ocean? The only time I was ever on a boat it was a canoe at scout camp and I tipped it over and almost drowned."

Ernesto shook his head. "No, you'd need a sailboat. A catamaran would serve you best."

"Thanks," Wyatt said. "But I wouldn't even know how to put up a sail."

"I could show you. Before... this..." He motioned to the sunless sky. "I was a fisherman. It seems like someone else's life now, but it's all up here." He tapped his index finger against the center of his forehead.

Ernesto looked to Roo with pleading eyes. "We're going

walkabout anyway. Let's go to the coast. I'll find these boys a boat. Show them how to use it."

Roo remained quiet, her eyes bemused and calculating.

"You'd do that for us? Help us, I mean?" Wyatt asked, somewhat taken back by the man's kindness.

"We're all in this together, right? You seem like a couple of good kids."

How funny that word sounded now. Kids. When their journey had begun he'd felt very much like one, but after everything he'd lived through, it seemed a joke.

"Or you could come with us," Wyatt suggested.

Ernesto ran a hand through his thick hair. "I don't know, man. I mean, the ocean does sound nice. It has been a long time since I've been on the big water." His voice sounded almost wistful. Then he looked to Roo, and beyond her, to the others. "But, it's safe here, with my people. And I love them."

Wyatt thought about it. He knew it was a long shot, asking Ernesto to go with him and his brother. With strangers. But he also knew taking a boat onto the ocean wasn't as easy as Ernesto was making it seem. There was no way he and Seth could be taught what to do, even if Ernesto spent days showing them how everything worked.

"We'll keep you safe," Wyatt found himself saying. Immediately he regretted it. He hadn't been very good at keeping anyone safe. He thought about everyone that had died on his watch. It was a long list and only growing.

But he let the promise stand anyway.

Ernesto smiled. "I'll think about it, man. Think while we walk."

"To the coast?" Roo asked and Ernesto nodded.

She shrugged. "I suppose it's as good a place as anywhere." Roo looked to Wyatt. "Looks like you're staying with us after all. At least, for a good while."

5

The hike to the coast was long and monotonous. Wyatt didn't realize just how far away they were. If he had, he might have second-guessed the plan, but after several days, he accepted it and took the new days as they came, grateful there was always another one.

Grateful for being one day closer to their goal.

But now it was just Seth and him, bringing up the rear.

Supper looked at him, cocking his head as if reading his thoughts.

What did he actually have to be grateful for?

He scratched the dog behind the ears, calming his nerves. Supper dropped his head back onto Seth's lap as Wyatt continued to push.

"At least one of us is getting some exercise," Wyatt muttered as he shoved on. "I still don't know why the dog gets a free ride."

Seth tilted his head back and looked at Wyatt upside down. "This terrain would be hard on his feet, brother. Unless you've got some doggy shoes hidden away, don't be a hater."

Wyatt managed a smile. As the days passed some of the shock of Barbara's death wore off. He still cried himself to sleep each night, and he understood that it was only his constant exhaustion that allowed him to hold his grief at bay, but all things considered, he was proud of how he was pushing through. The Wyatt he'd been a few years, hell, a few months, earlier, would have been a blubbering, worthless mess.

The group of travelers helped. Even though Wyatt refused to become part of the gang, or even learn their names, they were kind and giving. They shared as if Wyatt, Seth, and Supper had been a part of their cadre since the beginning. As if they weren't planning on abandoning them as soon as they reached their destination.

The food they scrabbled together was tasty, if undefinable. They used roots and herbs in ways Wyatt never would have dreamed, but they never went hungry. There were even times, usually at night when his mind wandered, that he had second thoughts.

Maybe it wouldn't be so bad sticking with a group rather than striking out on their own and heading into, no pun intended, uncharted waters. But when morning came around he always found himself yearning for more. For blue skies and warm winds. For a world where life wasn't enveloped in a cloud of dreary, gray dust.

6

THE BREEZE FROM THE OCEAN WAS SO DAMP AND COOL IT slicked his skin and made him shiver.

It had been a long time since Wyatt had been to the beach. So many things were different, but the memories flooded back to him.

With the ocean so near their home in Maine, they'd vacationed there frequently before Seth's injury. Wyatt's father would hold him and wait for the waves to come, then would jump as if hurdling them and the duo would dissolve into laughing fits. Barbara would sit on the sand, reading and sunbathing. She had no interest in the cold waters off the New England coast.

Back then, Seth could run like the wind and he'd suspend most of the day vaulting sand dunes and building castles. Occasionally Wyatt would help, other times he'd do his best Godzilla impression and smash whatever Seth had constructed.

With the smell of the saltwater, with its hint of fishiness, invading his nostrils, it felt like everything was back to normal.

But he knew it wasn't.

The beach was dark, and not the midday storm rolling in kind of dark. This was the perpetual gloom that had become standard the last several years. Also missing were the families, the pretty girls in their bikinis, the lifeguards keeping an eye for a swimmer who'd gone out too far or got a cramp and needed rescuing.

There was no laughter there. No joy. Just the steady crashing of the waves as they broke across the beach.

There was nobody around to litter, but there was also nobody around to pick up the trash and Wyatt was surprised at how much had washed up ashore. Chunks of wood, pieces of boats, metal barrels, discarded clothing, fishing nets. And plastic. So much plastic.

The various shades of it turned the beachfront into a mosaic of color. It could have been beautiful, from a distance, but up close it revealed its truth. It was a dump. Just like the rest of the planet, or what Wyatt has seen of it. Man might be mostly gone, but his litter would remain for eons.

A sidewalk stretched along the beach and Wyatt was spared having to push this brother's wheelchair through the soft sand. He'd worried about that for days, knowing Seth would get frustrated and the scene it would cause. Thankfully that potential misery was spared.

Now they needed to find a boat.

Or try.

Ernesto seemed to think plenty would await at the docks. He also seemed to think he knew where said docks were, but after another mile or so, Wyatt had his doubts. He bit his lip and didn't question the man out loud, but was already steeling himself for yet another failure when--

"Over there," Ernesto shouted, pointing at something Wyatt's younger eyes still couldn't see. "Our boat!"

Wyatt leaned down his spine popping, and whispered in Seth's ear. "Do you see a boat?"

"I think the guy's gone loco," Seth said.

Ernesto had broken into a quick jog and Wyatt struggled not to fall too far behind. The wheelchair shuddered and shimmied across the uneven concrete and Wyatt knew it might not be too long for the world. But, maybe they wouldn't need it for a little while. Not if they were ocean-bound.

Another hundred yards and Wyatt finally saw what had got Ernesto so excited. Tied to a small, weathered dock were three boats, all of which still floated.

"Well I'll be dipped in shit," Seth said.

Ernesto was already on the dock, which swayed precariously under his weight. Wyatt half-expected the man to fall through and wasn't about to push Seth and his chair into that old wood without trying it himself.

"You okay waiting here for a minute?"

"Brother, I was going to suggest that same thing. You go be a test dummy while I work on my tan." He rolled up his sleeves to soak in the nonexistent sunlight.

Roo and the others had already flopped into the sand, cooking up some food. Supper was with them, eager to partake in the communal sharing of grub.

Ernesto led the way toward the boats as Wyatt took note of the many empty spots where he assumed boats used to be. As he got closer, he saw a bit of white fabric breaking the surface of the water.

He peered past it, straining to see into the murky depths, then realized he was looking at a sunken ship. He wondered how many others were down there, or had broken their tethers and floated out to sea, captained by ghosts.

He was careful to step lightly, not wanting to break through the dock and plunge unto the water, but he worked his way to Ernesto who had sidled up next to one of the largest boats and was looking it over. It stretched about thirty feet in length and the thought of trying to handle something of that size made the hair on his arm stand at attention.

Ernesto turned back to him and waved him over with a thick, brown hand. "Wyatt, come look, this one seems to be good," he called out. "It's a catamaran."

The dual hulled boat wasn't the largest Wyatt had ever seen -

that would have been a yacht he's spied from Bar Harbor during one summer vacation - but it was close. The sails were tied to the mast, a towering white finger stretching skyward. Ernesto popped a door and stepped into the cabin. Wyatt followed.

It was spacious, luxurious even. There were cabinets filled with pots and pans, but no food. Several fishing rods were stacked in a corner. A bedroom was located in the rear and there were enough bench seats that sleeping space would be ample. As Wyatt surveyed it, he thought it was probably nicer, and larger than some apartments.

"So this is the one?" Wyatt asked.

"All things considered, I think it'll do."

Wyatt took another look around and couldn't help but feel intimidated. "And you know how to drive this thing?"

Ernesto laughed. "Yeah, I can *drive* it. I need to make sure everything is okay underneath, but it's still floating, so I think we're in good shape."

"Underneath?" Wyatt asked.

Ernesto grinned. "Come with me," he said, jogging out.

Wyatt shook his head and followed the excited old man who stopped at the port side, one leg already over the railing. "C'mon, let's take a dip."

"A dip?" Wyatt asked.

"Yeah, in the water. You can swim, right?"

Wyatt didn't know why, but he felt uneasy. Sure, he had gone in rivers and lakes in the past months, but something about the ocean seemed different and intimidating. It was like when he was a kid, he was afraid he was going to step on a jellyfish. Or something even more dangerous, like a snark. And now it was worse. With no people around, and the nuclear bombs, and whatever else, who knew what was down there?

"Is it safe?"

"Wyatt, it's fine."

"What about like, a Kraken or something?" Wyatt asked.

Ernesto looked at him as if he were the biggest idiot he'd ever met. "You're not serious, are you?"

"Well, I mean, what if something mutated and is just down there... Waiting for a good meal?"

"Waiting for some random people to come along? For five years, this close to the land? And I'm pretty sure the Kraken is like Norwegian or something, man."

"I saw Godzilla," Wyatt said, still unsure.

Ernesto rolled his eyes. "You know what?"

Before Wyatt could ask *what*, Ernesto shoved him over the side. Wyatt hit the water with a splash. The cold water took the breath out of him, but it also felt invigorating. Refreshing. Wyatt was mad for the shortest of seconds and immediately forgot all of his worries.

He surfaced and spit out the salty water, then exhaled and shot more from his nostrils.

"See. No Kraken," Ernesto said before diving in headfirst with the perfect form of an Olympian.

Wyatt followed him down, underneath the boat. It was dark, but as their eyes adjusted Ernesto made sure Wyatt could see what he was trying to show him. There were *things* attached to the bottom of the boat. The hull, Wyatt guessed it was called. Ernesto extracted a knife and used it to pry one off, then swam away.

As they broke the surface, Ernesto held up the anthropod. "Barnacles," Ernesto said, shaking water from his hair as would a wet dog. "But we'll call them dinner."

"You eat them?"

"You don't have to, but I'm not one to pass up seafood. Either way, we'll still need to get them off so the boat doesn't drag ass in the water. Other than that, it looks like there's no major damage."

"So we're in business?" Wyatt asked.

Ernesto grinned. "We're in business."

7

WYATT STARED OUT AT THE WATER, FEELING THE BREEZE against his skin as the catamaran sailed on the open sea.

After scraping the boat, fixing up the minor patches that Ernesto discovered while doing it, and making sure the sails and mast were in good condition, they had shared a meal of barnacles with Roo and the others. Wyatt couldn't believe how good they were. Not quite lobster-level, but close. After a few goodbyes, the groups split apart and Ernesto, Wyatt, Seth, and Supper shoved off.

Ernesto didn't seem to mind leaving his people. He kept telling the boys about his sea legs and that being on land for so long had gotten tiring. And as the land disappeared behind them, Wyatt thought he could see the man growing younger by the hour. He knew that wasn't actually happening, but the freedom of the ocean seemed to transform Ernesto. The man's youthful exuberance made Wyatt even more convinced this was the right decision.

Now, they were alone. Just the four of them. They were quite the bunch. Wyatt had no idea what he was doing, although he never wanted to admit that to anyone. He'd grown accustomed to being something of a leader, but now he was a student and there was so much to learn.

As he breathed in the salty air, he couldn't help but think of the others that hadn't made it but had helped to get him this far. He wished they could all be there with him. Trooper, Allie, Barbara, hell, even Pete and Alexander. Even River.

They were all good people in the end. But he knew their sacrifices would mean so much more when they made it to the end. When the plan came to completion and Wyatt and Seth were safe, at a place they could call home, away from the gloom and constant threats.

The boat sailed on and jumped a large wave, causing him to steady himself against the rope around the side. The water was rougher than when they had set sail, which was what Ernesto said would happen, but Wyatt felt his stomach roil.

It's no worse than turbulence on an airplane, Wyatt told himself as he tried to dissuade his body from doing what it so wanted. At least a little rocky water didn't make him think they would fall from the sky and die in a fiery inferno. This would be fine. He was sure of—

Wyatt leaned over the rope railing as the hot bile rushed up his throat. The puke splashed into the water below and he wiped his mouth. He felt better until—

It happened again.

8

Seth had always been analytical. Calculated. An elementary school teacher had once warned his parents to be careful or their seven-year-old son would be outsmarting them. He knew he was smarter than Wyatt, but had never told him that. Not even in their worst of fights. Doing so would have been a low blow. Besides, sometimes he preferred to be underestimated.

He watched Wyatt looking out at the sea and knew his brother was lost in his own head. Probably thinking about everyone who was dead. Seth did his share of that too but tried not to live in the past.

He knew what had happened at the casino was going to be the hardest hurdle to overcome in mending their relationship. And there were times when he wondered if things would ever be normal between them again. Would Wyatt truly forgive him?

Seth hoped so, but a part of him, a gnawing, nagging voice inside his head, said he didn't need to be forgiven. That he'd done nothing wrong. What happened to Allie wasn't really his fault and he didn't want to feel guilty about it.

But he did. He blamed himself for everything. For believing in Papa when the man was no better than a carnival barker. For not trusting Wyatt when he wanted to flee. If only he'd have listened, Rosario, Allie, their mother, all of them would be alive.

Now it was just the two of them. Of course, there was now Ernesto and Supper, too. But at the heart, it was just them. The brothers.

Seth glanced as Supper who was sprawled on his side, eyes cast toward the ocean. He wondered what the dog was thinking about. If dogs could understand the difference between land and sea. Or was it all the same to them? Supper looked at him as if he could hear Seth's thoughts mention his name.

Then, Wyatt's barfing drew both of their attention. As he watched his brother regurgitate their barnacle feast, Seth barked out a loud laugh. He just couldn't help it. After everything, they'd been through. Not eating, watching people die, watching people eat people, this was the tipping point. A few waves made his brother puke.

Wyatt was seasick and Seth continued to belt the laughter out. It was just so ridiculous.

After another round of projectile vomiting, Wyatt turned to Seth, glaring, his face twisted as if he were wounded by his brother's outburst.

"What the fuck, Seth?" he asked, wiping his mouth.

"Dude, you're such a pussy," Seth said, still laughing.

Wyatt's cheeks flushed pink with embarrassment, but then he joined in the laughter. He must have seen just how ridiculous it all was, too.

The breeze stopped and the boat continued to coast, but at a much slower pace. Ernesto emerged from the cabin, his brow knitted in concern. "Wyatt, you okay?"

"Just a little—"

"Wyatt got seasick!" Seth shouted, giddy.

Wyatt shook his head, then realized some of his vomit had splashed onto his shirt. He peeled it off and tossed it to the deck.

Ernesto grinned. "Yeah, I've seen it happen before. Looks like we're gonna be without wind for a bit, so the rocking should ease off. It'd be a good time to take a dip if you guys are up for it," Ernesto said. He quickly shot his eyes over to Seth and frowned. "Sorry, I didn't think when I said it."

Wyatt sprinted to Seth. "Nothing to be sorry about," Wyatt said.

"No! Don't you fucking dare," Seth said. But he knew it was coming. Wyatt slipped behind him and shoved his chair to the edge where the railing was gone. Seth felt the chair tipping, and before he knew it, he was falling face-first off the boat.

Seth hit the water with a splash. The water was cold but felt amazing. He came up for air, treading his arms in the water.

"You fucking asshole, I'm swimming in your puke down here," Seth spit a mouthful at his brother.

Wyatt jumped off the boat and did a cannonball next to Seth. The splash of water reached the deck of the boat. Supper got up and walked to the edge, looking at the two of them.

"Come on in, Supper," Wyatt called.

And like a good boy, Supper jumped. Seth could have sworn that the furry guy had a smile on his face when he was in mid-air.

Life was good.

Seth hadn't swum in years and had forgotten how free he felt when he did. In the water, he didn't feel like a cripple. He could move with as much ease as anyone else. It felt like flying.

It was the best feeling in the world.

Seth thought, at that moment, if they never made it to the south, he'd be alright. Maybe they could just sail forever.

He would never be that happy again.

9

After a long swim, the brothers lounged on the deck as Ernesto put the fishing rods to good use. He'd already reeled in three and showed no signs of slowing down. The man's skill set out here was amazing.

Wyatt sat next to him as Seth laid in the sun and let the breeze dry his body. Not that there was actual sunlight, but he was certain that it did seem marginally brighter.

"You know, my two boys really liked to be on the water, too," Ernesto said.

It was the first time he had mentioned a family and Wyatt's ears perked to attention. "Oh yeah?" Wyatt said.

Ernesto nodded. "Yup. My two guppies I would call them."

Wyatt watched the older man smile, reminiscing about his past.

"The two of you remind me of them. I mean, they weren't as old as either of you, but they had a similar relationship. Would needle each other all the time. Someone that didn't know any better, they would think they were fighting. But really, it was the way they loved each other."

Wyatt smiled. It was a great description of them.

"I could see them being just like the two of you if they had been able to live so long."

And there was Ernesto's tragic past. It seemed like everyone had one in this new world. It was inevitable at this point. Wyatt knew they would never meet anyone that hadn't suffered a loss this far after the wars and the bombs had changed everything.

"I'm sorry about your boys," Wyatt said. He was curious as to what happened, but he didn't want to pry. A man was allowed his secrets.

Wyatt thought about their decision to leave Maine. The attack had been the catalyst, but even if that never happened, the slow threat of starvation would have forced them out of their home. Barbara was right about that.

He considered telling his story to Ernesto, to bond in that way survivors do but thought better of it. Maybe it was time to leave the past in the past.

"Sorry," Ernesto said as if he realized his comment had changed the mood. "But I felt them right in the moment, you know?"

"You don't need to be sorry for remembering anyone. Let them live inside you. And share them as you see fit."

Ernesto grinned at Wyatt. "I forgot how insightful and emotional young people can be."

Wyatt flashed a bashful smile. Ernesto reached to Supper who laid nearby and gave the dog a rough scratch on the head. "You know, Wyatt, if I never met you two, then I would have never come out here. I would never have set foot on a boat again. And that would have been a boring life."

Wyatt shook his head as he watched the fishing line drift in the water. "You never know. Maybe you would have decided to do it on your own."

"I wouldn't have. I was safe with Roo. And safety leads to complacency. I had people with me that helped and we survived together. Maybe the closest to family I thought I was going to find. But that would have been it for me."

Ernesto patted Wyatt on the leg. "I guess I'm saying, thank you. You and your brother saved me in a way. You let me reconnect with what I loved. You let me remember my family. My real one, I mean. Whatever happens after this, just know that I'm grateful to you both."

"Of course," Wyatt said. "And I don't think I can ever thank you enough. For bringing us along. For teaching us."

"De nada," Ernesto said as he stood. "I gotta take a piss."

10

Nearly a week passed without event. Sailing and fishing. Eating and sleeping. It was a sort of lazy calm that Seth struggled to accept after the past months, where danger - and excitement - seemed to be around every turn. He couldn't acclimate to this newfound peace and, a part of him felt he didn't deserve it.

He felt like he deserved to die at the casino. Maybe shot by one of Papa's guards. It would be his penance for causing so many deaths. So much pain.

While Ernesto steered the boat and Wyatt fished over the port side, Seth sobbed. Supper wriggled further into his lap, shoving his wiry muzzle into Seth's neck. His rough tongue dragged across the boy's cheeks as he licked away his salty tears.

Usually, Supper could make everything better, but not now. And when Seth kept crying, the dog unleashed a scolding *Yip* in protest.

"Quiet," Seth ordered, but it was too late. Wyatt's attention had gone from his fishing line to his younger brother and before Seth could collect himself, Wyatt caught him crying.

He hurriedly reeled in his line and set the rod aside, going to him.

Wyatt's hair was a bird's nest from the constant salt spray, jutting out at wild angles and giving him the look of a carefree surfer or beach bum if it wasn't for the lingering sadness in his eyes.

"You need to stop this," Wyatt said, kneeling.

Great, Seth thought. Just what he needed. He could take the ballbusting, the teasing, the cut downs, and whatever else. That's what brothers did. But the last thing he needed was to feel shame or, worse, pity.

"Leave me alone," Seth said, sitting up and turning his back to his brother. He tried to wipe his eyes, but the tears kept coming.

"Seth, this is enough. Stop it already," Wyatt said again.

"You tell me to stop it one more time and I'm gonna punch you in the dick, Wyatt." Seth tried to sound intimidating, but between the sobs and tears, it was a poor act.

Then he felt Wyatt's hand on his shoulder. It was soft and caring. It wasn't a shove or punch like Wyatt was messing around. And Seth wasn't sure if it made it better or worse.

"What's so fucking hard about giving me some privacy?"

"You want to cry, cry," Wyatt said. "But I'm not going to keep watching you beat yourself up." Wyatt suddenly grabbed him by the face, his grip hard and stern. He twisted Seth's head, forcing them to come eye to eye.

"What are you doing?" Seth grunted as his brother pulled him in close for a rough embrace.

Then Seth finally said the words that had wanted to come for weeks. "I'm so sorry, Wyatt."

Seth could see from the watery corner of his eye that his brother was shaking his head, looking out at the water.

"Wyatt, I—"

"Don't," Wyatt said. "You don't need to explain anything to me."

"I need you to know. I need you to f—"

"It wasn't you, Seth."

Seth's mouth went dry and wordless. He pulled away and met eyes with his brother. He expected so much anger. He expected to be yelled at. He *wanted* to be yelled at. Hell, he wanted Wyatt to beat the shit out of him. Keep hitting him until his hands hurt and there was nothing left of Seth to pummel. He deserved so much worse for what he did. For what he let happen.

But instead, Wyatt was being Wyatt. Loving him unconditionally. Letting him off the hook. Seth wasn't sure he wanted that.

"I know it wasn't your idea. You would never have let anything happen to anyone we cared about." Wyatt pushed his hair out of his eyes. "You made some bad choices. Especially when it came to the... the sacrifices."

"I know," Seth said. He had bought into Papa so much. He was so blinded by being loved and power that he didn't see the bullshit that was truly going on. He'd believed the man was the savior he claimed to be. And Seth had loved him like a father and he felt the love in return.

Wyatt grabbed Seth's shoulder, bringing him out of his memories. "You're still my brother."

"I fucked up. A lot. Papa... he made me feel like I mattered, Wyatt. And you don't know how long it's been since I felt like anything more than a burden. The things he said, the way he treated me, it made me think I could actually be someone important. That I could be more than a cripple. That I could be a person people looked up to instead of down on. Someone like you," Seth said, his throat tight as he let out the truth he typically cloaked in sarcasm and bravado.

"What are you talking about?" Wyatt asked.

"Don't you see it? You have everything, Wyatt. Everyone we've met since leaving Maine has looked to you as our leader, even when Trooper was still around. You were eighteen, but they saw it in you. You're strong. They all respected you. You even get the girl without hardly trying." A smirk crossed Seth's lips. "Even though you're the less handsome brother."

Wyatt looked away, toward the water. It was his turn to feel self-conscious.

"It's always been you, Wyatt. I'm just the brother that can't walk. The one you have to protect. The one that drags everyone else down. I've never been one to believe in," Seth finished and it felt like a boulder had been lifted from his back.

Wyatt's face twisted in confusion. "Seth, none of that's true. I don't give a shit if you can walk or not. I'm just your older brother. You could be five inches taller and built like a Greek god and I'd still try to protect you. That's what brothers do."

"Well, I am five inches bigger where it counts," Seth said, unable to curtail his true nature.

Wyatt barked out a laugh but soon returned to serious. "You were never an anchor to drag me down, or anyone for that matter. You were a reason to keep fighting. A reason to push on. So what if you can't walk? You're the smartest of all of us. And you're like a pit bull in a fight. I've always wanted to be more like you," Wyatt said, pushing his finger into Seth's chest. Wyatt had his own set of tears in his eyes now.

Seth laughed, wiping the tears away, hopefully for the last time. While it felt good to get his feelings out, he had never felt more vulnerable in his life. "God damn, Wyatt."

"What?" he asked.

"You and me are a couple of the biggest pussies I've ever seen," Seth said.

Wyatt laughed and leaned in, tilting their heads together. And despite how ludicrous it sounded, Seth believed what Wyatt had said. He wasn't sure how exactly they were going to move forward. Forgiveness couldn't be that easy.

11

Wyatt laid on the cushioned bench in the cabin of the boat. It was pitch black outside and he drifted in and out of sleep as gentle waves broke across the stern. One minute he'd be out lost to the world. The next awake and in a fog of delirium.

Each time he woke he thought he was still in his real bed, thinking all of this new reality was but a nightmare, only to have to accept again and again that all his losses were real. That everyone was dead and not coming back.

He preferred the lies of sleep.

There, he dreamed of his mother making them breakfast in the morning. The sun shining through the kitchen windows blindingly bright. There was food - eggs and sausage and pancakes and bacon and hashbrowns - more than they could eat in a month. And laughter. And peace. And his mother's sweet voice singing to him.

Blue skies, shining on me...

He dreamt of his father, pushing through the door after his early morning jog. His University of Orono tanktop near black with sweat, his face flushed with exertion. And his broad, toothy grin as he cracked some dad joke they'd heard a thousand times but still made them laugh.

It was Sunday morning and nobody had to leave for work or school. They could just spend the day together, as a family. It was perfect, just the way life used to be.

When he woke from those dreams, he felt the heavy sadness. It was so nice to go visit, and he was happy to have those moments. Those memories. But he knew that would never happen again. He knew that his mother and father were gone. He might get to see them in another life, but that wasn't going to be for a long time.

He also dreamt of Allie. The feel of her silken skin against his own. The taste of her lips, salty and wet. Sometimes they talked about a future that would never come. About dreams unrealized. She was the woman he loved, the one he'd never expected to meet. But there she was. Just waiting to be found by Wyatt. The two of them had been so good together.

He dreamt of what was, but mostly about what could have been. In those dreams, they found a place to live together. A place where the sun always shined and the weather was always perfect. They were on the coast, in a cramped bungalow steps from the beach. They didn't need much. Just each other. And no worries.

That was the connecting thread in all his dreams.

Never having to worry again.

The happiness, the fulfillment, the peace.

But it didn't last. When he opened his eyes, slowly drifting back to reality, those feelings left him with a gaping hole, with such deep sadness.

That was the bad part of dreaming.

He yearned to return to sleep, even knowing that, at some point, he would have to wake for real. That he would have to face the day ahead. Reality was going to come crashing in, and he'd have to deal with it.

Still, he longed to experience just a few more minutes of fantasy.

Those delusions ended for good when he heard the footsteps.

12

Wyatt bolted upright. He knew the footsteps weren't from Ernesto as the man's snoring wafted in from the helm. And even though Seth preferred to sleep on deck, he certainly wasn't up and walking around. And to disprove the only remaining possibility, he saw Supper pacing the cabin floor, moving in a circle, occasionally stopping to stare at the closed hatch leading to the deck.

"What is it, buddy?" Wyatt whispered.

Supper glanced at him, ears perked, the scruff on his neck standing at attention. The dog turned back to the hatch and let out a low growl.

Who the hell could be up there? They were in the middle of the Atlantic and hadn't seen another boat since leaving shore.

So what was going on?

Wyatt scanned the room, but there was no real weapon in sight. He didn't even know if he needed one. What if some fat pelican had landed on the deck and was flopping around? Wouldn't he feel like an idiot?

The more he considered that prospect, the more rational it

seemed. In fact, it was the only theory that made sense. Still, he knew he had to check it out and satisfy his curiosity.

As Wyatt rubbed sleep from his eyes and reached for the hatch, Supper whined, his body tensed.

"You want to see what's up there?" Wyatt asked the dog. "You want a bite of a super-sized seagull, boy?"

Another whine, that one even more anxious.

"Okay, let's go exploring." Wyatt swiveled the handle and popped the hatch. Then he paused, holding his breath without realizing it.

Nothing attacked. No one lunged, grabbing at him. No one dove into the cabin ready to tear him to shreds.

Wyatt shook his head, bemused over his paranoia. "See, nothing but empty skies," he said to the dog.

Above, the black, starless night swallowed everything but the objects nearest. He almost closed the hatch again, then looked to Supper. "Maybe you should go take a leak. I don't want to go back to sleep, only for your bladder to wake me up again in an hour."

Supper jumped against Wyatt's legs as if saying he agreed that was a swell idea. Wyatt bent, grabbed the dog around the waist, and hoisted him into the air. He was ready to pop him up and onto the deck when he heard not footsteps, but a voice.

"Atar al lisiado!"

The voice was rough like it came from a mouth that chewed glass instead of gum. Wyatt strained to see, his eyes too slow to adjust to the stygian night.

Then Ernesto's snores came to a sudden, choking stop. "Who ar-_"

There was a crack, then a thud - a sound Wyatt immediately recognized as a body hitting the deck.

Wyatt let go of Supper, pointing a finger to indicate *stay* and the dog obeyed. Then he slowly, silently, eased himself through the small opening and onto the deck.

What he saw made him wish he was still asleep. Even a

nightmare would have been preferable to the reality going down on their peaceful, perfect catamaran.

Seth was on his back, a rope crossed through his mouth to gag him into silence. His face was dark and wet and, Wyatt realized, covered in blood. One eye was swollen shut but the other was almost absurdly wide open. Full of panic and pain and fear.

A man who was no more than a hulking shadow had one knee on Seth's back, pinning the boy to the deck while he bound his hands behind him. Another man stood beside them, holding something long, but slender. He seemed to be the one in charge.

"Rapida!" he ordered.

"Yo soy," the bigger man said as he finished tying off Seth's arms. Then he stood.

Toward the bow came a raucous commotion and Wyatt's eyes followed. He saw a third man dragging Ernesto's limp body toward the others.

"Viejo hijo de puta es pesado," the man with Ernesto said as he dropped the legs he's been using as handles.

"¿Hay alguien más?" the leader asked the others.

Then, as if a psychic connection was birthed by the words, all three of them looked toward the hatch.

And saw Wyatt.

Where did they come from? How did they board the boat without anyone hearing?

Wyatt cursed himself for becoming so comfortable, so lax, so careless. This would have never happened on the road where even a leaf crunching was enough to send him on red alert. Damn him for being such a good sleeper.

None of it mattered anymore. He was going to have to deal with it... But how?

As the three men rushed toward him, he dropped back into the cabin. Supper, now also aware that danger lurked above, dashed about, barking and snarling, slobber flying from his jaws.

At least one of us is ready to attack, Wyatt thought.

Wyatt realized he was more than just outnumbered. He was wholly unprepared for a fight. He had no weapon. He had no backup outside of the three-legged dog. Hell, he wasn't even wearing shoes. The few short weeks on the boat had softened him and allowed him to become complacent.

He heard the strangers close in above, but he wasn't going to go down without a battle. Hell, he wasn't going to go down at all. He had dealt with worse than these assholes. He'd faced cannibals, he'd taken down a cult. And he'd always survived.

Wyatt grabbed a fire extinguisher, long past its intended usefulness, off the wall, and held it, ready to strike.

The first man, the biggest man, dropped into the cabin. Supper lunged forward, diving for the man's leg but the dog was awkward and the man dodged, then kicked out with his foot. He connected with Supper's ribs and the dog gave a pained yelp as he skidded across the floor before crashing into the wall.

That was enough to push Wyatt into the red zone.

"If you get the fuck off our boat right now, I'll let you bastards live!" Wyatt found himself saying. His voice didn't waver. He believed himself.

The big man snarled and, from above, the others laughed. Not just chuckles either. These were hearty guffaws like Wyatt was giving some grade A zingers at the Friars Club roast.

As the big man came toward him, Wyatt realized he wasn't holding a baseball bat. He was holding a sword.

A sword? Wyatt thought. Do these guys think they're pirates or something?

Then the other two men dropped into the cabin and Wyatt realized they too were armed with long blades. It looked so absurd he almost laughed, but he had enough sense to stay quiet.

They didn't all come at once. Maybe because they underestimated the kid standing before them, or maybe because they thought three men charging wantonly with four-foot blades had the potential to end badly. They moved single file, biggest to smallest.

The first in line raised his sword clumsily, lunging forward, blade leading the way. Wyatt parried with the fire extinguisher and saw a bright, orange spark as the two metal objects collided. Before the man could swing again, Wyatt was ready with the canister, bashing it into the man's face with a teeth-shattering crunch.

The big man groaned and let out a loud *oof*. Along with the sound came bits of teeth that fell into the cabin floor with a clatter.

"Gilipollas!" the man grunted. Then, he smiled, baring his broken mouth.

Wyatt returned the smile. His own heart beating so hard he could hear it in his ears. As much as he didn't want to fight, as much as he just wanted to be left alone, something about this, about surviving, felt natural. Maybe, even, welcome.

The man lunged again and Wyatt dodged again. Except this time, the man didn't put his full force into it. It reminded Wyatt of a basketball player fake pumping the ball up to the hoop.

When Wyatt dodged, the man pulled back and hooked one of Wyatt's arms with his own. Using his momentum and his body weight against him, the man swung Wyatt into the cabin wall face first.

As he tried to brace himself, to stop himself from falling, Wyatt let the fire extinguisher drop from his hands. He managed to stay on his feet, but when the big man grabbed him from behind, he knew he was in trouble.

He thrashed and flailed, trying to break free, but the man had six inches and probably close to a hundred pounds on him. He was so strong Wyatt felt like his shoulders were being dislocated as the man bent his arms at angles they weren't supposed to bend.

Wyatt's grand plans of saving the day flew out the window as the man lifted him like a rag doll, carrying him toward his cohorts. And Wyatt knew it was only a matter of minutes before he'd be tied up and gagged. Or maybe they'd just ram one of their swords through his belly. Send his guts to the cabin floor so he could watch himself bleed out.

So much for being a hero.

Before Wyatt's visions could become reality, he heard Supper barking. Then he heard the big man yelling. Wyatt craned his neck to look back and found Supper's teeth buried in the man's right ass cheek as the guy bellowed in renewed pain.

Wyatt had seen what Supper could do when keeping them safe. The viciousness that his best buddy could unleash when the situation called for him. A part of him almost felt sorry for the man.

Rather than come to his aide, the other men laughed at their friend's predicament. Wyatt was enjoying it too, until he saw the tallest of the men, the leader, grip his sword harder. And Wyatt knew as soon as the man grew bored of watching his amigo's ass get chomped on, he was going to turn Supper into a shishkebab.

There was no way Wyatt was going to let anything happen to his dog.

"Supper," Wyatt called out, stern and commanding. "Stop it."

And the dog let go of the big man's ass, obeying his master.

The big man released one of Wyatt's arms, reaching behind himself to explore the wound on his rear end with his fingers. Wyatt used the momentary distraction to kick back with all his force. His bare foot collided with his captor's knee, folding it backward with an audible snap.

The man fell to the floor, ass bleeding, knee hyperextended, fixated on his own pain, and out of commission. Wyatt wanted to turn and finish him off, but there were two more. Two men who had no injuries.

When the next man came at him, Wyatt was ready. As he lunged at him, Wyatt grabbed hold of his arm which was twice as thick as Wyatt's. He could feel hard muscle rippling under his dark flesh and knew if it came to a battle of strength, he was bound to lose.

But Wyatt was quick. And he used his advantage when he could. He dropped backward and that act, coupled with the man's forward motion, caused him to fall with him.

When the man lost his footing, Wyatt swung his fist. It made hard contact with the man's jaw and Wyatt thought he might have broken his own hand. But there was no time to pity himself. He thrust his knee up, into the man's gut.

As the second attacker hit the deck with a loud thud, Wyatt was feeling pretty good. Two men hadn't been able to take him down. He was going to win this thing. He was going to save everyo—

The world surged black as the back of his head shot heavy with pain.

The surge lasted a split second, but when he regained his sight he was on his knees and surrounded.

"You can fight really good, gringo," the third man said from his flank. The man was so tall he had to stand stooped over as to not hit his head on the cabin ceiling.

Supper barked, then growled, saliva flying from his jaws but none of the intruders paid the dog any attention. They were already pulling out the rope with which to tie Wyatt up. And Wyatt's world was still spinning from the blow. He felt hot blood dripping down his back.

"Three on one isn't exactly fair," Wyatt said, still trying to focus.

"Who promised you fair?" the tall man asked.

Supper continued to bark, in a frenzy now.

"Shut the mutt up," the first attacker said, pushing straggly, black hair out of his eyes with one hand and lazily waving the sword at Supper with his other.

"Don't you fucking hurt him!" Wyatt shouted. "He's nobody's meal."

The men paused, exchanged a glance, then burst out laughing.

"You're a bit morbid, man," the tall man said. "Shutting someone up doesn't mean we're going to kill him. And we won't be eating him either. What you think we are? Savages?"

Wyatt put a leg up, trying to climb to his feet. The act made a galaxy of stars appear in front of him. "Fuck you," Wyatt spat.

"No, boy, we don't swing that way," the long-haired man said.

"He's right," the tall one said. "We want you for something else."

Before Wyatt could stand, the leg of the other man, the one who'd been silent so far, flashed in a quick arc. It was on a collision course with Wyatt's face and so fast he had no chance of dodging it.

He hit the deck, lying flat on his back, and saw the world fade completely to black this time.

13

When Wyatt's eyes opened again, he'd almost forgotten what that had happened. But the pain brought it back to him.

How he wished he was still in dreamland. Just as he was before the attackers arrived.

He was now on the deck of their catamaran, and the boat was moving, fast. There was no breeze to speak of though, and the sail hung limp. So how was that possible?

Then he heard a noise he hadn't heard in years but recognized instantly.

An engine.

His eyes sought out the sound and he saw a smaller boat ahead of their own. He couldn't see the rope or chain or whatever tethered the two, but he realized what was happening. They were being towed.

He looked over and saw Seth sitting against the railing, his hands tied behind his back, just as Wyatt's were. His leg was stretched out (no need to tie his feet together, as they'd done to Wyatt's) and his mouth was still gagged.

Pain radiated from Wyatt's head in steady waves and he wondered why he'd ever tried to fight. All it had earned him was a splitting headache - maybe a concussion - and a humiliation at the hands of his attackers. Sometimes he couldn't comprehend how he'd managed to stay alive so long, being so dumb.

He scanned the catamaran for the rest of his companions and found Supper lounging, his head resting on a stack of life vests. Apparently, the dog had more sense than to carry on the fight. More sense than his owner. Wyatt breathed a little easier knowing that the man hadn't lied about that, at least. Then Supper looked at him, finally noticing he was awake.

He started barking, the sound high pitched and piercing even to Wyatt's ears. It also drew the ire of the man Supper had bitten.

"I said shut that mutt up," he yelled as he strode toward the dog. He had a devious grin plastered to his face, baring ragged teeth that Wyatt could barely make out in the darkness. There was no humor in that grin. Only hate.

The man limped when he walked, still favoring the ass cheek Supper had munched on. As the man approached, Supper growled, then lunged, but that time the man was prepared. His timing was perfect as he kicked Supper in the stomach. It was hard and Wyatt could hear the contact made from yards away. The dog skidded across the slick deck, yelping.

Wyatt's blood boiled. He screamed against the cloth shoved in his mouth. He tried to get up, but his hands were tied around the railing, preventing him from going anywhere. The man looked to Wyatt and cackled.

Supper lurched to his feet, not barking anymore, his fight gone. Instead, the dog limped to Wyatt and laid his head across his lap. Wyatt leaned forward and put his head against the dog's. With his hands tied, that was all he could do to make him feel better.

"Chinga tu madre puto!" the tall man shouted, leaving his station behind the wheel and loping toward his companion.

"Se lo merecía!" the man with the long hair muttered. "Perro me-_"

In an instant, the tall man was on the scene. He didn't wait for the sentence to be finished. He didn't wait to say another word to his cohort. He only drew his sword.

The blade slid into the kicker's gut, then out his back His mouth opened in a wide O of shock and his eyes blazed with confused betrayal.

The tall man stared back, cold, emotionless. Kicking Supper had sealed the dying man's fate.

"Fernando," the long-haired man gasped. He grabbed on the tall man's - Fernando's - shirt, the blade still jutting out from his back.

"Shut the fuck up and die." Fernando jerked the blade out of his friend. Blood dripped from the sword, falling on the deck in fat droplets.

The dying man covered the wound in his stomach with both hands, went unsteady on his feet, then fell to a knee. He coughed up a mouthful of blood, then spat it onto Fernando's shoes.

Fernando looked down at the mess, then tossed his sword to the side with a clatter. He grabbed the man under his arms, effortlessly hoisted him into the air, then dropped him over the railing.

Wyatt watched him bob in the black water, but as the boats moved, he was soon out of sight. When he was nothing more than a speck, Wyatt gave up on staring and looked to Fernando who examined him, his own face blank.

Their eyes locked, then Fernando gave a barely perceptible nod. With that, he turned and returned to the wheel.

Wyatt wondered why a man so quick to kill his own companion had spared him. It was obvious that he didn't hesitate to kill, so he must have other plans.

Where were they being taken, and why?

Hours later, after night had transitioned to what passed for day, Wyatt got his answer.

A ship that dwarfed the catamaran loomed ahead and the two smaller boats headed straight toward it. A large sail flapped in the morning breeze and atop its mast was a flag Wyatt recognized instantly. A skull and crossbones.

Wyatt looked to Seth who'd been sleeping and still was. He kicked his feet hard against the deck and his brother's eyes fluttered, then opened. Wyatt tilted his head in the direction of the ship and Seth followed his gaze.

The brothers stared in confused dread.

And awaited their fates.

Helpless.

14

After sidling up next to the pirate ship, a small crew peered down at the catamaran and tugboat. A few moments later a rope ladder dropped down and a man whose skin was as dark as midnight descended it. He jumped the last two yards, onto the deck of the catamaran, and headed straight for Fernando.

"Been a while Nando," he said, pushing a thick hand out for a shake. His voice was heavy with a French accent.

Fernando obliged. "Almost two months."

"You get lazy on me? I pay you too good maybe."

"You? You're the cheapest son of a bitch I ever know!"

After that, both of them shared a jovial laugh and it was easy for Wyatt to discern that this was far from the first time something like this - whatever *this* was - had gone down.

The black man's head swiveled as he took in the catamaran and its contents. "What do you got good for me today?" he asked.

"Plenty," Fernado said as he headed for the bow. "A fine boat, for one. Plenty of fresh water still in the tank too."

The black man shrugged. "Little small, don't you think?" He motioned toward his own boat. His *ship*.

"For you maybe, Elon," Fernando said. "But you could sell it to someone less privileged."

Elon grunted, unimpressed.

"Then maybe this will do," Fernando said, bending at the waist and dropping out of sight. He reemerged dragging Ernesto and deposited him at Elon's feet.

Elon peered down at Ernesto who was hogtied. Blood had dried on his forehead, but his eyes were open and alert. Wyatt was relieved to see the man was still alive.

"What else?" Elon asked, but he was already looking at Wyatt and Seth, and he stepped toward them.

Fernando stayed close on his heels. "Two young ones," he said. "Strong. White. Not many miles on either of them."

Elon crouched beside Seth. He made no effort to hide that he gawked at the boy's stump. "What happened to you, son?"

Seth grunted through his gag and even though he couldn't actually speak, Wyatt knew his brother was making his best attempt at cursing.

"Not sure what's up with that one," Fernando said. "Think he's half lame."

To demonstrate, Fernando picked up Seth's foot, then let it drop to the deck. Dead weight. Motionless.

"You a cripple, son?" Elon asked.

Seth bent forward at the waist, his face red with rage. Spittle frothed from his mouth.

"Top half still works anyway. That's good." Elon grabbed Seth's chain with his ebony hand, his slender fingers stroking Seth's flesh.

"Not even any whiskers yet. You're just a baby." He looked to Fernando, a wild grin crossing his lips. "There's always a use for the young ones, am I right Nando?"

The two men laughed, the kind of laugh shared after a ribald joke and Wyatt knew what sort of *use* Elon was insinuating. His chest rose along with the anger inside, and in short order, he too was seething.

The heavy breathing drew Elon's attention.

"I didn't forget about you." He moved to Wyatt's side. As he looked at him, his eyes narrowed, then he swiveled from Wyatt's face to Seth, then back again.

"You are brothers?" Elon asked.

Wyatt gave a reluctant nod.

"You're not a cripple too, are you?" Elon poked Wyatt in the legs.

"No," Fernando said. "This one's a fighter. Took on two of my men and came out on top. For a short while, at least."

Elon's impressed smirk revealed gleaming, white teeth. "I like me a man who can fight. Always in demand." He reached out and tousled Wyatt's hair in a fatherly way.

A way that Wyatt loathed.

Elon stood, twisting at the waist in a hard stretch. "I'll take the boys and the boat."

Fernando's face fell. "What about the man?" he asked, glancing at Ernesto.

Elon returned to them and took another look. Then, in one smooth motion, he withdrew a pistol from beneath his shirt and pointed the barrel at Ernesto's forehead.

No more than a nanosecond passed, but it felt like an eon to Wyatt who watched Ernesto's eyes flare wide and fearful. He wanted to jump to his feet and go to his friend's rescue. He wanted to scream and beg for his friend's life. He wanted to do something - anything - to stop the inevitable.

But there was no time.

Elon squeezed the trigger and a bullet ripped through Ernesto's forehead. Bits of blood and bone and brains blew out a much larger hole that appeared on the rear of his skull. Then he collapsed.

As Wyatt felt tears streaming from his eyes, he remembered what Ernesto had told him. That he was grateful for Wyatt and Seth getting him back out on the water. Getting him connected to his family again. He remembered how happy Ernesto was, and what a good mentor he'd been. He remembered all of their carefree days on the boat when they had no idea it would end like this.

Elon holstered his pistol. "We'll use him for chum," he said. "Maybe catch us *Jaws*!" Then he motioned for more of his friends to join him on the deck of the catamaran. They did, hurriedly collecting their newfound bounty.

And there was nothing Wyatt could do to stop them.

15

The world was pitch black and empty. All sound was muffled, sounding a thousand miles away.

Soon after Elon's men boarded the catamaran, they threw a thick sack reeking of spoiled potatoes and cheap booze over Wyatt's head. After that, all he knew were the hands holding him, the arms grabbing him, as he was herded like an animal.

He wasn't sure why they even bothered to blind them. The brothers had seen the ship and the men already, but he wasn't going to push the issue.

He breathed heavily as they led him further into the boat and, after a screech of metal hinges, inside a room. There were stairs and low ceilings. He knew because they shouted to him to duck so he didn't clunk his head. It only took one time of slamming his forehead against a steel beam to realize this was the time to obey.

He knew he should be scared worried about his own life and Seth's. But all he could focus on was the bag. Where had the disgusting thing been before? He doubted anyone bothered to wash them in between hostages. Who was the last guy to wear it? And what had happened to him? Maybe, Wyatt thought, the man died wearing it. Maybe some of his blood was still there, brushing against his own lips now.

What the hell was wrong with him?

There were better things to fret about, but maybe he wasn't too worried about them because they had kept him alive and there must be a reason for that. Or maybe it was because he had been through so much shit and survived that he'd begun to turn into an optimist.

Besides, being captured by pirates? Hell, at least it was a good story.

Hopefully, he'd live long enough to tell someone all about it.

He was ushered through another door which clanged shut behind him. Whatever room he'd just entered was filled with murmurs, random breaths, and body odor. The smell was so rank the bag he was wearing now seemed like a good thing because it filtered out some of this new, ripe stench.

And then someone ripped it away and his nostrils caught the full assault of the room's aroma. It wasn't just BO from hell. There was feces and urine and vomit mixed in.

As he tried not to barf, to not add his own awfulness to the bouquet of offensive smells, he saw a dozen or more people in the room. Most were men, within a decade of his own age, but there were two women and one young boy too. Everyone was bound in one way or another - either tied to posts and beams or trussed and lying on the floor.

They were captives, Wyatt realized, just like him.

He risked a glance behind and saw four pirates, and Seth, wheelchair and all. Then Fernando grabbed a fistful of Wyatt's hair, wrenching his head backward. Wyatt tensed, ready to fight, but had no way of doing so.

As if reading his mind, Fernando chortled. "Sit down and relax, gringo. Save your strength. It'll come in handy later."

To Wyatt's surprise, Fernando removed the gag from his mouth. But before he could get out a word, the man shoved him forward and he tripped over the outstretched legs of a woman with ice blonde hair. With his own arms tied behind his back, he had no chance of stopping himself or preventing his fall, and he landed in a heap on the floor, his cheek smashing into a pile of someone else's barely formed shit.

That made Fernando and the other pirates laugh even harder.

Wyatt looked to Seth. His hands were tied in front of him and another one of the pirates removed his gag.

Seth stretched his jaw. "Where are fu--"

The pirate who had untied his gag punched him across the face. Seth's head snapped back and his chair rolled a foot before hitting the wall.

Wyatt rolled onto his knees, eager to defend his kin, but Fernando grabbed him by the hair again.

"This can be an easy trip if you do what we tell you. Or it can be hell if you don't. Got it?"

Wyatt looked to Seth who wiped blood from a split lip. Seth gave a little nod, signaling he was okay. And Wyatt realized this wasn't the time to let his ego take over.

"I got it," Wyatt said.

"Good," Fernando said. "You get fed once a day. If you don't eat it, one of them will." He motioned to the other captives.

"What about my dog?" Wyatt asked.

Fernando rolled his eyes, overly dramatic. "That dog never had it so good. He got a full belly and better quarters than you, I promise."

As Fernando left the room, his men secured Wyatt with shackles and chains. Then, they left too, eager to be away from the fetid aroma.

When they were gone, Wyatt looked to his fellow captives, took in their filthy, frightened faces. Most of the people cowered low to the ground and refused to make eye contact. Some constantly rocked back and forth, mumbling unintelligible words to themselves, lost in their own trauma. And all of them looked defeated and hopeless.

He wondered where this ship was heading, and what awaited them once they got there.

16

THE JOURNEY HAD BEEN LONG AND MISERABLE.

Kept in near-constant darkness, Wyatt couldn't tell day from night, but he kept count of the meals. It was day thirty-two.

There had been moments where he plotted how to break out. He thought maybe he could rally the others to take pirates hostage, steal the keys to their locks, then break through the door. If only they could get out of this room, they could fight. And if they could fight, they had a chance.

Then he realized that even if they won the fight and killed all the pirates, they'd be adrift at sea, and without Ernesto to handle the boat, he'd be at the mercy of the waves.

Besides, any plan would involve talking to the others. And most of them got spooked if you looked at them. He hadn't got more than a dozen words from any of them, and most hadn't spoken at all.

They were quite the fun bunch of prisoners.

Prisoners.

Wyatt hated to think of himself that way. Helpless. Hopeless. Even Seth had grown quiet and sullen as their fate sunk in.

But, on day thirty-two the door opened and a beam of light cut through the darkness of their prison. Everyone cowered, hiding their faces and Wyatt turned away too.

Not because he was scared, but because he was blinded by the light.

He couldn't remember so much brightness in... how long? It must have been years. This wasn't the light of the fluorescents in the casino or the light of a campfire.

It was sunlight.

And Wyatt hadn't seen sunlight since he was fourteen years old.

He forced himself to look into it even though doing so made his retinas burn. The feel of the sun on his skin was like static in a thunderstorm. Alive. Electric.

"You," a guard named Henry, said, pointing his sword at Wyatt.

"Yeah?"

"Stand up," Henry ordered.

Wyatt did as told and another pirate moved behind him and unlocked his restraints. With the heaviness of the chains removed, Wyatt felt freer than he had since being ushered onto the ship weeks earlier.

Wyatt stood there, waiting for his next order. It came soon enough.

Henry pointed his sword to a five-gallon bucket in the corner. It was supposed to be the toilet but had been overflowing since their arrival.

"Bring the latrine," he said.

Wyatt eyed the bucket and the flies swarming it. He let out a long sigh and trudged to it. He tried to breathe through his mouth, but that was worse because the smell had a taste.

He gagged and heaved, swallowing back the bile that came up in his throat and scorched his tongue. It was a blessing in disguise, overpowering the smell and taste he already had.

"Come on," Henry commanded.

Wyatt lifted the bucket and stuck his face into his shoulder. He hurried behind the guard, making eye contact with nobody. He was sure that nobody would be willing to trade him places, but he was glad to do it. It got him up top so he could figure out where they were.

When he stepped outside, he felt the cool breeze come off of the sea. He lowered the bucket and stopped to stare in amazement.

The sun was out and shining.

There were no clouds.

No grey skies.

He looked around and saw everything. The colors. The brightness. It was like they turned the contrast up on the television. Everything was so much more intense.

Everything had life in it.

"Dump it over," Henry said, pointing his side over the ledge. "And you spill a drop, you lick it up."

As he peered across the ocean, taking in the idyllic, sunny day, Wyatt couldn't hold in his grin. Even carrying the bucket of shit couldn't change his mood at that point.

His mother had been right all along.

There was a better place, she'd said. A place where the sun still shined and the skies were blue.

And they had found it.

He hoisted the pail and tilted carefully, not wanting to have to lick up months old, festering feces, then allowed the chunky, grotesque contents to rain over the edge of the ship, spilling into the cerulean waters below.

But he didn't watch them splash. He was too busy taking in the brilliant day, the sun gleaming in the sky. And, in the distance, land.

Henry tapped his sword on the rail, drawing Wyatt's attention to it. He followed the blade up to the man's face and realized what he'd before taken to be a dark complexion was actually a deep, golden brown tan.

"What are you grinning about?" Fernando asked, appearing from the side.

"I told him to empty the shit bucket. Don't know why--"

"I was talking to him," Fernando said to Henry. "Go to the kitchen and help Pedro."

Henry shrugged, then left them.

Fernando sidled up next to Wyatt, his hot breath prickling the younger man's skin. "Now answer me," he said. "Cause I don't think hauling shit is a reason to be happy."

His tone was gruff, judging, but Wyatt didn't care. Nothing could spoil his good mood.

"Look at it!" he said, gesturing to the horizon. "We're south of the equator, aren't we?"

Fernando furrowed his brow, his eyes narrowed to slits. "Far past it. Why do you care?"

"The sun," Wyatt said. "I forgot what it looked like."

Fernando's expression softened. "I forgot you were from the north." He leaned into the railing, joining Wyatt in peering out at the water. "Been a while for you, huh?"

"Too long. Way, too long."

Wyatt felt his pant leg jerk sideways, looked down, and saw Supper pulling at the denim to get his attention. That made his smile grow so wide he felt like his face might split in half.

"Hey, boy," Wyatt said, crouching to pet the down. As he did, he realized that Supper's usually rough, dirty fur was sleek and glistening. And that his three-legged friend had put on some weight.

"He's a good dog," Fernando said.

Wyatt's eyes burned as tears threatened. He did his best to fight them off as he looked up at the man who'd taken him prisoner. "Thank you for taking care of him," Wyatt said.

Fernando smiled. "Don't get too happy."

"Why?"

"Because it's a different world here."

"No shit," Wyatt said. "Where I'm from, it's a wasteland. This is…" He swallowed hard. "Amazing."

Fernando shook his head. "Don't expect to find civilization, even down here." His eyes were on the spot of land gradually growing larger in the distance. "And especially not there."

"What do you mean? Where are you taking us?"

Fernando wouldn't meet his eyes. "I don't know what it was called before. And nobody there has a name for it there. But we call it, Isla de Pecados."

Wyatt did not know much Spanish. Being from Maine he hadn't been a need for it. And his silence tipped Fernando to his cluelessness.

"Island of Sins," Fernando said.

As far as names went, it made an impression, and some of Wyatt's good cheer faded. "Is that where we're going?"

Fernando nodded.

"Why?"

"That's where the auctions are."

"Auctions?" Wyatt asked. "For food and stuff?"

"There's no shortage of food there."

"Then what do they sell?"

"Everything," Fernando said, then he spat into the water below.

17

The pirates had lined up Wyatt and Seth with the rest of the captives on the top of the deck. It was still bright out - blindingly so - and Wyatt could tell that the rest of the people were just as mesmerized as he was when he first saw it.

The boat was moored at a weathered, gray dock, swaying with each push of the ocean. Beyond it laid the island and, past the sandy beach, Wyatt could see the tops of what appeared to be a large city. But, after what Fernando had told him of where they were, he wasn't eager to check the place out.

Not that he had a choice.

"Everybody get to walking," Fernando called out from behind them. Supper was at Fernando's side, although he didn't seem happy that Wyatt was chained up, which made Wyatt feel a slight victory. At least his buddy was still loyal to him.

All of the prisoners did as they were told. The chains rattled between them all as they walked the narrow wooden gangplank between the ship and the dock. Wyatt pushed his brother as Seth held the chain up so it didn't drag on the ground between them. The last thing they needed was for it to get caught in his wheels and have them topple off the side, bringing the rest of them overboard into the ocean. As much as he didn't want to find out how bad the island was, he also would rather not drown.

They made their way off the docks and set foot on the solid ground. The first thing that Wyatt saw was a giant statue of Jesus. He held his arms up to the air as if he was calling out to God himself.

Except this Jesus had been defaced.

Other than the random graffiti that was sprayed all over him, and what looked like dried blood splashed about, someone had taken a chisel to his hands. The digits were broken off, and instead of holding his hands out, welcoming God and whoever else, he held up two middle fingers. It might have been clever if it wasn't so jarring and offensive, but Wyatt supposed that was the point.

As they crested a small hill that led to town, Wyatt saw how filthy the area was. Trash was strewn everywhere like the entire place served as one huge garbage dump. He had to be careful where he stepped so as not to have his foot land on a broken bottle or rusted-out chunk of metal. It was obvious there was no care for the environment here, which was ironic considering what was happening in the northern hemisphere.

"It's worse than a third world country," Seth whispered.

That was an oddly true realization. In the north, they were starving and freezing, barely able to scrape by. Most places were deserted, crops couldn't grow, animals had died off, and people were dying everywhere. And half the survivors they did meet were cannibals who only wanted to kill and eat them.

Now, here they were. A place of light and bountiful goods. But it was soiled, apparently by people who didn't understand how lucky they were.

"It's much worse," Fernando said, past them, continuing up the line of shackled people.

They followed him down the alleys leading to wherever the hell it was they were going. People in the streets gawked and leered. Some of them grabbed with lecherous hands. One caught Wyatt by the groin, the man's fingers fondling his genitals. Wyatt tried to kick him away but his tether prevented doing so and the groper brayed a laugh and gave his balls a hard squeeze.

The chain gang continued on, dragging Wyatt away with them as he suffered through the throbbing ache.

Others watched them, hooting and jeering. They sucked liquor from bottles, spilling much of it down their unwashed clothes. One man, who looked to be about a hundred years old, pushed a brown carafe at Seth.

"Drink, lisiado!" the old man crowed. "Drink!" He poured alcohol into Seth's mouth and Seth drank.

Then, he spit it back up.

"It tastes like piss!" he shouted. Spitting repeatedly to cleanse his pallet.

The old man did a monkey-ish dance, waving the bottle in drunken celebration.

"It probably was," Wyatt said.

As they continued, they came across drunks passed out on sidewalks and in the streets - some they had to climb over. There were drug addicts too. A couple smoking something off a piece of foil, a man stumbling about with a needle dangling from the crook of his arm. And another that looked dead, a pill bottle still clutched in his hand. Judging by his gray flesh, he'd been lying there a long while and no one bothered to move the body.

The world continued to move on. One dead junkie was not going to stop anyone here from doing whatever they pleased.

The smell of the place wasn't as bad as the room where Wyatt and the others had been kept prisoner, but it was close. Rotting food mixed with vomit and bodily fluids. Rats the size of small dogs scurried about, enjoying their all they can eat buffet.

They turned the corner, moving further into the city. There were no more drunks or druggies there, but this section of town offered a different kind of nastiness. Dozens of prostitutes, equal numbers men and women, lined the streets, cooing toward the pirates and beckoning them with flashes of breasts and cocks.

One of the women sauntered up to Henry and ran long, delicate fingers through his coarse chest hair. Henry seemed to be enjoying it until Fernando shouted something in Spanish, then he moved on.

"Buy one get one free," shouted one of the women to the pirates.

Seth eyed her up and Wyatt saw his little brother grin. She looked vaguely similar to Rosario, Seth's murdered lover.

Only this woman looked at the boy in the wheelchair with disgust. "Fuck off, perdedor!"

Seth lost his smile. "What was that about?"

Wyatt shrugged. "Probably 'cause of these," he said, holding up his chains.

Most of the prostitutes sported sores and growths that oozed disease. Wyatt saw one that seemed like she was either new at hooking, or had struck the lottery on not catching anything. Then she turned around and he saw she was pregnant. Very pregnant. Her neck had a mustard-colored rash that looked rough as sandpaper and Wyatt quickly averted his eyes.

As they made it down the street, there was a man standing in front of a woman. She was on her knees, her head bobbing back and forth. The man held his head back, blissful as she serviced him. There was no shame from either of them. Wyatt glanced to the side and made accidental eye contact with the woman. She looked back with a thousand-yard stare.

He wondered if she was earning money by choice, or if she'd come to her position in life the same way that Wyatt found himself in his.

Finally, they made it past the alley where the bulk of the hookers did business. Wyatt was relieved to be out of that place, finding it more tragic and depressing than arousing.

They marched through what looked like a normal, albeit dirty and cluttered, market where vendors lined up selling different foods. There were carts with fresh-caught fish and others with different fruits and vegetables. There were even multiple carts filled with fresh meat - everything from chicken to steaks to bacon.

No wonder the pirates had laughed at Wyatt when he thought they were going to eat his dog.

Wyatt spotted a vendor selling a variety of fruits. Bananas, oranges, apples. It had been so long since he'd had fruit not from a can that he was tempted to swipe something.

The glistening, red skin of an apple called to him and his hand darted toward the cart, only to be swatted away by a pirate's sword. The blade grazed the back of his hand, and he knew it would be worse if he tried anything like that again.

So much for a refreshing snack.

Wyatt's stomach growled as he watched a hulking, muscular man stride toward the fruit vendor. Accompanying him was a smaller fellow with a stingy mustache, one that dangled past his upper lip like a spider's legs. The two approached the cart of fruit, conversing between themselves, then, the plus-sized man put both of his hands on the edge of the cart and leaned in to examine the merchandise.

The vendor looked at the hands planted on his cart and, before Wyatt even knew what was happening, the fruit seller had lashed out with a machete. His swing was harder and more purposeful than what Wyatt had received from the pirate, and it resulted in the big man's right hand being severed from his forearm.

The man lifted his arm and grabbed at his wrist. Blood spurted from his new stump, pumping into the air as he screamed. It reminded Wyatt of Alexander's grisly fate.

The big man dropped to his knees, bellowing in pain as he tried to cover his gushing wound with his shirt. To Wyatt though, the worst part of it all was the mustachioed friend. Rather than coming to his wounded pal's defense, the man only laughed, pointed at the stump, and muttered something unintelligible.

The vendor put the machete away, smiling.

Wyatt was immediately thankful that the pirate had swatted his hand away lest he meet the same fate.

Here, the world continued on. People died in the streets. People had their hands cut off. Their friends laughed at them, and no one cared.

If that was what happened to the people who were free, what was going to happen to him and Seth?

18

After seeing what the city had to offer, Wyatt and his other compadres made their way to a group of warehouses. The sun hit the metal roofs and sent a glare into Wyatt's eyes. He squinted through the blinding light, still getting accustomed to a land not sheathed in darkness.

A large garage door was open to one of the many gray, featureless buildings and they stopped in front of it. Fernando went to the other pirates who had marched alongside them.

"Unlock them," Fernando ordered.

Once freed of his restraints, Wyatt rubbed his flesh where the heavy metal had etched grooves into his skin. Freedom felt wonderful, but he had a feeling it would be short-lived.

"Everyone listen good," Fernando said loudly. "You're going to be told once where to go. If you do not obey, there will be consequences."

Wyatt opened his mouth, ready to ask a question, but Fernando pointed to him.

"I know this isn't what you were expecting when you left wherever you were from. But you'd better get used to it. This is your life now. It may be unfair. You may not deserve it. But nobody promised you fair," Fernando said. "Just be grateful you're alive."

Wyatt kept his mouth shut, but he wasn't about to accept a fate that kept him in chains. He knew a chance would come along, the sooner the better.

He was nudged in the back to get walking. He did and they filed into a massive line at the garage door. There, he made small steps every few seconds, pushing his brother with him as the line plodded forward.

He spied Supper with Fernando. Although the dog was healthier than ever, his ears were tight to his head and his tail hung low and unmoving. As if even the dog knew this was a bad place. Seeing Supper look so dejected made Wyatt feel even worse.

After half an hour they neared the front of the line. A woman who looked young, possibly around Wyatt's age, was told to move to the right of the room. She did. Then the man behind her was sent to the left. To each side stood empty cages that looked fit for an elephant.

Wyatt felt his stomach tighten. The uncertainty of what was going to happen, and happen soon, had him ready to jump out of his own skin. As his eyes met Seth's he saw the same look of apprehension on his brother's face.

"You okay, Seth?" Wyatt asked.

Seth nodded but didn't say anything, a sure sign he was scared. And Wyatt wanted to take any chance possible to keep him safe. So, he quickly slid around his brother's wheelchair and took his place as the next in line.

The man directing the captives eyed up Wyatt with a cursory glance. His lips were thin and chapped, revealing teeth that looked as if they'd never met a toothbrush.

"To the left," he said.

Wyatt looked back at Seth and gave what he hoped was a reassuring wink. He stepped to the left, moving with the speed of a slug so as not to put much distance between the two of them.

The man crouched down so his face was level with Seth's. He grabbed Seth's lone foot and wrenched it sideways. As it had no feeling, Seth never even flinched.

The man directing traffic gave a chuckle, shaking his head. "To the right," he said, then looked to Fernando. "You fuckers are crazy."

Fernando grinned, but Wyatt didn't see the humor. He needed Seth to stay with him. Besides, the line was being divided up by gender. Men to the left. Women to the right. Sure, there was a woman or two to the left, but there was something different about them. The women in his group were bigger, more fit. They looked like athletes.

With a sickening dread, Wyatt realized they weren't being sorted by gender after all.

"He has to stay with me," Wyatt said.

Henry, the nearest of the pirates, immediately hit him across the face with a hard, closed fist. Wyatt took the punch, biting back the pain. He looked past Henry, to the man calling the shots.

"He's my brother," Wyatt said, keeping his voice firm.

The man shrugged his shoulders and gave a tired sigh. "I don't give a shit. Workers to the left. Holes to the right."

"Holes?" Seth said loudly. "What the fuck are you talking about?"

Henry abandoned Wyatt, grabbing the handles to Seth's chair and lurching him to the left. But he didn't make it a yard before Seth lunged toward the shot caller, snatching a dagger from the man's waistband.

Before anyone could react, Seth thrust the dagger over his shoulder where it plunged into Henry's face. His eyeball burst in a splash of blood and vitreous fluid then was ripped from the socket as Seth yanked the dagger free. Chunks of it clung to the blade as Henry stumbled backward, fell, his body twitching on the floor.

A few pirates pulled their swords in response. Seth deftly spun his chair around and thrashed out, holding them at bay.

Seth's face was feral, frenzied, and Wyatt half-expected his brother to take on all of them at once, but he wasn't going to let that happen. Seth wasn't going to fight alone. He stepped to join in the fray when--

Fernando wrapped an arm around his neck, holding him firmly but not choking him.

"Your brother's on his own in this one," he said in his ear.

The shot-caller grabbed Seth from behind and pulled his arms back. He struggled, but the man had leverage.

One of the pirates came in close enough to grab the dagger from his hand, but not before Seth twisted the blade and carved a deep gash into the man's forearm. The pirate responded by swatting Seth across the mouth with his bleeding paw, leaving behind a streak of dripping, crimson war paint on the boy's face.

"Leave him," Fernando ordered before his men could do anything else to Seth. "We don't get paid if he's dead."

"He killed Henry!" one of the pirates whined.

Fernando's eyes narrowed as he considered it. "Okay. One hit each."

The pirates each took a turn punching Seth in the face. Four punches in all. Seth took them in stride, gritting his teeth, never coming close to crying or showing pain. He spat a wad of blood out when they were finished.

"The cripple has some cojones," the shot caller said with a respectful smile. "I like it. Put him with the workers after all."

The other pirates grabbed their dead friend and dragged him out the garage door while Seth wheeled himself to Wyatt's side of the crowd. There, more men pushed the brothers and the other fighters into the waiting cage. The door clanged shut behind them, then locked.

As he peered through the bars, Wyatt thought they were no better than animals. Waiting for whatever was going to happen next. Waiting for their commands.

Waiting and helpless.

19

They were given no orders, no directions, but each so-called worker was provided with an ample portion of food. Oatmeal and a piece of fruit far past its sell-by date. Still, Wyatt wasn't complaining. He doubted he'd ever complain about food again.

That night, just as a few of them had begun to fall asleep, the garage door clanged open and revealed a crowd of onlookers gathered outside.

Amongst them, Wyatt spotted Fernando and Elon, but none of the other pirates. Everyone outside the warehouse seemed different in a way that took him a few moments to process. They didn't look like hookers and drug addicts. Not thieves and vendors.

They looked like rich people. Fine, clean clothes draped their bodies. Many wore outlandish jewelry, thick gold necklaces and bracelets. Some carried suitcases, others designer bags. Wyatt had a moment to think that his mother would have loved one of those bags before Elon's voice boomed out.

"Alright everyone, you know the rules. We'll start with the big money items. No refunds. Everything sold as-is. Caveat emptor."

Big money items? No refunds?

It finally clicked for Wyatt and he realized they were going to be sold. But it was more than just sold, they were going to be auctioned off to the highest bidders.

His mind immediately went to a swift talking man with a gavel, but there would be no such theatrics. Elon stood in the expanse of the doorway, prepared to lead the auction himself. Wyatt smiled as he saw Supper with him, still being taken care of.

"Bring the rest in!" Elon yelled.

Wyatt waited for them to open the cages, but nobody did. Instead, he watched workers wheel other cages, these full of animals into the warehouse. There were cows, pigs. Then more exotic fare. Tigers. An alligator. Even a tank filled with exotic fish.

They were going to start selling the animals first? That was the big money?

Wyatt wondered what human life was worth to anyone at that point.

Fernando brought out each animal, one by one. It was agonizingly slow and there was nothing for the captives to do but sit and watch as the animals were sold to various bidders. The cows brought in huge numbers. One exceptionally hefty heifer went for ten thousand. Dollars? Wyatt wasn't sure what the currency was in this strange, horrible place. Or why anyone wanted money in a world on its last legs.

But they did. There was a society set up. There was a civilization or an attempt at one.

Once all of the animals were sold, the holes went next. They sold for far less than the livestock, but several of the bidders seemed delighted with their haul.

And then they were up. Elon waved at the last cage, grinning wildly.

"I hope everyone is ready for the workers now!"

There was nothing but a small grumble. Many of the bidders had left already and it seemed the remaining crowd wasn't as enthusiastic as Elon had hoped.

"Open the cage. Everyone out. Line up, side by side in front," Fernando commanded.

The cage was unlocked and opened. Armed guards were everywhere, so there was no chance of running and they all knew it. Instead, they did as they were told. Wyatt grabbed Seth's chair and pushed him so they were all lined up, just as commanded.

Wyatt looked around at his fellow captives and thought it was a pathetic-looking bunch. And the faces in the crowd seemed to indicate they shared his low opinion.

"Should we start the bidding? Maybe two hundred," Elon said, pointing to the first captive in the line. That man was in his thirties, broad-chested, but almost emaciated.

A portly man with a wild mass of facial hair raised his stubby index finger.

Fernando quickly pointed to him nodding. "Good, good. Two hundred to Monger. Who wants to go three?"

Nobody raised their hand.

"Two fifty?" Elon asked to no takers. "Alright. Sold to Monger. Two hundred."

Wyatt watched as the man at the end of the line was ushered to his buyer who hurriedly bound the hands of his new purchase with rope.

"Maybe what we need is a little demonstration," Elon said.

He walked to Wyatt and grabbed him by the arm. He set him out in the open space of the warehouse and whispered in his ear. "Sorry to do this to you kid, but I gotta make a big sale."

What the hell was that supposed to mean, Wyatt thought.

Then it came together for him. Fernando pointed to another man, the biggest guy in the bunch. Tall and thick with the build of a lumberjack.

"Go at him," Fernando ordered.

"You want me to fight *him*?" Wyatt asked.

"It's not to the death. Just put on a show for the crowd. Give them a reason to get excited," Fernando said.

Wyatt looked up to the lumberjack who appeared more than ready for a battle. Fernando tossed two broom handles to the ground between them.

"Grab your weapons," Elon said.

The big guy grabbed his, but Wyatt hesitated, unsure. Was this really what his life had become?

"We don't have to do this, man," Wyatt said to the lumberjack. "If we don't fight, they can't—"

The lumberjack swung his stick and nailed Wyatt in the cheek, flaying open his skin. So much for playing peacemaker.

"Oh come on!" a woman shouted from the crowd. "The boy has no spirit. We want to see a real show. Put him against Uno," she continued.

Fernando shook his head. "There's no competition against Uno."

Wyatt paid no attention to them. He had a much bigger problem to deal with.

He dove for his own broom handle, catching it in a rolling tumble. The lumberjack swung again but Wyatt rolled out the way a second before the stick slammed into the concrete floor, breaking it in two.

The remaining piece was jagged and sharp. A spear instead of a blunt object.

Wyatt bounced to his feet, sidestepping in a circle like he's seen boxers do in the ring but never expected to have to do himself in real life. Not when it mattered.

They moved in sync almost like a strange, tribal dance. It went on for a good thirty seconds and the crowd grumbled with bored displeasure. Wyatt risked a glance toward Elon, hoping he'd call this off now that it wasn't going as he'd hoped, when--

"Wyatt look out," Seth shouted.

His head snapped back in time to see the lumberjack barreling toward him, his new spear at gut-puncturing level.

Wyatt jumped sideways, like a matador dodging a charging bull. He felt the air break as the mass passed him by.

The lumberjack was all brawn, no brains. And Wyatt realized he had to fight back to end this.

As the big man tried to stop his forward momentum and rotate back to the fight, Wyatt was on him. He slammed his broom handle into the back of the lumberjack's thigh, a blow that rocked the man and dropped him to his knees.

He pushed his hands into the floor, trying to regain his footing, but Wyatt was quicker. He brought the handle over the big man's head, then pulled it tight against his throat. He let all of his body weight drag him down, resulting in a sick, choking noise from the lumberjack.

Wyatt kept pulling, harder and harder. But the man flexed his neck, making the muscles and tendons pop, creating a nearly impossible force to compete against. But Wyatt tried.

Then, before Wyatt realized what was happening, the lumberjack threw himself backward and took Wyatt with him.

With a pained groan, they hit the floor. Wyatt's back slamming into the concrete while all of the huge fighter's weight fell atop him. The pain was so sudden that Wyatt wondered if something inside himself had ruptured, but he refused to let go of his broom handle, which was still against the lumberjack's throat.

Then the man sat up and used the weight of his body and flung himself forward. Wyatt somersaulted over the man's head, landing flat on his back for a second time. And losing his stick in the process. He stared up at the brute, his neck black and blue from Wyatt's attack.

The lumberjack slammed his fist into Wyatt's nose, exploding it in a sea of red. Wyatt grabbed his face, hot blood coursing through his fingers. The brute grinned down at Wyatt and walked away.

Wyatt rolled onto his side, blood gushing from his broken nose, and then onto his knees. He forced himself to his feet even though his head was swimming. He felt Seth's hands on his waist and was relieved for the added support.

"Wyatt, are you okay? Wyatt?" Seth asked, his voice sounding high and childlike for the first time in years.

"I'll live," Wyatt said.

"Alright, looks like someone has earned a little extra attention, haven't they?" Elon asked the buyers.

Wyatt looked to them and saw a little more interest in their previously dull eyes. They stared at the lumberjack with admiration.

Nobody said the fight's over, asshole, Wyatt thought.

As bidding began, no one saw him grab his stick from the ground. All of the focus was on the brute who'd just kicked his ass. And Wyatt wanted to change that.

He screamed as loud as he could, the sound echoing through the metal building. All eyes went to him - the buyers, the guards, the prisoners, and the lumberjack.

Wyatt charged, his stick raised in the air. The guards rushed forward, ready to intervene, but they couldn't catch Wyatt in time. He kept his focus on the brute, watching his face twist into confusion, then realization. He tried to react.

But he was too late.

Wyatt struck the lumberjack hard across the temple and it was like a switch flicked off. His body went rigid, then limp.

Everyone watched the huge, muscular man fall over, slamming into the concrete. He was out cold. Fernando rushed in, hurriedly checking for a pulse. Five seconds later he smiled and Wyatt was able to relax. He had maimed the man but hadn't killed him.

The guards were at Wyatt, ready to grab him, but Elon put up a hand. Wyatt stood there, looking down at the opponent that he had just bested. He felt like an animal. He was covered in blood, his heart racing, blood frothing from his mouth.

"Five thousand," the woman's voice called out, shattering the silence of the room.

Elon snapped into money mode again. "Five thousand?!" he said loudly. "Is there anyone else?"

"If there is, they'd better be ready to face Uno right here, right now," she said.

Murmurs and grumbles came from the crowd. Wyatt strained to locate the woman who'd just bid on him.

And he found her.

She was exquisite, with coal-black hair pulled into a loose ponytail, bronze skin, and emerald eyes. Tall and fit, she made him think of an Amazon warrior and her steely gaze gave him no reason to believe she wasn't willing to kill anyone that annoyed her.

Behind her was a man that was even taller and more muscular than the lumberjack Wyatt had just fought. He looked like he was sculpted out of stone and Wyatt guessed he was the Uno person the woman kept referring to because nobody dared to make eye contact with him. Or maybe that was because the man had only one eye. Where the other should be laid a deep cavity, scarred with purple flesh that glistened in the light.

"Sale to Rainha," Elon said. "Although, next time, let some other play too, okay?"

Rainha, Wyatt's new owner, stared at Elon and the man's perfect smile faded to nothingness.

"I don't play," Rainha said. "I only win."

Elon swallowed hard but didn't respond otherwise.

Wyatt still stood there, his labored breathing heaving his shoulders up and down. Up and down.

"Come to me," Rainha said to Wyatt.

Wyatt examined her, then turned to Elon. The man shoved him away, but Fernando came to him, leading him toward the bidders.

"You go with Rainha and do not misbehave, for your sake. Good luck, amigo" Fernando whispered to him and sent him on his way.

She grabbed Wyatt's shoulders and looked him up and down. She was a few inches taller and ran her strong hands over his body, feeling his build, his muscles, such as they were. "Good, I can work with this," she said.

Then she lowered her hand and grabbed his cock. Wyatt jumped back in surprise, but Rainha only smiled. "I can work with that, too."

Wyatt decided it was best not to say anything and stood between the woman and Uno as the auction went on. He watched his fellow captives be bought and sold, few breaking even one thousand. Even the lumberjack only went for twelve hundred.

Wyatt hated to admit it, but he was proud of being the most valuable.

Finally, Seth was up.

"We have something a little different now. We saved him for last because we know he has many different uses," Elon said. "Should we start at a hundred?"

Nobody said anything and Wyatt knew his brother would be devastated if no one wanted him. Instead of bidding, the remaining buyers ebbed away, with no interest in buying the boy in the wheelchair.

"Let's go," Rainha said, turning to Uno.

"Wait, what about him?" Wyatt said, pointing to Seth.

"Bite your tongue," Uno said, striking Wyatt across the face, battering his still throbbing nose. Uno hit a lot harder than the lumberjack. Another one of those punches and Wyatt didn't think he'd still be standing.

Rainha gave Wyatt a pitying smile. "I've got no use for anything like that."

"He killed one of our men," Fernando said, grasping at straws. "He's a real fighter."

Wyatt widened his eyes and nodded. He didn't want to say anything else and risk being hit that hard again, but he wasn't ready to just give up on his brother.

"How about fifty?" Elon asked.

Rainha laughed. "I wipe my ass with more than that."

"Why not have your own slave to wipe your ass instead," Elon said.

Anything to make the sale, Wyatt thought. And he hoped it worked.

She considered for a moment then looked down at Supper who sat next to Fernando, the dog almost frowning. "You throw in the dog?"

Elon glanced down at Supper whose ears had perked up. He nodded. "Deal."

20

Wyatt, Seth, and the other slave Rainha had bought were marched toward a mansion that sat high on a hillside above the town. Although, if pressed, Wyatt would have described it more as a compound than living quarters. It was concrete, utilitarian, and void of all character. It looked futuristic and ancient simultaneously.

But the slaves weren't taken to the mansion. Their journey brought them to the bottom of the hill where Uno unlatched a locked gate. He swung it open, revealing a sprawling field and, although there were no lines marking out the sections, Wyatt was certain it had been a soccer field in an earlier life. A fence, topped in barbed wire spanned the perimeter, and a low, droning hum signaled that it was electrified.

Wyatt was still adjusting to a land where the sun not only shone and food was plentiful, but where cars still ran and electricity still existed. It disgusted him that people with such bounties had still descended into a primitive, cruel lifestyle.

He felt Seth tugging at his pants and glanced down. He didn't have to be a lip reader to get the question.

What the fuck?

He shrugged, every bit as clueless as his younger brother.

Behind them, the gate slammed shut, the noise so loud that, coupled with the uncertainty, Wyatt flinched.

That made the other slaves, a thick, brutish man with a scraggly goatee stretching to his exposed nipples, laugh.

Wyatt considered speaking up and asserting himself, but Uno stepped in before he could. He backhanded the laugher across the mouth, wiping the grin off his homely face. Not laughing now, the man spit two broken teeth into the dirt, but even he knew better than to fight back.

A few dozen men emerged from stables. All were scarred and bruised, muscular and fit. They were Rainha's other slaves and they came to inspect the new purchases.

A group of four guards, all armed with automatic rifles and clad in green and brown camouflage fatigues, joined the party and, when they neared Rainha, bowed. She responded with a curt nod and breezed past them, continuing on to midfield where she stopped and turned to her newest toys.

"If you have not realized it yet, you belong to me now. I own you and you will do as I please."

The day had been exhausting and as much as Wyatt wanted to learn more about their new station, he also wanted to sit, to sleep. He struggled to keep attention on her words.

"This is Uno," she said pointing to the man with one eye. "He is going to train you."

"Train us to do what?" Seth's voice interrupted.

One of the guards stepped toward him, but Rainha stopped that with a glare.

"Questions are natural," she said. "I understand this is all new to you so I'll elaborate."

Rainha spun with her arms outstretched, like a model on a game show revealing a coveted prize. "This is my training ground." She looked at each of the new slaves, holding eye contact for a long moment before moving to the next. "Where you will be transformed from men into warriors."

She stepped toward the men, close enough to touch. Wyatt could smell a fruity, delicate aroma wafting from her body. Perfume. And despite the situation, he felt his skin prickle with goosebumps as she stood before him.

"You have potential," she said, seeming to direct the words at Wyatt alone, but then she was on to the next man and Wyatt suddenly felt less special.

"But you'll need training. Battling isn't the same as brawling in the streets. It's an art. And you must study to succeed."

She stepped to Uno, wrapping one hand around his oversized bicep. "Uno is the undefeated champion. He will be your instructor and I expect you to learn from him."

Rainha simmered with excitement as she continued. "Every weekend there are battles. That gives you five days to prepare for your first. And, know now, that I will not tolerate anything but your best. When the battles begin, you don't stop until I permit it. Those who win will be rewarded. Those who don't will not like the consequences."

Wyatt swallowed hard, the idea of rest now far away. Did she mean he was supposed to be some sort of gladiator now? What was this, Thunderdome?

"Bend over and I'll give you a reward," the man with the scraggly goatee called out to her. A few laughs followed it, and even a wolf-whistle.

Rainha was stunning, albeit in an unconventional way, but she also exuded a *Don't fuck with me* aura that any sane man could see a mile away. She wasn't the type of woman who took kindly to catcalls, but apparently, there was no shortage of idiots in this world.

She surprised Wyatt by laughing loudly. "I love the cajones. I really do. And, believe me, some of you may be lucky enough for me to show an interest." She winked at Wyatt whose mouth went dry as a desert.

"I didn't see who the caller was though. Who felt the need to speak with their cocks at this moment?"

Nobody said a word.

"Now you turn shy? Just moments ago you were rock hard, wanting to fuck me. And now? Did your pecker tuck his little turtle head back in his shell?"

Awkward giggles came from some of the men. Seth and Wyatt kept their mouths shut.

"Okay, tell you what Don Juan, you step forward and fight me. If you win, I will take off my clothes right here and let you have your way with me. And when you're finished, you're a free man." There was no mistaking her confidence. Her words didn't waver at all.

"You'll just have your giant lap dog step in and save you," the goateed man said.

She smirked. "I don't need any man to save me." She turned to Uno "No matter what happens, you stay out of it. You understand?"

Uno nodded with a grunt.

"Now then. You were saying?" she asked.

The man pushed past Wyatt to get at her, muttering, "Get ready to watch a real fight, asshole," as he did.

Wyatt was already making friends. Great.

Rainha looked her challenger up and down. He was roped in lean muscle and looked like someone willing, hell, eager, to fight dirty. That matched his appearance and odor as he looked and smelled like he hadn't bathed in a year.

"You're the man with the big mouth? I'm surprised your words can get through that weasel's nest on your face."

That made the slaves, even Wyatt, laugh.

"What's your name?" she asked.

"Javier."

"Good. I like to know a man's name before I kill him. It makes it more memorable."

Not dissuaded in the least, Javier grinned, revealing teeth stained shit-brown. "You've got a lot of strong talk in you, bitch."

"That's not all. Trust me," Rainha said. Then she signaled for Uno to kick things off. He did so by tossing a sword in the middle of the field between them, but closer to the man. The blade sunk a foot into the ground as he landed.

"What's this?" Javier asked.

"Your weapon. I assume you want one, though you're probably not used to handling something so big," Rainha said.

Javier snatched the sword from the dirt, clutching it in both hands. "Nothing for you?"

"I'll take it from you when you're finished with it," she said.

He narrowed his eyes and charged at her. He was sloppy with nonexistent sword skills and Rainha used that to her advantage. Wyatt watched her closely and saw her gaze locked on her opponent's eyes rather than his weapon. He was giving her every advantage she needed just by where he looked.

She dodged each swing as if it was a choreographed dance. He would swing right, and she'd step left. He would slice high and she'd duck low. After a few moments of that, with each bob and weave, she began to step closer and closer to him.

Javier was already tired and Wyatt could see it. Sweat flew off his forehead with each increasingly weaker swipe of the sword. And worse, he was becoming frustrated. His face reddened and he narrowed his eyes.

"Stay still you punta," he said.

Then she was right in front of him. His last swing had gone wide and she grabbed onto his arm, wrenching it back, bending the elbow at an angle it wasn't meant to bend. Then Rainha threw her forehead into Javier's face which exploded in a shower of blood.

The sword fell from his hand but she didn't want it - yet. Instead, she brought her knee into his cajones, garnering a pained squawk. Then she yanked his arm, which had gone limp as an overcooked noodle again. That time he cried in pain, his eyes squirting tears and his mouth twisting in misery. He stumbled backward a step, fell onto his ass, then momentum carried him onto his back.

Now, Rainha grabbed the sword. In one effortless motion, she plunged it through Javier's sternum, the blade passing all the way through his body and planting itself in the ground. Blood bubbled from the dying man's lips, intermingled with the matted fur on his face, and ebbed down his cheek as he stared up at the woman who'd just ended his life.

Rainha stood over his dying body and kicked his face to the side so that he looked at the other slaves as he took his last breaths.

She wasn't even winded. "Do not mistake my words. There are only two ways out of here. You challenge your way out and win. Which Javier did not. Or you die and are left to rot. Which he did, and will."

21

Wyatt was exhausted and sore from long days of training. Uno was a sadist who didn't speak more than necessary, but the man knew how to run an operation. Wyatt imagined this program was like boot camp on steroids where the only rule was to keep going or die.

Great motivation, Wyatt thought.

He peered toward the field where Javier, the man Rainha had slaughtered, still laid on the ground. The corpse was already bloated to the point where it looked more like a blow-up doll version of a man than the real thing. Flies dive-bombed, laid eggs and feasted on the graying mass and it wouldn't be long before it burst, spilling millions of maggots into the dirt. It was there as a reminder of what would happen if they disobeyed.

The sun had set, but the moon hung full in the sky and Wyatt watched as Uno pummeled a wooden dummy posted in the ground. The man was hulking, but also possessed fast fists that landed like cannonballs.

The man never seemed to lose his stamina, a far cry from the others who either sat or laid in the dirt, too tied to even crawl to the stables where their beds of moldy straw awaited.

Some of the men were snoring, claimed by sleep. As beat as Wyatt was, he couldn't imagine resting and knew a long night awaited.

He was anxious because they had been informed that their first battles would be the following day. And these weren't boxing matches where the loser went on to fight another day. These battles were to the death.

As Uno told it, they'd be battling other slaves with most of the town watching, cheering, and jeering away. It seemed impossible that humanity had fallen so far so fast. The world was a nightmare that would never end. At least until he died.

"Seth, you awake?" Wyatt whispered to his brother.

Seth had his eyes closed and hands folded behind his head as he laid on the ground. Wyatt watched him turn his head. "Yeah. Too wired to sleep. I feel like I drank four pots of coffee. You think you'll get any z's?"

"I doubt it."

Without a beat, Seth asked, "You think we'll die tomorrow, brother?"

So caught up in his own training and adjusting to this awful new normal, Wyatt hadn't even thought about the battles from Seth's perspective. About how much harder it was going to be for him. "No," Wyatt finally answered.

"I do," Seth said. "I mean, I know we can fight. We've done it before. But that was all life and death shit. We were killing bad people. Tomorrow, we're going to be fighting guys in the same fucked up situation as us. They didn't do anything wrong. They didn't attack us or hurt our family. They've just got bad luck."

"Seth, you can't think like that."

"Why?" Seth asked. "It's the truth."

It was.

"You're focusing on the wrong thing," Wyatt said. "We need to figure out how to get out of here. Out of this prison. Off this island."

Seth rolled onto his belly and propped himself up on his elbows. "How are we gonna do that? The fence is topped with barbed wire and is electrified. And those guards carry uzi's or something and you know they're just itching to go all Tony Montana with them."

"We'll figure it out. It's just going to take time."

Seth chewed his bottom lip. "Time's not exactly on our side, brother. Tomorrow, we have to fight. We have to kill someone, or die."

Wyatt considered it. His brother was right. He was looking at the big picture when he needed to prepare for the immediate future. If they died in the arena, then all the hope of escaping wouldn't matter anyway.

He wondered if it would be possible to convince the other slaves to refuse to fight. If they banded together, what choice would Rainha have other than to acquiesce to their demands?

The men were rough and crude, not a civilized fellow among the bunch. It would be a Herculean effort to win them all over, but Wyatt had faith that they could do it because the alternative was unimaginable.

"How close are you to the others?" Wyatt asked Seth.

"I know their names, but I won't be sending birthday cards if that's what you're getting at," Seth said.

"But you talk to them?"

Seth nodded. "Sure. It's what I'm good at."

"Then tonight, when we're bedded down, you need to tell them that we're not fighting tomorrow. We just need to buy some time, then we can find a way out."

He watched skepticism cloud his brother's face and was ready to continue on with his barely formed plan when--

"You fucking idiots," a voice muttered.

Wyatt turned his head toward the nearby stables where a trio of men sat in the dirt and played poker with a tattered pile of cards.

None of the men paid any attention to Wyatt or Seth.

"Are you talkin' to me?" Wyatt asked. He wasn't interested in a fight with anyone, but he wasn't the same docile kid that left Maine, scared of his own shadow. He had been through enough that he would say his peace if he so desired.

"Fuck yeah, I'm talking to you," one of the men said, finally turning his way. In doing so he revealed his deformity. He had no nose. It had been bitten or sliced off in some previous battle. In its place was a chunk of wood, whittled into a vaguely nose-like shape. It was held in place by a strap of leather that circled around his skull.

"What's your problem?" Wyatt asked.

The man stood, so tall his head almost hit the stable ceiling. "You two gringos aren't as smart as you think you are. Maybe you can get one or two fools to join your little escape party, but it ain't gonna get you anywhere."

"What do you know about it?" Wyatt asked, climbing to his feet and stepping toward the stable.

"Pino, save your air," another of the poker players said. "He'll be dead before it matters."

"Pino?" Wyatt asked.

The man grinned. "Short for Pinocchio. I lie a lot," he said sarcastically, his voice nasally and thick. "I'm just warning you kid. You won't make any friends in here if you get them all killed with your fantasies of escape."

"Why are you so convinced it won't work?"

"Look around," Pino said. "There's no way out. This place is locked down tighter than a nun's snatch. And let's say you do manage to get out. Where the fuck are you gonna go? We're on an island."

Seth had climbed into his chair and wheeled himself behind Wyatt. "Anywhere's better than this shithole," Seth said.

That made Pino and the others laugh.

In between hearty guffaws, Pino managed, "If you believe that, you haven't been many places."

"You'd rather live like this?" Wyatt asked in disbelief. "Forced to be a murderer for some sick bitch's enjoyment?"

Their laughter ended when he insulted Rainha. The men made Wyatt feel like a cocky, blowhard kid without a clue. But he knew he was right.

"Bite your tongue lest you lose it," Pino said. "Rainha takes care of us. She feeds us. She rewards us. Maybe it's not the same as what you grew up with, but you have it better than most on the island and that's all because of Rainha."

"How so?" Seth asked, wheeling toward their game.

"She's the one who keeps this place in line. Without her rule, it would be chaos, robbery, murder. There would be no consequences. Rainha keeps people from turning into animals."

Wyatt was shocked at how much respect Pinocchio had for Rainha. It was almost like he admired her. He began to wonder how long he had been her fighter. Was he suffering from Stockholm Syndrome? Were all of them?

"You act like she's a queen," Wyatt said.

"She is," Pino said. "Or as close as we have to one." He stepped into Wyatt, so close Wyatt could smell the tarter on his teeth. "Listen, boy, and take my advice. You could have it so much worse. Worse than even in your nightmares. Don't give that up because of some silly notion like freedom. Because, boy, ain't no one really free no matter where they live."

Pino sat back down, rejoining the poker game, but taking one more glance at Wyatt. "All you need to do is win fights and don't piss off Rainha. If she wants something, you make sure she gets it. She's very generous with those of us who make her proud."

"Hell yeah," one of the other players said, slapping on Pinocchio's shoulder. "Gonna get me some good, young pussy after my next win."

Pino smirked and shook his head. "As you can see, there are benefits, especially if you're a fucking pervert like Chester here."

"Just because I like them hairless don't make me a pervert. And I hate that fucking nickname," Chester said.

Pinocchio shrugged. "You get called what you are." He looked Wyatt up and down. "We'll have to come up with something for you. I heard about your fight with a big fucker at the auction. Keep that up and they'll be calling you David - the giant slayer, or something."

"That's kind of a shitty nickname," Seth said. "And *Chester?*"

"The molester," Pino said.

Wyatt wasn't interested in nicknames. He didn't want to become like Pinocchio or Chester, complacent and grateful. He was going to find a way out. He knew that this wasn't the best that his life had to offer.

"I tell you, kid. The thrill of the arena. There's nothing like it. People will cheer you on. People will chant your name. Nothing better than that. And I know that, if I die, at least my name will be remembered. It will stay on the tongues of those that watched me for years. I won't be forgotten. And that's the best we can ask for," Pino said.

Wyatt didn't want to listen anymore. He was sick of it. He thought the people at the casino that believed Papa's bullshit was crazy. This was a whole new level.

"You can make a good living here," Pinocchio finished. He looked over to Seth and looked back down. "I can't say the same for the crip, though. You made a mistake bringing your brother here. Should have let his hole get stretched. Doc's never gonna clear him and, when that happens, it's a trip to the worm farm."

And Wyatt immediately thought that Pino was right. Seth had a better chance of escaping from a brothel than he did from the compound.

Had he given his brother a death sentence?

22

The morning escaped too quickly from the night and Wyatt hadn't slept at all. Instead, his mind cycled over and over again with the words Pinocchio had spoken. That they were better off in Rainha's stables than anywhere else. That they could have a good life if they played by the rules. And most of all, that Wyatt might be okay, but Seth wouldn't.

He couldn't let any of that happen.

He couldn't forget who he was.

He couldn't just become another fighter, doing it because he was too scared to see what the world outside had to offer. He would play along as long as he had to... until the moment came where he could escape.

There was still time, though. There was the trip from the stables to the arena Uno and the experienced fighters had talked about. From what Wyatt could gather, it was over a mile away. Plenty of time, plenty of distance, to make something happen.

He mulled it over while he ate a breakfast of hard-boiled eggs and potatoes. Compared to the dreck on the ship, this was a feast. He didn't want to enjoy it, but he couldn't remember the last time his belly was so full of warm, nutritious food.

The seasoned fighters ate too. But their menu was more expansive. They had bacon, sausage, bread, and a variety of juices. And the men left not a scrap.

Wyatt knew the score. They had to prove his worth in the arena before they could get the super-sized menu. But how many more times would he have to prove himself? He thought he'd done that at the auction, but that wasn't good enough. He had to do it again.

And he had a feeling that it was only the beginning.

Once breakfast was over, a guard stepped into the stable. "New guys, line up. Gotta see the doc before you fight."

There was no point in being stubborn and making waves this soon. Having the guards on his case would mean less of an opportunity to make an escape if and when the time presented itself.

He would be a good, little slave until then.

They were directed to a room off the training ground where the most peculiar man Wyatt had seen since his old pal River waited. The doc was short, not even topping five feet, and wore huge, round glasses that made his eyes look crazed and beady. White hair grew in wild patches atop his bulbous head and, as he walked to Wyatt, he had an obvious limp.

When Wyatt's gaze drifted, he realized the doctor was missing a leg from the hip down. Flesh and bone had been replaced with a steel rod, gears, hinges. At the bottom, what looked like an industrial spatula was welded fast, serving as a foot. He looked back up at the man and was met with a grin.

"Lost it some time back. Fabricated this myself," he said, knocking the rod where his calf should be. It clanged like a coin against a bottle.

Doc hobbled to a table where a slew of tools awaited. The man's leg moved robotically and Wyatt realized it was motorized. Doc picked up an otoscope, flicking the light off and on, studying it as if he had never seen one before.

Was this guy for real?

"Just gonna take a quick look," he said.

He pushed the cone into Wyatt's ear with no regard for comfort. Then did the other ear, moving quickly.

"Can you see my brain with that thing?" Wyatt asked. But then Doc put a stethoscope to his chest, leaning in close and listening to his heart.

The Doc placed a finger against his own mouth and kept listening. When he seemed satisfied, he stood as tall as possible and looked Wyatt in the eyes through his thick Coke bottle lenses. He blinked a few times, saying nothing.

"Doc?" Wyatt asked.

The Doc finally shook his head. "Seems to be a good ticker. And no, can't see your brain. Apparently, it's gone missing."

He broke into a toothy grin, clueing Wyatt in that it was a joke.

"Wouldn't surprise me," Wyatt said.

"I expect not. Heard you took on a big oaf at the auction. Almost got your clock cleaned."

"I came out on top in the end," Wyatt said.

Doc nodded. "So you say." He set the medical instruments aside. "Alrighty then. Seems to me you'll make a fine warrior. I'm sure Rainha will appreciate you." Then he gave an exaggerated wink. "If she doesn't already."

Wyatt wasn't in the mood for innuendo and motioned to Seth behind him. "This is Seth. My little brother."

"I'm not little where it matters," Seth said, rolling toward Doc.

The Doc nodded. "Good for you."

Wyatt leaned into Doc, lowering his voice to a whisper "I, uh, heard that if he doesn't check out, he'll—"

"Be sent to the slaughter, yes. That's right."

"So, it's true. He won't even get a chance to defend himself?" Wyatt asked, feeling seconds away from barfing up his filling breakfast.

"Yes. Rainha buys those who seem to be worth something, but looks can be deceiving. She put me in charge of giving the go-ahead and deciding whether they're fit. If they aren't sick or weak, first-timers join the junior ranks. There you battle other rookies. It's a level playing field, that way." He grew visibly excited at the talk. Bouncing as he spoke like some malfunctioning children's toy.

"But I don't put anyone in those battles that wouldn't be able to handle it physically," Doc said. "Wouldn't be sporting. Besides, the crowds get annoyed."

His matter of fact tone was jarring to hear, especially with Seth in earshot. Wyatt looked to his brother who watched on, stone-faced and stoic despite it all.

"My brother needs to fight. And he can. You have to believe me." He twisted his face, trying to let Doc know he wanted him to pass him through, worthy or not.

"If he's anything like you, then that's exactly where he will go."

"And if he's not?"

The Doc cocked his head and frowned. "Then he gets put to the slaughter. I already said this. Maybe I should check your ears again."

He reached for the otoscope, but Wyatt stopped him by grabbing his wrist. "What is *the slaughter*?" Wyatt asked, not really wanting to know.

"Crowd pleasers," Doc said. "They're different every time. Usually, it's man versus animals. Lions, bears, wild dogs. Quite exciting!" Doc said, still smiling. "There's betting on those. Not as much as a real fight, but Rainha still fares well."

The idea of Seth going up against a wildcat or bear made Wyatt want to punch Doc out, grab his brother, and make a run for it. He'd rather they both die in a hail of gunfire than see Seth shredded in front of a screaming crowd of bloodthirsty onlookers.

"Doc, can't you just skip the exam and give my brother a pass? No one will know."

"Oooooh," he said, finally understanding what Wyatt wanted.

"That would be against protocol. No, no, no, no, no. Can't go against Rainha. I've made my way up to this point by doing the job the way she wants it. No exceptions."

"What do you mean, *made your way up*? Like promoted? Like this is fucking corporate America?"

Doc laughed. "I guess you could say that." He knocked on his leg. "With my knowledge and expertise, I avoided the slaughter and earned myself a vital position in the operation."

"You're a slave, too," Wyatt said. It wasn't a question, just a realization.

"Time to move on," the Doc said, pushing at Wyatt. But Wyatt only stepped past the table and waited as Doc leaned into Seth.

Doc examined him in the same way he had done Wyatt, making the same befuddled expressions and nods. Then, he finished. "Everything looks good here."

"Good," Seth said.

"But—"

Fuck, Wyatt thought.

"You plan to fight?" Doc asked Seth.

"Of course. What's it to you?" Seth asked, then squared his shoulders. That same attitude, never letting anyone talk down to him.

The Doc nodded his big noggin. "Usually, someone like yourself doesn't even make it this far." He walked around Seth's chair, mumbling to himself and fidgeting with imaginary tools. "This is fascinating."

"Welcome to my life. Just full of interesting tidbits," Seth said sarcastically.

The Doc looked up, meeting Seth's eyes. "That's just it. I've never seen someone like yourself come through here. I'd have expected you to be sold to the brothels. And that's only if they didn't simply kill you rather than bring you on board. Trust me, I've known it to happen."

Doc tapped his chin with his finger. "For the pirates to spare you, you must have made quite the impression."

"Killed one of their men," Seth said, puffing his chest up.

The Doc grinned. "I love it. I love it. How did this even happen to you?" He dropped down and began to look at Seth's stump.

"I stepped on a rusty nail. Infection traveled up my leg. Had to lop it off before it spread any further." He made a karate-chopping gesture where his leg ended.

"Interesting. That's not very likely. I mean, not being able to walk and all, but here we are. Who am I to question? I'm just a kooky doctor."

Truer words had never been muttered.

"Your brother was trying to talk me out of putting you to the slaughter."

"That's considerate of him," Seth said, glancing over to Wyatt.

"Yes, yes. But that's not his choice. It's mine. I'm in charge of directing fighters from here. When I saw you, I was quite certain you were destined for it. People would love it. Watching animals rip you apart. Blood and guts for all," the Doc rambled. "Once, they had an alligator. Must have been twenty-five feet long. What a spectacle that was..."

He blinked, getting himself back on track. "But you have an abundance of spunk and I admire that. Other than the unfortunate situation with your legs, you're in tip-top condition, so..."

Wyatt just wanted to hear it already.

"You're going with your brother."

Wyatt let his fists relax. He had dug his fingernails into his palms so hard they had cut into the skin.

"Do me a favor," the Doc said. "Don't die."

Seth looked at the Doc like he was the craziest person in the world. Wyatt didn't think he was far off. "Sure thing, Doc. Just because you asked."

The Doc smiled again. "Good, good. I've got some plans for you. Some real good plans. And remember, don't die. It would be bad for both of us if you did."

Seth nodded and wheeled past the Doc who seemed downright

exuberant. Now they didn't have to come up with a half-cocked plan. They only had to survive the arena until they could figure out what to do.

23

The men had been correct about it being a mile-long trip, but they left out the fact that the voyage wasn't made on foot. A thirty-year-old pick up truck towing a wheeled cage hauled them to the arena and all the while the would-be fighters breathed in rancid exhaust fumes.

The arena itself wasn't what he expected either.

It wasn't the grand, Roman Colosseum. Nor some ancient Mayan battleground. Instead, it was a generic sports stadium, filled with enough rows of seats to fit around a few thousand spectators. Wyatt could hear, but not see them, as he and the fellow fighters were taken in through a tunnel in the rear of the building.

From there, they were funneled to a locker room that reeked of sweat and body odor. The gray concrete floor was stained dark brown with long-dried blood. It was clear to Wyatt that this place had been used for these exact purposes for years.

Once inside the locker room, the guards unlatched their shackles. Now, they were the team, ready to literally kill the other players. And Wyatt still struggled to believe it was real.

Uno and the guards watched over the men, but Wyatt had

already realized there was no place to go, no escape. They could refuse to fight, but Wyatt had accepted that he'd never be able to convince the other fighters to join. Maybe one or two, but not the lot of them.

He was going into the battle, whether he wanted to or not.

Uno's voice snapped him out of his thoughts.

"This is Akeldama. On the field, you will have a chance to prove yourselves worthy. I envy you in your journey." Fire burned in his eyes as he spoke. He eyed Wyatt and Seth, plus two other men who had arrived a few days later. They were the rookies. "You four will fight first."

"Like a warm-up act?" Seth asked in a question no one acknowledged.

"You'll fight as a group and must work together to crush your opponents. Take what I have taught you, and do Rainha proud."

Uno opened the door that led down the hallway. The four of them walked out, nobody looking confident, except maybe Seth. The light at the end of the tunnel grew brighter as they approached it and Wyatt couldn't help but think that it was an appropriate metaphor for what he was about to face.

"I'd wish you luck, but you sorry motherfuckers will need a lot more than that!" Chester cackled from behind.

"Use the cripple as a decoy," Pino added to the laughter of the other, experienced fighters.

As the light intensified, so did the raucous noise of the crowd. Cheering, screaming, stomping. Wyatt tried to tell himself this was an ordinary sporting event. That the people would be lounging in the stands, sucking down beer, chomping on hot dogs and nachos. That they didn't want to see men kill each other at all and that they were there for nothing but a good show. But their cries said otherwise. They were ravenous for the blood that was about to be spilled.

As he broke from the tunnel, the first of the men to do so, he felt his feet sink as the surface underfoot transitioned from cement to dirt. Wetness oozed through his shoes and each step through the dense muck was laborious. As he wondered how Seth would ever get his wheelchair through that mud, he realized there were bigger problems.

The dirt of the field wasn't simply wet, it was saturated and deep crimson. It was soaked with so much blood the ground couldn't absorb all of it.

My God, Wyatt thought, how many men have died here.

Then the smell hit him like a hammer.

And he found the source at the far end of the field. Bodies were piled ten, twelve men deep. The corpses closest to the ground barely resembled humans anymore, they were so rotted and withered. A few were mere skeletons, bones picked clean by insects and scavengers. The bodies nearer the top of the pile were green with decay, skin sloughing away. And those on top, the newest additions, were all too fresh.

Wyatt knew there would be more added soon enough. He just hoped that he and his brother were not amongst them.

He tried to ignore the stench of death and rot. Tried to block out the drone of the corpse flies that swarmed the pile. Did his best to not hear the chants from the crowd.

Fight!

Kill 'em!

No mercy!

He had to focus on staying alive.

"That's what we have to look forward to if we die," Seth said as Wyatt pushed him through the slog of bloody earth. "Lovely."

"That's why we won't die," Wyatt said.

Seth rolled his eyes. "As if I needed another reason."

One of the other newbies, a man named Ricardo who was tall and lean but didn't have much else going for him, pointed to the death pile and the crowd cheering behind it. "Those are the cheap seats. I don't know how they can stand the smell. Dios mio."

Wyatt glanced at him and observed the look of abject horror on Ricardo's face. "You knew about this?"

Ricardo nodded. "I've been here three years. A farmer bought me to work his fields, but the spring was dry. He lost everything, including me. I was sent to auction to pay down his debts." He ran slender fingers through his ink-black hair. "I never thought I'd end up here though. Dios mio."

The fourth man in the group, Juan, didn't say a word and, judging by his expression, teetered on the verge of a nervous breakdown.

What a team they had.

"Up there," Ricardo said pointing to the stands. "She's watching."

Wyatt looked past the people sitting on the bleachers - there were thousands of them - and to a fenced-off section of the stands which Wyatt immediately recognized as the luxury box.

Inside it stood Rainha, her arms planted on the edge of her booth, never letting her eyes off her fighters. Others, all men in fine clothes, joined her in the box, chatting, drinking, smoking. But Rainha seemed separate from even them. Above them. Superior.

From the other end of the arena, four men emerged from a different, but identical tunnel.

Their opponents.

He thought they looked fierce, ferocious. Ready to fight. Ready to kill.

But that was in his head.

The men looked scared, desperate, confused. Just like Wyatt and his team.

Wyatt pondered the odds of convincing those men to join his team in ending this madness. In refusing to kill senselessly. Maybe, eight men from different worlds banding together could make a difference.

Then a bell rang, and the battle began.

24

THE MEN ACROSS THE FIELD SCATTERED.

Wyatt saw the other two from his team do the same. Then he realized what everyone was running to.

Four motorcycles, each with its own sidecar, were parked in the corners of the field, just waiting for riders.

But Wyatt didn't want to fight.

He cupped his hands to his mouth and screamed. "We don't have to do this. If we make a united stand, nobody can force us to fight."

No one listened. Men boarded motorcycles, kicked them into gear. As the engines roared to life, smoke billowed from the machines. Then they were moving. Then they were coming for him.

Seth yanked Wyatt's shirt, snapping him out of his fantasy that all the coming violence could be avoided.

"Get your head out of your ass, brother," he spat. "Nobody gives a shit about peace and love here. Get us to that fucking motorcycle before we get killed."

Wyatt followed Seth's finger, which pointed to the last unclaimed cycle.

This wasn't what he wanted to happen, but it was what he had to do. He realized that now.

Pushing the chair through the bloody soil was impossible, so Wyatt dashed in front of the chair and knelt. "Climb on," he said.

Seth wrapped his arms around his neck and Wyatt stood, hoisting his brother into the air. Then he ran, his feet splashing and kicking up sprays of blood.

One of the fighters from the opposing team was close, twenty yards away. Wyatt wasted no time and, when he reached the motorcycle, dropped Seth into the sidecar without a bit of grace. Seth landed hard, groaned, but didn't protest. He wore his game face as he strapped himself in and grabbed a hatchet from beside the seat.

But it wasn't an ordinary hatchet - it was a chunk of steel cut from a car's wheel, then ground into shape and sharpened into a double-bladed instrument of death. And Seth looked in love with it as he gripped in on both hands.

"Ride!" Seth ordered.

Wyatt hopped onto the motorcycle, ready to do just that. He'd ridden a dirt bike a few times when he was a kid, but this was different. As he bucked the kickstand back, the weight of it brought that home. How was he supposed to drive this and fight at the same time?

"Let's go!" Seth shouted, staring at the oncoming bikes.

Wyatt started at the switches and dials, trying to remember what to hit first. Choke lever, cut off switch. He flipped a coin in his head, hitting one, then the other.

"Wyatt, hurry the fuck up!" Seth screamed over the roar of incoming cycles.

He hit the start button.

Nothing.

Fuck.

Then he remembered the clutch. He squeezed it in, tried the start button again.

The engine cranked.

Hallelujah.

Wyatt looked up at the approaching motorcycle and the man in its sidecar. The fire in the rider's eyes was a drastic change from how unsure and timid they'd looked moments earlier. The man in the sidecar held a spear at the ready, prepared to impale Wyatt or Seth as soon as they got close enough. Which was going to happen in seconds.

Wyatt twisted his right hand on the handlebar, and the motorcycle took off, just barely avoiding a strike from the oncoming attack.

"Jiminy crick-fuck," Seth shouted. "That was too close."

"No shit," Wyatt said, still focused on the ride. The engine screamed but sounded anything but smooth. He thought it might stall at any moment.

Then he remembered the choke and throttle, closing the former and opening the latter a bit at a time until the engine purred. He rode away from the others, wanting to get a feel of the machine between his legs before he tried to fight. He heard the crowd jeer at him, annoyed by his cowardice, but he cared not.

He made a lap, coming a bit too near to the pile of rotting bodies. In the process, he saw a white lion mixed in with the dead men, its fangs bared in perpetual fury. This place only got worse.

As he circled back, Wyatt saw Ricardo and Juan and was relieved to find they were having no issues with their ride. He closed in on them. Too close.

They shouted, but Wyatt couldn't hear over the rumbling engines and the din of the crowd. Seth was shouting something, too. But again, the noise was too much.

Before Wyatt knew it, he clipped the side of the motorcycle Ricardo was driving. Miraculously, nobody spun out or flipped over, but both of their engines cut out.

Juan shook a sword at him from the sidecar. "Learn how to fucking drive!"

Wyatt shook his head, trying to get his bike going again. "Sorry, I've never done this before."

Ricardo gestured frantically at his own motorcycle as he started it back up. "Turn that, squeeze that. Push that button. Slow down, push this, and squeeze that. Then ease up. Easy."

Wyatt nodded as Ricardo fired up his bike and took off. He had watched everything that he pointed to and listened as best as he could. He repeated them and his engine fired up.

He barely had time to let out a relieved exhale before Seth was clawing at him, dragging him down and nearly off the bike.

It was just in time as a spear soared through the air where Wyatt's head had been a split-second earlier.

Wyatt looked sideways at his brother, the lifesaver. "Thanks."

"Thank me later. Drive, now."

Wyatt did and, surprising even to himself, he wasn't bad at it. Having the sidecar made balancing relatively easy, but with all the panic, he was still proud of himself for actually picking up on the orders Ricardo had barked at him.

As the machine increased its speed, Wyatt stole a glance at Seth and saw him, ready for action. Wyatt reached down, trying to grab onto a spear that sat in the sidecar with Seth. The bike started to wobble and veer toward the wall.

Seth swatted at his hand.

"Don't crash us, asshole! You get me close to them, and I'll take care of the rest," Seth said.

Wyatt had seen that look in his brother's eyes a few times. And every time, it ended with someone dying in a horrible way by Seth's hand. He had complete faith that Seth would get it done.

He turned back to the field, the tires of the bike kicking blood and dirt into the air. The opponents were circling around as they tried to chase down the other members of Wyatt's team. But Wyatt was going to change that.

He drove, heading straight toward the rider that had launched a spear at his head. He brought the bike within a foot of theirs as he rolled up beside them. So close they almost touched.

While he focused on not crashing, Seth went to work.

He swung the halberd down, chopping the blade directly into the man in the sidecar's collarbone. It buried itself in the man, too deep to free, and Seth let go of it, not willing to risk crashing them if he held on.

In near slow motion, the man's body peeled apart at the cut. The heavy blade cutting deeper and deeper into his chest.

Half of the dead man's bisected, bleeding body slumped forward, while the other half slung out the side of the car, pulling the weight of the bike to the side.

Wyatt steered away from them as the driver tried to stabilize his ride with little success. The bike wobbled, then it pulled a hard right and Wyatt heard the man scream as he slammed into the wall. His body flew over the handlebars, somersaulted in mid-air, then he face-planted into a concrete barrier.

There was no getting up from that.

In fact, Wyatt wasn't sure where the man's face ended and his ass began. His body looked like an accordion, closed sloppily and too fast. The bike burst into flames, its rear-wheel still spinning as it burned.

And the crowd cheered at the carnage.

Two men down.

Wyatt kicked his motorcycle into gear and turned around, no time to take a victory lap. There were two left and, if he let his guard down, he and Seth would end up just like that slug against the wall.

As he circled around, he realized his teammates were in trouble. A spear jutted from Ricardo's shoulder and blood spurted from the wound. The bike wobbled and weaved as the driver bled out, then toppled off the bike.

That left the motorcycle without a driver. Juan stood up in the sidecar, stretching to grab the handlebars, but it was too late. The front wheel snapped sideways, throwing the bike end over end and sending Juan soaring. He rolled over and over and over again and even above the chaos, Wyatt was certain he heard his arms and legs breaking.

When he finally came to a stop, Juan rocked back and forth, trying to get up despite his body being a pulverized mass of misery. He moaned and cried out in pain. His legs were behind him, his feet twisted backward. His arms were above his head, shattered in multiple places. The man was covered in blood. Both from the field and himself.

He screamed louder than the crowd could cheer.

Then the opponents returned, swinging their own halberd his way, silencing his cries in one fatal swoop.

Wyatt didn't know Juan or Ricardo, but they were just like him. They didn't want to be there. They didn't ask to be put in the fight. They had seemed just as scared as he was when it all started. They were part of his team if that meant anything.

Wyatt knew he had to finish the fight. And avenge their deaths.

"Seth, be ready," Wyatt said, revving the throttle.

He took off before his brother could say anything. Wyatt set his eyes on the driver of the other bike. He saw them coming and smiled. He headed straight for Wyatt.

Wyatt was not going to be intimidated.

It was a game of chicken.

And Wyatt was determined to win.

"Wyatt! Wyatt!" Seth screamed as they got closer, nearing a head-on collision.

Wyatt was in the zone. He couldn't be broken.

Seth pulled at Wyatt's hand, causing the bike to veer just slightly to the right. The two sidecars grazed each other, kicking out sparks.

The fighter in the other sidecar had his spear ready, but Seth leaned back and out of the line of fire. In the process, he grabbed the spear and put all his weight into it, jerking his hands as he did.

The man in the sidecar was pulled out and onto the bloody field. One of the man's legs snapped in the fall and he brayed in pain, drawing more cheers from the crowd.

They chanted, "Finish him! Finish him!"

The spectators wanted the man to die. And Wyatt was going to make that happen.

He circled around, giving Seth a good amount of space to take care of business. And Seth did.

He swung the spear like a baseball bat, connecting with the side of the man's face. It exploded in a bloody mess.

Seth rubbed his hands which they shook from the strike. "Jesus that hurt," Seth said.

"How do you think he feels?" Wyatt asked. He looked at the man, now dead, face down in the center of the arena.

All that was left was the driver of the motorcycle.

They passed each other again, like a medieval joust. Seth launched the spear, but he didn't hit the man. Instead, the pole flew right into the front wheel of the motorcycle.

In the blink of an eye, the bike locked up and the man went over the handlebars. He flew high and far, just missing the wall, then landed in the front row of the stands, in the laps of the spectators.

Wyatt had never seen such frenzied excitement.

And he had never seen so many bloodthirsty savages.

The crowd showed no mercy as they grabbed and punched and clawed at the fallen fighter. More joined in, dozens, maybe a hundred. Some had his arms, some his legs. They pulled in opposing directions as they ripped the limbs from his body.

Then, they went to work on his head, not stopping until it was torn free of his neck. They hoisted it into the air like the lucky fan who'd just caught a foul ball.

They were insane.

Wyatt leaned over the bike and threw up his still undigested breakfast.

What a victory.

Then he looked past the savages in the stands, to the luxury box, to Rainha.

Even at a distance, he could tell she was smiling and staring intently back at him.

25

"Ungratefulness will result in punishment," Uno said, pacing back and forth in front of them.

Chester and Pino had survived, winning their fights, as had all of Rainha's other warriors, but it was Wyatt and Seth who seemed to be the heroes, getting congratulations not only from the other men but from many onlookers who filtered out of the arena after the battles had ended.

There had been high hopes for Wyatt, mostly because of the show he'd put on at the auction, but no one had expected Seth to survive. In fact, everyone had feared Seth would be an anchor for his brother, dragging him down and getting the both of them killed.

Yet they not only survived but dominated.

Now, they were told they were to be rewarded, but the brothers had been separated from the other fighters, taken away by Uno who now rattled off threats to them.

"If you make Abuelita feel uncomfortable in any way, you will die. If you make Rainha angry, you will die. If you try to escape--"

"Let me guess," Seth interrupted. "We'll die."

Uno glared at him with his lone eye. "Do you understand me, funny boy?"

Seth, still high off victory, nodded. "Sure thing, bossman. We'll be on our best behavior. Now, why don't you tell us what the hell is going on? And what's an Abracadabra? Are you going to put on a magic show for us? Because I fucking love card tricks."

Wyatt was confused too but worried Seth's swagger would bring a fast end to their relief over surviving the battle.

"Abuelita," Uno said.

"Aboo-who-ta?" Seth asked.

Uno tensed, glared. "Abuelita is Rainha's mother."

Seth and Wyatt exchanged glances. Her *mother?*

The door to the mansion swung open. Uno quickly spun around and his posture shifted from threatening to relaxed. He even looked... happy. Wyatt strained to look around the giant man to see what or who was coming.

What he found was a stooped, ancient woman with long white hair and a peaceful, warm smile spread across her small face. Her eyes were soft and inviting and Wyatt couldn't recall the last time he'd seen someone who immediately provoked such feelings of comfort and kindness. Maybe his own grandmother, who'd passed away when he was barely out of diapers.

"Are these the boys I've heard such good things about?" Abuelita asked.

Uno nodded. "Yes, ma'am."

Ma'am? Aside from Rainha herself, Wyatt had never heard Uno be respectful, let alone deferential, to anyone. What sort of power did this elderly woman hold to make Uno turn into a giant teddy bear?

"Come closer." She waved her hands for them to enter the mansion. "Let me get a good look at you."

Wyatt pushed Seth's chair, taking them both closer to the woman. She was so bent with age that she was at eye-level with Seth and she put hands twisted with arthritis on his shoulders and gave him a squeeze.

"Handsome, you are," she said with a serene smile.

Wyatt half expected his brother to come back with a quip. Something sarcastic and off-color, but Seth surprised him by being polite.

"Thank you. It's nice to meet you. I'm Seth." He cocked his thumb over his shoulder. "And that's Wyatt, my brother."

"Brothers!" Abuelita exclaimed. "No wonder you worked so well together. Or so I was told." She backed away, into the house, and beckoned them with a wave. "Come."

They did.

"They all call me Abuelita, although it makes me sound much older than I feel. That means Granny if you aren't aware."

Wyatt was not.

"I'm not, though. A granny, I mean. My daughter is barren. But, I suppose all the fighters look at me as their nana, so I'm okay with the nickname. It could be something worse, I suppose."

The interior of the mansion was as sterile as the outside. It was more modern, New York City apartment than quaint, country home. Wyatt was unsure what he'd expected, but it wasn't this.

There were decorations - abstract paintings and sculptures - but it was largely utilitarian. Concrete walls, floors, ceilings. An occasional animal skin rug was strewn about, along with random chairs and couches. But it was far from homey.

They followed Abuelita into the dining room, where the smell of a freshly cooked meal hit him and stoked an appetite he'd lost forever after the battle. He wasn't sure what was cooking and he didn't care because it smelled amazing. He needed some of whatever it was.

When Abuelita moved into the kitchen, the men remained in the dining room.

"When was the last time you boys had a good, home-cooked meal?"

Wyatt pondered the question but couldn't recall. He glanced at Seth for an answer, but his brother was equally clueless. It must have been five years or more.

Their silence was answer enough.

"That long?" Abuelita reemerged carrying a large stockpot. She walked with a slight limp but didn't seem in pain and when Uno stepped toward her, arms reaching for the pot, she shook her head. "I'm quite capable, Uno."

He backed away, shoulders slumped and looking cowed for the first time ever so far as Wyatt could tell.

Abuelita set the pot on a sprawling, butcher block table where five settings of plates and silverware were already in place. Also on the table were silver trays, still covered. It reminded Wyatt of the dining tables in movies about kings and queens and he began to feel out of place.

Seth didn't have that problem. "It smells fantastic! When do we dig in?"

"After you wash your hands," she said and motioned to the kitchen.

The men moved into it, scrubbing their filthy paws in the sink, fragrant soap cleansing weeks' worth of dirt and sweat, mud and blood. The water ran black at first, then cleared as their sins were washed away.

Seth grabbed a dishrag off the counter and dried his hands, then passed it to Wyatt. Uno loomed over them and, even though the man was in a rare good mood, his very presence made them uncomfortable. It was like sharing an intimate moment with your fifth-grade teacher looking over your shoulder.

Wyatt didn't meet the man's eyes as he handed him the towel.

"Thank you," Uno said.

Wyatt was so shocked he almost stumbled backward in shock. Those were the first two kind words Uno had spoken to him, and he suspected they might be the last.

"You're welcome," Wyatt croaked in response.

Then Uno left them. Wyatt and Seth exchanged a befuddled look, then followed him back into the dining room.

They sat and Abuelita began spooning delicious-smelling stew into soup bowls. Then she placed one in front of each of the men.

Seth snatched up a spoon, ready to dig in until Uno cleared his throat. "Not yet!"

Seth froze, hand trembling, the silver spoon making a rat-a-tat sound against the fine china. Seth looked as if he expected Uno to murder him on the spot and Wyatt wouldn't have been surprised either.

Everyone sat in stony silence. And then Wyatt heard it.

Footsteps descending a nearby staircase. All eyes went to the sound and found Rainha gliding down the stairs.

She was still clad in the same skin-tight, white leather outfit she'd sported at the arena. Seeing her up close, Wyatt realized she should have been a top model strutting down a catwalk in the old world.

Everything about her was larger than life and extraordinary. Her height, her cheekbones, her makeup, her body. Especially her body. Michelangelo couldn't have sculpted a more perfect figure.

"Uno, have you turned my mother into a serving wench?" she asked as she reached the landing and glided toward the dining room.

Uno's eye grew wide, his face flushing red. If Wyatt hadn't been so scared himself, he might have laughed.

But, it was Abuelita who laughed instead. "Nonsense, Rainha. I will not have my guests serve me. In fact, I had to order this one to keep his hands off my cookware." She winked at Uno and some of the tension left the man's face.

Rainha shook her head but smirked. "You coddle them too much."

"As they should be," Abuelita said. "A touch of home, a touch of kindness. It goes a long way. You can't have these men living with no hope. That's needlessly cruel."

"Enough, mother. We've had this discussion. I won't have it again," Rainha said.

Wyatt didn't know why, but he was surprised by the family drama. It seemed so... normal. It was hard to believe she was actually a human being. With family. With quarrels. And quite possibly, with feelings?

Wyatt couldn't be sure about the last one.

His ears perked up to the sound of toenails clicking against the concrete floor. He quickly spun toward the sound and found Supper. The dog bounded toward him and, if a dog could smile, Supper was. Wyatt was too, one so big he thought his face might break as the dog bounced against him, licking furiously.

All his worries about his furry friend vanished. The dog was clearly well cared for and a red bandana was tied around his neck. He was healthy, happy, and living a better life than Wyatt. Rainha was treating him well.

"He loves you," Rainha said.

"Me too, I hope," Seth said, patting his thigh. Supper left Wyatt and went to him, bouncing into the boy's lap and washing his face with his tongue.

"You keep winning in the arena and you can see the dog anytime you'd like. Both of you," Rainha said, spooning herself a bowl of the aromatic stew, then sitting at the head of the table.

"What are you waiting for?" she asked them. "Eat."

Everyone did.

Wyatt and Seth had their first serving devoured in under a minute and, after cleansing his palate with a swallow of wine, Seth unleashed an ear-splitting belch. The room went silent and if looks could kill, Uno would have destroyed him.

"Sorry," Seth said.

"Do not apologize," Abuelita said. "I take it as a compliment."

"Can I have some more?" Seth asked.

"But of course. Fill your bellies. That's why I made it."

Seth refilled his bowl, then Wyatt did the same.

"You were the big surprise of the day, Seth," Rainha said. "I bought you for my own amusement. I never imagined the Doc would let you fight with the men. When I saw you there, I thought I'd have to execute him for his incompetence, but you proved him correct."

"I try," Seth said, chewing open-mouthed.

"And I'm grateful. It was a prosperous and rewarding day."

Wyatt hadn't started on his second bowl yet. Talk of the battle brought his thoughts back to his dead teammates.

"And what about Ricardo and Juan?" Wyatt asked.

Rainha cocked her head, curious. "Who?"

"The men who fought with us. Who died in the arena."

The woman shrugged, nonchalant. "Not every investment pays out. I accept that. You should too, Wyatt."

That's all they were to her. Investments. She didn't care if they lived or died. Only that she got her money's worth.

"They were scared. They didn't volunteer to be thrown into that madness. None of us did. But I'm glad that most of your investment paid off," Wyatt said, his words backed by attitude.

An awkward silence filled the room. Uno planted his hands on the table, just waiting for the order to attack. Wyatt knew he had crossed the line, but he was pissed and tired of keeping his opinion to himself.

"Enough," Abuelita said. "No bickering at the table. Here, we are all friends. Correct?"

She eyed Wyatt, who nodded, albeit reluctantly. Then she stared down Uno and her daughter, Rainha. Both acquiesced.

"Uno, please pass me the stew," Abuelita said.

Uno stood, holding the pot for Abuelita as she spooned more food into her bowl. Steam still billowed from the stew and the pot was scalding hot. Despite that, Uno didn't use a potholder and his hands had gone scarlet, yet he showed no sign of pain as he stared at Wyatt.

Wyatt broke eye contact, staring instead at his own food, even though his appetite had vanished.

Tension lingered in the air, and Abuelita still worked to diffuse it. "You boys remind me of my own son," Abuelita said. "Rainha's brother, if you hadn't put it together."

"Where is he now?" Seth asked.

As soon as the question was proffered, Wyatt sensed it was an unfortunate one. Abuelita's smile faltered.

"Unfortunately he's not with us anymore," Abuelita responded.

"I'm so sorry. I can't even imagine your pain" Seth said, sincere.

Wyatt wondered if he'd picked up that empathy from Papa, and supposed not everything about the big man had been bad. He was able to connect with people at a level foreign to most.

"It was many years ago, but thank you," Abuelita said. "Tell me about you. Where are you from?"

Wyatt continued to eat. Seth continued to talk. They all continued to exist on the surface. Wyatt made sure not to push Rainha's buttons anymore. And everything had seemed to be alright. For the time being.

Many stories were exchanged, and a bit of laughter. Laughter from Rainha and Abuelita. Uno wasn't much for smiles or any sort of emotional outburst other than anger, but even he seemed to relax as the feast went on.

Wyatt realized, with some discomfort, that it felt like it was a real family experience. Something he desperately missed and longed for. He had to keep reminding himself that Rainha was a psychotic and violent slave owner that controlled every move they made.

A knock at the door interrupted a story Seth was telling about how he'd become paralyzed. That one involved a camping trip and a bear attack and was complete bullshit, but Wyatt enjoyed seeing his brother fool the others and wasn't about to spoil his fun.

Rainha went to the door, chatted with someone for less than a minute, then returned to the room, her face all business.

"I have some matters to attend to. Sorry, mother, but dinner is over"

"Nonsense," Abuelita said. "There is still food. And as long as there is food, the meal goes one. Besides, look at Uno. He needs to eat. He's a growing man."

Wyatt didn't think that Abuelita was joking. He was in peak

physical form, and so muscular he probably burned a thousand calories each time he farted.

Rainha shrugged and headed to the staircase from which she'd earlier emerged.

"Fine. Uno, when this is over, take Wyatt back to the stables. A guard will arrive shortly for Seth. The Doc needs him."

"Thank you, dear," Abuelita said.

"Rapido," Rainha said. Uno nodded.

Wyatt was amazed that anyone had influence over Rainha, let alone a woman so small she could snap her like a pencil if she was so inclined. Maybe there was actually something human underneath her tough shell, something he could work with.

Or maybe he was fooling himself.

But he knew he couldn't lose hope and become another lackey, doing what he was told and being happy with scraps. That wasn't his destiny. He was certain.

26

Wyatt didn't like being separated from his brother, especially in this place where everything was so uncertain and dangerous. But life was different here and he had no choice. All that put his mind at ease was that his brother had proven himself in the battle, and he trusted Rainha would not want anything untoward to happen to one of her good investments.

Was that supposed to make him feel better?

It was a crazy world they lived in now.

Uno escorted Wyatt back down the hill and to the stables and despite the shitty company, it was a pleasant walk. The weather was humid, but he didn't care because the sun was out, shining high above in the blue sky.

After so many years of not even seeing a glimpse of that yellow ball of fire, he was certain that he'd never tire of that sight. It could be his worst day - his last day - and so long as the sun was shining down on him, he'd be all right.

Of course, while on the walk, Wyatt plotted ways he could escape. The pathway from the house to the stables was open and no guards were to be seen. He could make a run for it, maybe even outrun Uno. The man was fast with his fists, but Wyatt had never seen him sprint and he thought he could take him.

But Seth wasn't there. And Wyatt could never leave his brother behind. He'd rather die.

So he played nice.

For now.

As the two approached the gate to the stables, Wyatt saw Rainha there, talking to a man Wyatt remembered seeing at the auction. He wore a red, silk coat that almost touched the ground and sported a ponytail of bleached-blond hair.

The two stood in front of a trailer hitched to the rear of a truck. It looked like the cage that had taken the fighters to the arena, but smaller. A white tarp covered the contents, giving it a covered wagon look.

"Who's that?" Wyatt asked Uno, gesturing to the man in silk.

"The Drip," he said, his tone flat and emotionless.

"Doesn't anyone here have a real name?"

Uno took a breath and let it explode out as if Wyatt was exhausting him. "He owns the brothel. You can assume what you want from the nickname."

It took a few moments before it clicked.

"Oh. *Oh*. That's... disgusting." Wyatt thought about Chester and his predilection and fought back a shudder. "What's he doing here?"

Uno shoved him toward the stables, hard enough to push Wyatt off balance. He stumbled before steadying himself.

"What Rainha does is none of our business, slave" Uno said, stepping into Wyatt and directing him away with his massive frame.

Wyatt obeyed, shuffling along but stealing glances at Uno along the way. The man was strong and confident, but Wyatt also knew their stations weren't that far off.

"Aren't you describing yourself?"

Wyatt thought he saw a flash of emotion in Uno's eye, but it was extinguished before he could read it. Was it anger? Defiance? Or something else entirely?

"When the Drip has whores who are too used up to keep working, he sometimes sells them to Rainha. Fodder for the slaughter. Cheap meat for the animals. And sometimes she sells to him."

"She sells us?" Wyatt asked.

"As I said, sometimes," Uno said. "Say, a man is a good fighter but comes up with a lame leg. He's no good to her after that, yet he still has value. That's the way it works here. You go to whoever can use you. When there's no one left, it's to the slaughter."

Wyatt nodded as he watched Rainha and the Drip converse, and was now close enough to hear snippets of the conversation.

"I want him," the Drip said. "I pay five hundred plus the new man."

Rainha shook her head. "I already told you, no."

"One thousand!"

"He's not for sale," Rainha said. "Wheelchair boy has proven his worth. He's staying with me."

"Two!" the drip pleaded.

"Just because I got him for a steal, doesn't mean you can take him. Without my training and the show he put on today, he would be nothing to you. Now, if you ask again, I'll take all my brothel business elsewhere."

The Drip gasped, his movements, his gestures, even his breathing were overly dramatic and theatrical. "You wouldn't dare!"

"I would," Rainha said. "We've done business for many years. I always treat you fairly and pay above going rate. Do you wish to throw that away over a boy with one leg?"

The Drip folded his arms, furrowed his brow. After a long pause, he shook his head. "I do not."

"Good. Then our deal still stands. Now show me what you've brought. He better be impressive after wasting all this time."

The drip went to the trailer, casting aside the tarp to access a padlock. He unlocked it and began to open the door.

"Go inside," Uno said to Wyatt, who'd almost forgotten he was there.

Rather than wait to make sure Wyatt obeyed, Uno stepped between the Drip and Rainha, protective.

"It's okay, Uno. Our friend has brought us a man who he says can fight."

Uno didn't move, continuing to play the bodyguard.

The Drip leaned into the trailer and, when he reemerged, was holding a rope with both hands. He yanked on it and a man stumbled out, his hands and feet bound, a sack over his head.

He was shirtless, tall, solidly built, and clearly unhappy with his predicament. He strained at the ropes holding him, which resulted in the Drip kicking him in the groin.

With a muffled *oof,* the man dropped to his knees.

"Stay down or I cut your throat!" the Drip ordered and the man remained on his knees.

Rainha stepped closer, looking the prospect up and down. She seemed impressed. "He looks strong."

The Drip nodded, flinging his hair to and fro. "Quite strong. He'll do well in the battles. But his cock…" The Drip wrinkled his nose, then held up his thumb and index finger, keeping them about an inch apart. "No good to me."

Rainha laughed, throwing her head back. "You men, so obsessed with what's between your legs when tongues do such a better job."

She reached out, grabbed the sack, and ripped it off the man's head.

And Wyatt's heart sank.

The strong jawline.

The salt and pepper hair.

The piercing eyes.

He recognized him immediately.

Franklin.

The man responsible for Allie and his mother's deaths. The man who tried to kill him. The man he hated more than anyone who ever lived.

How could it be? He was supposed to be dead in a ditch on the other side of the border, in what remained of the states.

But here he was, very much alive and, as far as Wyatt could see, no worse for the wear. Franklin blinked, his eyes adjusting to the light. Then he looked around, taking in his surroundings. He saw the Drip, Uno, Rainha. Then he looked past them.

And saw Wyatt.

And he smiled.

At the sight of that smug grin, the same smile he'd flashed as Allie died, Wyatt knew what needed to happen.

Franklin had to die.

After that realization, Wyatt lost his mind. He bellowed from the pit of his stomach, like a war cry. And that's exactly what he felt like he was doing. Going to war.

He charged forward and everyone turned to face him. Uno actually seemed startled. The Drip looked on the verge of shitting his pants. Rainha stepped back, away from the man Wyatt was rushing.

And Franklin kept smirking.

He knew exactly who was coming for him.

Wyatt flew past the others and tackled the man on his knees. Both of them skittered a few yards across the hard dirt. As they rolled, Wyatt flailed with his arms, reigning blows on Franklin's body, punching him in the face, clawing at his eyes.

And Franklin's response? Laughter.

Wyatt's knuckles burned from the pounding he was delivering, but it felt so good to be doing it that he couldn't stop. Wouldn't stop.

Wyatt brought his fist back one more time, ready to smash in Franklin's aristocratic nose, but didn't have the chance.

Uno had grabbed his arm in mid punch. He flung Wyatt onto his back, then picked him up and slung him over his shoulder like he was a sack of potatoes.

Wyatt struggled, but it was no use. Everything people had said about Uno was true. He was unbeatable.

When they were at the entry to the stable, Uno flung him into the hay, then grabbed a handful of his hair and punched him in the face. Wyatt dropped to the ground like a paperweight. A galaxy of stars clouded his vision and he could feel consciousness running away from him.

But he stayed alert long enough to see Rainha appear over him. She stared down with displeased, steely eyes.

"You do not fight unless I order you to," she said. Then, she kicked him in the jaw and Wyatt's lights went out.

Franklin had managed to crawl onto all fours, blood spilling from his mouth like water from a faucet. He looked like a shell of the physical specimen he'd been moments earlier.

The Drip looked at Rainha, anxious, worried. "Our deal's still on, right?"

She gave him a curt nod, then looked to Uno. "Get him to the Doc. See if he can be salvaged."

Uno grabbed Franklin by his hair and dragged him away.

27

Seth sat in front of the Doc as the man tinkered with a pile of metal and tools. He mumbled to himself as he inspected Seth's worn and beat up wheelchair. He tightened some screws, removed others. Every so often he would mutter a syllable that sounded close to a real word, but Seth couldn't decipher it through the jabber.

"Care to try English, Doc?" Seth asked, growing tired of being the lab rat.

"Hmm?" the man said, casting a furtive, distracted glance at Seth's face.

"What's all this about? Rainha said you wanted me."

The Doc grinned. "Oh yes, yes. I do. I made something while you were away. I wasn't sure you'd be back, but I couldn't wait. Couldn't wait. Just had to make it anyway."

He hobbled with his metal leg into a small side room. Metal clanged, something fell. Doc muttered more nonsense. Then he returned.

Pushing a wheelchair.

At least, that's how Seth's eyes identified it at first glance, but this was something else. Something special.

"What the freaking fuck?" Seth asked, half bewildered and half awed.

"It's your new chair. Perfect for fighting and getting around. You can leave that hunk of junk behind now." The Doc was pointing at the chair Seth sat in. "Here, let me help you."

The Doc wheeled his Frankenstein chair next to Seth and extended his hand. Seth grabbed on, wrapping his free arm around Doc's shoulder, and between the two of them, he was up, out of his chair, and into his new ride.

Seth bounced as his butt hit the amply padded seat. The back support was equally comfortable and, from the feel of it, ergonomic. Seth felt like he was floating.

"How's the fit?" the Doc asked him.

"Perfect," Seth said.

"There's much more." The Doc grinned, thrilled to be sharing his weird, yet wonderful creation. "You'll notice the simple weapon storage on the side. You can keep knives or hammers in there for use in hand to hand combat."

Seth observed the pouch he was talking about. It seemed useful but paled in comparison to the rest of the chair and its attachments.

Doc continued. "I fabricated two major weapons. The one on your right side, there's a switch on the armrest for it. You see, the tube curves down around the back, and it comes out here." He pointed to a cylinder that emerged over Seth's shoulder. It looked like, and was, an exhaust pipe from a car. "Please don't push the switch now, but when you do, a high-temperature flame will shoot out approximately eight feet."

"You put a fucking flame thrower on my wheelchair?" This was amazing!

The Doc nodded. "It runs off a separate tank from the one that powers your chair itself—"

"The chair is motorized?"

"Of course," the doc said, matter of factly, as if there were any other options.

Seth examined the wheels and saw a variety of belts and gears connecting them all. The tires themselves were knobby and rugged. No more getting stuck in the mud. From the looks of it, he could scale the Andes.

Doc went on. "If you flip the switch at your left hand, anyone that is near or more specifically, on your chair, won't be there anymore. At least, not in a singular piece."

Seth looked at the nob at his left hand. He didn't know what it did, but he knew he wasn't going to be flipping the switch to find out while what seemed to be his only friend was nearby. "It is a bomb?" he asked.

Doc shook his head. "No. That would be dangerous. Shrapnel and all that. I'll let you find out when the opportunity presents itself."

Seth nodded, that was fine. He was overwhelmed with it all, still trying to grasp that this was all for him. "Why do all this work? For me? I don't even know your name other than Doc," Seth asked instead.

The Doc took his glasses off and wiped them with his shirt, studying Seth. "Because small disabilities shouldn't hold anyone down. I don't let it."

"Your leg," Seth said.

"That, but more. Some people call me Doc. But others call me Eunuch. I'm sure you can put it together yourself. Doc the Eunuch, that's me." He smiled, half-heartedly. "People like you and me need to be stronger than the rest. Instead of being weighed down by our disabilities, we need to find ways to use them to propel us forward."

For the first time, Seth saw the Doc as a person with thoughts and feelings, not just a man that wanted to make gadgets and be weird. And he liked him, even if he was a crazy, old bastard.

"You'll need all of it too. Because you have an encore tomorrow. Don't worry, though. I made sure it is unstoppable."

Seth swallowed hard. He hadn't known he'd be entering the arena again so soon.

28

As punishment for his outburst, Wyatt spent the night alone. He'd been kept separate from all the others, in a small, cramped room that stank of piss, some of it his own.

Before throwing him in what Wyatt had come to think of as a cell, Uno had told him he was on probation, that he'd spent his one strike and he wouldn't get a second. Then he left him alone, with his thoughts.

It was a long evening and night and gave him too much time to think. He regretted attacking Franklin - to an extent. If he'd been successful and killed him, it likely would have bothered him much less.

Knowing that he'd failed, again, to end the man who'd taken so many people he loved... It was hard to feel like anything but a loser.

When morning came, Uno freed him and gave him the news that the day would be filled with fights. After a sleepless night, he could barely fathom it, but he had no choice, and he knew better than to protest.

Now, he sat in the dugout at Akeldama, the field of blood. Wyatt wondered what it had been called before the world fell apart.

Fenway Park, Wrigley Field, something along those lines? He supposed it didn't matter.

His hands and feet were bound in chains. Not because anyone expected him to try to escape, but to humiliate him, to make a spectacle of him. To show him that he was at the bottom of the totem pole, below all the others. Even Chester the Molester.

But he couldn't worry about that now. What mattered was that his brother was on the field, preparing to fight alone, in danger of dying any second, and Wyatt couldn't do anything about it.

"Hey, Wyatt, your brother is looking good on that hot road. I bet he lasts five, six minutes before he gets killed," Pinocchio said.

Wyatt stared at the noseless man who brayed nasally laughs. "I hope you die today," he said.

Pino lost his smile, turning serious. "That's a little rude, amigo."

"That was the point," Wyatt said, pushing him out of the way so he could get a better vantage point, trying to see what Pino was talking about when he referred to Seth's hot rod.

Then he saw him at the east side of the field. Seth aboard a wheelchair, but one far from his usual ride. The machine he rolled around in looked like a tank built for one or a Battle Bot come to life.

"What the fuck is that?" Wyatt said to himself as he took in the chair with its chunks of metal, various tubes, motorized wheels. It looked like a formidable machine, and he was relieved Seth had it, but how had such a thing been created?

Then he looked to the west side where two men waited with machetes. Wyatt shuffled his chains dragging all the way to Uno. "Two versus one? It's supposed to be a solo match!"

Uno acted as if he didn't exist.

Then the bell rang out over the loudspeaker.

The match was on and all Wyatt could do was watch.

29

The bell echoed through Seth's ears. Echoed through the entire arena. Louder than all the shouts and cheers. But eventually, it died out and the screams were what was left.

The people in the stands wanted blood and they'd take it any way they could get it.

Seth's heart pumped hard inside his chest. He wiped his sweat-slicked hands on his pants. He'd been in plenty of fights before. Even as far back as middle school. Kids made fun of him and he brought them down to his level. Literally. He was right at sack level to the bullies he encountered. Sure, it was dirty, but so was making fun of some kid in a wheelchair.

And then there were the fights on the road. So many times he could have died. All to end up... here.

What a cruel joke life had become.

Now, he had to fight, not only to survive but to entertain.

He had done it once, but this time he was alone and that had knocked his confidence down a peg. Wyatt had always been there for him, but Seth hadn't seen his brother since leaving dinner and he'd heard the others talking about his fight with a new slave.

He wasn't sure what had gone down, or Wyatt would have attacked a stranger, but he was eager to talk to his brother and find out. That meant he needed to win.

What was supposed to be a one-on-one match had turned into a two-on-one when Rainha had seen his new chair. She told Seth she believed in him and that he'd win her more money if he could take out two opponents at once. It wasn't like he had a choice in the matter, so Seth assured her he was up for the task.

He just hoped that Doc's chair was as great as he made it out to be.

Seth was armed with a 28-inch machete, as were the two men across the field. It was the weapon of choice for their fight. That and whatever other scraps they could salvage from the field.

And there was plenty. Rods that could be used as clubs or spears. Chunks of metal that would crush a man's skull. Broken bones that would pierce throats and bellies. It was a veritable buffet.

Seth gritted his teeth and watched the two men charge his way.

"Let's see what you've got, beautiful," he said to the machine.

He grabbed the joystick and thrust it forward. The chair responded with so much force he bounced against the backrest, hopped in his seat. He felt like he was on a bucking horse. "Steady now," he whispered, settling in for the ride.

He was going faster than anyone had ever pushed his chair, speeding dead ahead twice as fast as the men moving toward him.

He pounded through a deep puddle of blood, sending rancid, red rain splashing up and over the wall, onto the first few rows of onlookers.

They loved it.

Seth's lips pulled back in a feral grin. The cheers and shouts of encouragement were pumping him up. He was going to win. Not only was he going to win, but he was going to be amazing.

The two men looked surprised at the speed that Seth was coming at them, eyes growing wide, but they still held their ground. After all, they were fighting a cripple, How hard could it be?

He'd show them.

One of the men took the lead as his partner planted his feet in the mud, and gripped his machete like a baseball bat.

Seth could see their plan unfold. The first guy would distract him, then the second would lop off his head as he flew by.

That wasn't going to happen.

Seth swung his machete as the running man came near, but as he did, the runner ducked at the last second. He lashed out with his blade which clattered against Seth's leg rest, where his missing leg would have been if were still attached and not in the bellies of some cannibals back in the States.

Shocked by the man's dexterity, Seth floundered. He was heading straight toward the Babe Ruth wannabe who was all too ready to turn his noggin into a home run. His instincts told him to veer off course, to race away from the man and circle back for another go, but something about the crowd's chants--

Kill!

Kill!

Kill!

He couldn't take the easy way out. He wanted to win and he wanted to do it hard.

Seth eased up on the joystick, cutting his speed in half. The guy waiting to take him out flashed a toothless grin. "You scared of me, boy? You should be!" Then he sprinted forward.

Seth let him get within three yards, then he flipped the switch on his right side.

He heard the hiss, then a click.

Then a blueish-orange flame kicked out over his shoulder.

The toothless man's face turned from determined and cocky to shocked. Then, as the fire washed over him, agony.

In seconds he was ablaze from head to toe and running spastically in irregular patterns. His arms flailed. His clothes melted off his body. He howled in misery.

"Should've paid attention in school, pal," Seth said. "It's all about stop, drop, and roll."

Instead, the man ran, collapsed, and died.

The sizzle of the fire being extinguished by the blood was just loud enough for Seth to hear over the frenzied crowd. He could smell the burning flesh. Somewhat sweet, and somewhat stomach-churning. It reminded him of the cannibal who'd been burned in a pyre at the casino.

Ah, memories.

But this wasn't the time to reminisce. Seth needed to turn the chair around, which was one of the chairs' faults. It didn't corner worth a damn. He had to make a wide, sweeping arc and before he got all the way around--

A searing poker of pain penetrated his left shoulder.

Seth screamed as he looked to the source and saw a three-foot length of rebar sunk just above his clavicle. It had entered from the rear, puncturing the backrest before plunging all the way through Seth's upper body.

He let the chair roll to a stop as he tried to move his left arm. Couldn't. The pain was excruciating but somehow welcome. At least it wasn't numb like his legs. That meant nothing was paralyzed. At least, he hoped.

"Not so good at the turns, eh?" the man who'd stabbed him growled. He was in his forties, bald on top and, Seth thought, looked way too old to be putting up such a good fight.

The man walked to the front of Seth's chair, making sure to stay clear of the flame thrower. "I'll just stay on this side after seeing your little show."

Seth lashed out with his machete, slashing erratically and pointlessly at the man, but it was useless. The old fighter saw it coming before Seth had even considered it.

The man grabbed Seth's wrist and wrenched his hand, causing Seth to drop the blade. Then he slammed a fat fist into Seth's nose which bent ninety degrees to the side. Blood exploded from both nostrils, drenching his shirt as pain ebbed out across his face. And that was just the beginning.

Punch after punch after punch followed and Seth was helpless to stop it. He felt blood fill his mouth, coughing, gagging on it. A mouthful sprayed onto the old man's face, but the attacker only laughed and licked his lips.

"Mmm. Tastes like cum," the man said.

Seth tried to punch back, but it was weak, harmless. He tried to grab the man's nonexistent hair and got his ear instead. He could work with that.

Seth closed his fist around the man's ear, twisting until he felt the flesh tear. Hot wetness soaked his hand as blood seeped, but the blood also slicked his fist and made him lose his grip. The man stepped to the side, his ear half-torn off, dangling by a chunk of skin, then he dove back in for the fight.

He landed a blow to Seth's throat, leaving him gasping for air. Then he grabbed the rebar, pulling, straining. Seth could feel the rough metal tearing through his body, could sense important vessels and muscles in his chest shredding under duress.

And he realized he was going to die.

It wasn't supposed to end like this. Not one and done. He was supposed to kick ass in these battles with the help of the new chair.

"I heard about your first fight," the old man said. "Guess you're not so lucky this time, even with the gadgets." The man was taunting Seth. He was toying with him.

The old man freed the rebar from Seth's torso, spun it in his hands, ready to finish him off for good. But he couldn't resist putting on a show. He turned to the crowd raising the rebar, which dripped blood, high above his head.

"You want to see death?" the old man screamed. "You want to see him suffer?"

The crowd went nuclear, their roars deafening.

"Then you watch what I'm about to do!" The old man spun back and jumped onto his chair, straddling it. He held the rebar like a javelin, prepared to ram the rod through Seth's head, skewer it like an olive. It would be a hell of a spectacle.

But Seth wasn't ready to die just yet.

He pushed the lever, launching his chair drive forward. Then he jerked the joystick back and forth, but the man hung on. The old man laughed. Laughed right in front of Seth's bloody, beaten face.

"I'm not letting go. You won't get rid of me."

Seth saw he wasn't lying. This guy could go eight seconds on a bull and then some. He made another attempt at a punch, but the old man caught his fist with his free hand. Then he slammed Seth's right forearm into the chair's armrest, snapping the bones against the metal frame.

Seth screamed in pain. He peered through the eye that hadn't swollen shut and saw his arm dangling in its skin. Useless.

What a pathetic sight I am, Seth thought. Legs no good. One arm was broken. The other, who knows. I may as well be a sack of dicks for as useful as I am.

"You ready to die, boy? No better way to go than in front of a crowd."

Seth twitched the fingers in his left hand, tried to move his wrist, but that sent pain rocketing up his arm and into his wounded shoulder, pain so intense he couldn't fight off tears.

"You fought well if that helps."

It didn't.

The old man wrapped his hands around Seth's throat and squeezed. He wasn't in a rush. He was enjoying his moment in the sun.

Seth tried his left hand again and felt his finger graze the trigger he'd almost forgotten was there. The mystery trigger.

His shoulder flared with pain. His throat closed in on itself as the man squeezed.

The world started to go black and the cheers began to fade in his ears.

Then, seconds before dying, he shoved his index finger forward, flipping the switch.

He heard snapping behind him as a compartment opened. That was followed with a high-pitched, grinding whine.

Out of the corner of his eye, Seth caught sight of a circular saw spinning on a metal lever.

It ripped a straight line from one side of the chair to the other, missing his own chest by mere inches. Boiling blood-soaked him and then the pressure released from his throat.

The world came back to him all at once and he coughed, spitting up more blood. Then his vision cleared and he saw the man's legs and lower torso still straddling him. But his chest, shoulders, and head were on the ground.

The Doc had delivered.

Seth was alive.

Barely.

The bell went off again, declaring Seth the winner, and the crowd was louder than ever. He tried to raise his left arm, to wave to them, to thank them for their support, but the pain was too much.

30

Wyatt felt his heart sink as Seth slumped over in his chair, bleeding, motionless. His brother had won the battle but looked like he was dying. Or maybe even dead already.

"Help him!" Wyatt screamed. "Get out there and help!"

He would have run onto the field himself if not for the chains keeping him in place. He tried anyway, straining at them, trying to pull the heavy bolts holding them to the wall loose. It didn't work.

"Calm down, amigo," Pinocchio said, shaking his head. "They need to clear the field for the next battle. Someone will be out soon."

Wyatt wanted to pummel him and the man must have seen the rage in his eyes and backed out of reach.

Then came the voice Wyatt had never wanted to hear again. "Aw, is little Wyatt worried about his baby brother? So sad."

Franklin mocked him with that same stupid grin plastered to his cocky, albeit bruised, face.

Wyatt felt the hatred burn inside of him. The asshole was still alive while Seth bled out in front of ten thousand screaming onlookers. And Franklin was enjoying every bit of Wyatt's misery.

But, what Franklin didn't realize was that he was within the range of Wyatt's chains.

Wyatt lunged at him, and finally, the bastard stopped smiling. He got in one punch, another.

"Hey Uno, Wyatt's beating on the pretty man again!" Chester shouted.

Wyatt stopped punching and wrapped his chains around Franking's throat, watching as the man's dreamy eyes bulged in their sockets. His face went purple as he strangled and choked.

Wyatt knew the man would be dead in under a minute, but as much as he wanted that vengeance, it would have to wait.

"Get my brother help!" Wyatt screamed. "Right now or I'll kill Franklin!"

Pino grabbed Wyatt from behind, taking him by the shoulders, trying to pull him off. But Wyatt threw back an elbow, catching the man in the face. He heard something snap.

"Bastardo broke my nose!" Pino yelled, stumbling backward as two chunks of wood clattered to the dugout floor.

Chester and another man joined in, trying to pull apart Wyatt and Franklin with little luck.

"Break it up!" Uno shouted, stomping into the fray.

But Wyatt wasn't quitting. Not until he got what he wanted.

He glared at the glowering man who looked ready to break him in two. "Help Seth, now, or I kill this motherfucker."

"Nah," Franklin croaked. "Barb... wasn't... my type." He gasped in another breath. "Too old... and ugly."

Wyatt's entire body quivered with rage. How could Franklin be so damn smug to insult his dead mother when he had chains around his throat? Now he wanted to kill the man out of spite.

But Uno was towering over them, ready to end it one way or another.

Wyatt expected to be killed. That Uno would reach out, grab his head, and snap his neck. And if Seth was dead out there on the field, maybe that was for the best.

Instead, Uno raised a booted foot and kicked Franklin in the face. The man went limp in Wyatt's arms and Wyatt stared at Uno, confused.

"Look," Uno said, using his square chin to gesture toward the field.

Wyatt followed and saw two men tending to Seth. His brother's head lolled, but he could see Seth was still alive.

"Anything else?" Uno asked.

Wyatt considered it. "Yeah. Take me to Rainha."

31

Rainha dipped a plump shrimp into cocktail sauce, then popped the whole thing in her mouth. It wasn't ladylike, but she didn't care. No one here was in a position to judge her. Without her strength, her vision, they'd all be dead at best.

She chewed, then washed the food down with the best wine in the land. She had her own bottle and no intentions to drink it all but enjoyed the jealous eyes as the other slave owners watched.

Her eyes drifted to the field where men prepared to battle. She had no stake in that match and cared not at all about the results. Everyone else's fighters bored her. They weren't trained. They were barely above animals, slashing and punching without a plan. Sometimes they got lucky, on rare occasions they even toppled one of her men, but it was like watching dogs fight. No style or substance.

She made good money from the battles, but what she earned by putting her men against these dregs was a pittance compared to her portion of the pot when her own men were pitted against one another. On those battles, she made a fortune because everyone wanted to bet. Everyone wanted to watch. Everyone wanted a piece of the pie. And her slice was always the largest.

Those battles were rare though. The men were her investments and there was no point in killing off her stock too often, even if it did bring in copious amounts of cash.

As the new battle unfolded on the field, she thought about the last match. About the boy in the wheelchair who continued to surprise her. She had expected him to die in his first match, but he had a feral ferocity that carried with it high hopes. That's why she was confident enlisting him on the two against one. Well, that, and the chair Doc Eunuch had created.

And he had won but looked far worse for the effort. She wondered how bad he was injured but, more importantly, how soon he'd be able to fight again.

Behind her, other slave owners conversed, laughed, cut deals. Occasionally they tried to drag her into their pointless niceties, but she could rarely be bothered. When it came down to it, none of them were as good as her. She owned half the island. She was what kept the monkeys from taking over the jungle.

"Wheelchair always puts on a good show," the Drip purred beside her. He was the closest to a friend that Rainha could consider. Although he was also her biggest competition. Not that any of them were true competition.

Deep down, she knew the Drip would kill her if the chance arose. He wasn't satisfied being second best. But she knew he'd never succeed.

"He barely survived," a different voice said from behind her.

Rainha lost her fake smile as she listened.

"It was a rigged match. If he didn't have the chair, he wouldn't have lasted ten seconds," the same voice whined.

"He is a cripple," the Drip said. "Having the chair made it fair. It was still two men against one boy. You're just a sore loser."

"He's a cheat! He should be dead!"

Rainha had heard enough. She turned around, never setting down her shrimp cocktail. Her eyes went to Monger, the local dairy seller, and the whiner. A few months earlier he'd decided to invest the money he made selling milk and cheese in fighters. But he knew absolutely nothing and it showed in his unending stream losses.

"Don't be so petty, Monger. My worst fighter just beat two of your men. Accept that you're out of your league."

Monger snorted. "We don't all have a mad scientist to rig the matches."

"You prefer hand to hand combat? No weapons at all? Give me your three best men and I'll put Uno against them. Think you'd have a chance then?"

Monger's eyes widened. "I thought he was retired."

"Hardly. The only reason I don't offer him up is because no one would challenge him. And no one in the stands would bet against him. There's no money to be made." She leaned in close to his oily face. "But I'll make an exception. For you."

She spun, walking away before he could respond, and heard the anxious whispers in her wake. Nobody wanted Uno back in the battles.

Rainha stuffed another shrimp in her mouth, ignoring them, ignoring everything until--

"Ma'am." Uno's voice came from the stairwell leading to the luxury box.

She looked and found Uno restraining Wyatt with a chokehold, despite the young man also being in chains. Wyatt peered up at her, his eyes bloodshot and pained, but there was something else there. Something that impressed her.

Defiance.

"What's the issue now?" Rainha asked Uno.

"He almost killed the new slave. Again. He demanded to see you, so I'm giving him what he asked." He tightened his thick forearm around Wyatt's neck. "Say the word and he's dead."

Uno's typically blank, stony face was eager. He wanted Wyatt dead, but Rainha wasn't sure that was the right decision. She moved down a step, closer to the men.

"Is that what you want?" she asked Wyatt. "Death?"

Wyatt didn't respond, or maybe couldn't. Either way, the steely resolve remained in his gaze.

"Let him go," she said.

Uno twitched. "Ma'am?"

"Do it. And go. I'll deal with him."

Uno did as ordered, but it was clear he was displeased.

Wyatt gasped, sucking in giant mouthfuls of air and coughing them out. His bound hands rubbed his neck which was chafed and raw.

"Where's Seth?" Wyatt asked in a froggy croak.

"Uno wanted to crush you. He still does. I didn't let him because my mother is fond of you and your death would wound her."

Wyatt didn't respond.

"But don't expect a permanent reprieve. My mother understands our business, our ways. I won't tolerate a burden."

"My brother had the shit beaten out of him and you left him out there. Bleeding, maybe dying, for minutes. Is that how you treat all of your *investments*?"

Rainha couldn't suppress a laugh. "Wyatt, you are so extreme. So emotional. Are you sure you're not a woman?" Her hand darted out, cupped his groin, caressed it. Her fingers rolled across his cock which hardened in her grip. "No, I guess not."

Wyatt stumbled back, away from her, almost tripping over his chains, but the ample bulge remained in his pants.

"Why wouldn't I care for your brother? He's won two fights. The crowd adores him. Doc will fix him up good as new. Better, even."

Wyatt gave a small nod. "Okay."

"But I can tell that your brother has enough confidence for ten men. That will be to his detriment. At some point, he's going to meet his end."

Rainha watched Wyatt clench his teeth. His face redden. It was a look of petulance.

"So, either he keeps proving his worth, and I don't know when he will be able to again. Or, I need something from you."

"What can I give you?"

Rainha's eyes went to his crotch, her tongue snaked across her lips. She didn't have to tell him when she could show him so she grabbed a fistful of his hair and pulled him into her. Their mouths met, hard, teeth smashing together. It hurt and that was how she liked it.

She forced his lips apart with her tongue, then invaded his mouth. He tasted like blood from his earlier fight, and she liked it.

Then he squirmed free.

"I-- I can't."

She grabbed his waistband, keeping him close, pushing their groins together. He was still hard and she was getting wet.

"I think you're perfectly capable," she said, laughing.

"No, I mean-- I had a--"

"Shut up. I don't care about the life you left behind. If you had a girlfriend or a wife or a family. Listen to me, and listen well. Your past doesn't matter because it's gone. Now, you belong to me."

She cupped his ass with one hand, grinding their genitals together through their clothes. Then she went in for another forced kiss, but Wyatt snapped his head away.

"I said no."

Such a child.

She released him, backed away, smirking at his unused hardon. "Enjoy the blue balls."

She'd never been told no before. And something about it was working for her. But that was going to be a very short-lived feeling. "I'll play your little game... for now. You act the innocent, chaste boy role. But I want you to know, I always win in the end."

She returned to the luxury box, grabbing her shrimp cocktail from the table. She thought about offering Wyatt one but decided that no slave, even one that she wanted to fuck, was worth sharing it with.

"I'll make sure Seth is tended to. He's already on his way to Doc Eunuch. But I expect to be tended to as well. Sooner rather than later."

32

Seth screamed.

It was pain like he'd never experienced before. Not when he was paralyzed. Not even when his leg was cut off.

He screamed until he couldn't scream anymore and then all he could do was moan.

He laid on a cold metal table as the doc injected something green and viscous into his shoulder wound. He emptied one syringe, then grabbed another and went to work.

The pain seemed to grow by the second and Seth just wanted it to be over.

"All right. I think I've got it numbed enough," Doc Eunuch said.

"What the fuck?" Seth asked. "That's supposed to be numb? I feel like my arm's being eaten by a wolverine!"

The Doc furrowed his brow. "It's the best we've got. Sorry, son."

He grabbed a curved needle and thread and went to work, starting on interior tissue, sewing up bits of muscle and tendon. Seth felt every prick, every pull, every tug and groaned through clenched teeth.

Seth knew Doc was trying to help, trying to repair him. The man was more focused than ever before and he trusted him to do a good job, but he longed to pass out so he could sleep through the process.

"Thank you Doc," Seth said, still biting down.

The Doc paused and looked at Seth for a moment, then quickly went back to work, sewing the large gash shut at skin level. "I don't get thanked much. Actually, I never do. It's nice."

Doc pushed a bottle close to Seth's left arm. Seth grabbed it and slowly lifted it to his mouth, taking care not to move too much so the Doc could still stitch him up. He poured what tasted like lighter fluid down his throat greedily.

"You're fortunate that the blade missed everything important. Just meat and skin, really. No arteries or major nerves."

"Just call me Lucky," Seth said. He looked to his right arm that still dangled freely in its skin sack. He made no attempt to move it, lest he want to give his left arm competition for pain level.

Seth stared above and saw his reflection in the shiny metal of the ceiling. What a wreck he was. One eye was swollen shut, the skin around it black, blue, and a deep scarlet. A myriad of cuts carved into his face and two teeth were snapped off from the beating he'd taken.

"I don't like what happened to you, Seth," Doc said as he worked, focusing diligently on his sewing.

"Same," Seth said. "I guess I need to learn how to focus." Truth be told, he didn't feel much like talking about the fight. He was lucky to be alive. If it wasn't for the Doc's chair, he'd be rotting on the mound of dead fighters, food for the carrion.

"I don't mean that." Doc stopped sewing and turned his face to Seth. "It's Rainha's methods I don't approve of. She should never have pitted you against two men while you were still learning how to use the chair."

"She shouldn't put any of us out there," Seth retorted. He hadn't thought much about it, but Wyatt was right. Nobody should be forced into this lifestyle.

"No, she shouldn't. But what she did to you was careless. Reckless. This isn't the first time either."

"Then why do you even work for her? What you did for me, making me that chair and now putting me back together, I really appreciate it, Doc. But why don't you quit and get the fuck out of here." Seth kept staring up at his own reflection as he spoke. "Is it the money? The safety? What?"

The Doc grabbed Seth's face with force. Not enough to hurt him, but enough to make sure Seth was going to hear him well. "Not everything is what it seems, Seth. Your definition of *working for* is a bit off. I wasn't always like this, you know."

He turned Seth's head so he was looking at Doc's mechanical leg. "I lost the real one in the arena. Except the only *Doc*, they had back then barely knew enough to declare a man living or dead. As a result, I was on my own. Either fix myself or be sent to the slaughter. I opted for the former."

"You were a slave, too?" Seth asked, the Doc letting his face go.

"Still am."

"Shit. I'm sorry," Seth said.

"Every worker you see in this compound is owned by Rainha. And we're the lucky ones. We had useful skills outside of fighting. The majority, the great majority... well, they're rotting in Akeldama."

Seth swallowed hard, trying to picture Doc fighting in the arena. "Have you ever considered leaving? Escaping, I mean?"

Doc put his hand over Seth's mouth. "Don't ever say that to anyone else. I don't care if it's another fighter or the slave girl who scrubs Rainha's toilets. Nobody is your friend in here and they will use your words against you. They would sell you out for a scrap of chocolate or a cold beer." He removed his hand from Seth's mouth slowly. "Do you understand?"

"You're my friend," Seth said.

The Doc smiled as he went back to sewing Seth up. This time, Seth managed to endure the pain.

"Perhaps I am," Doc said and Seth watched a tear run down the man's face. "It's been so long since I've had one, I've forgotten how it feels."

"There's a better world out there than this. I've seen places where people might be struggling and it might be dangerous, but they're free to do as they want."

Doc snickered as he tied the knot on Seth's latest round of stitches. "It's a nice thought, but how would we get out? I'm not much of a fighter these days. Not like you or your brother."

"We'll take care of you," Seth promised. "We just need a key to the back gate. Then we'll get out here, get to the water, and figure it out from there. And we'll be free."

Doc thought for a moment and let out a long, tired sigh. "It's been years since I allowed myself to so much as consider the theory of freedom."

Seth tried to lean forward, to look Doc in the eyes, but the pain kept him prostrate. "Do you think you can swipe a key?"

Doc nodded. "Possibly. The guards come in for regular checkups. I could dilate their pupils, blind one temporarily. Make an imprint of the key in clay and mold one from that."

"That sounds like a plan," Seth said.

"Can we really do this?"

Seth tried on a smile, failed. But the sentiment was there. "Trust me. The three of us will get out of here. We'll sail someplace better than this hellhole."

Doc grinned. "I'm in. Now let's set that arm."

Without a second's hesitation, Doc grabbed Seth's broken arm and pulled. The boy screamed as the pain again overwhelmed all of his thoughts.

33

Wyatt sat cross-legged in the moldy hay, which was fairly comfortable when compared to some of the places he'd slept. He'd expected to end up back in the cell upon return to the compound and was shocked when he was taken to the stables instead.

Rainha liking him had some benefits, it seemed. Not that he welcomed her affection.

So many thoughts ran through his head.

Was Seth okay?

How many more times would they have to risk death in the arena?

When was he getting out of here?

How was he getting out of here?

And most of all, why the fuck was Franklin still alive?

But he knew if he attacked him again, Rainha might stop giving him a pass, no matter how much she wanted him in bed. If he murdered Franklin, she might decide he wasn't worth the trouble and kill him too.

Maybe it was worth it.

He needed to clear his mind of the circular logic, he needed a distraction.

Wyatt climbed to his feet and left his stall, drifting toward the voices of some of the older fighters. He could tell from the chatter they were playing cards. Wasting time. Just another day in the life of a slave.

So pathetic.

If they could only understand how much power they would have if they banded together. They could take on Uno. Take on Rainha. Take on anyone else who wanted to strip them of their freedom.

But the men had been slaves too long and had become complacent. More than a few of them even enjoyed their life. He'd never convince them to try for something better.

Wyatt peeked around the corner and saw Franklin sprawled in a bay a few slots down. He shifted, restless, and in visible pain. And he was alone. Both of those facts made Wyatt happy. Or as happy as possible given the circumstances

Franklin hadn't made any friends here. He probably hadn't had the chance between the beatings Wyatt kept giving him.

And that was good. He deserved the worst that life had to offer.

As Wyatt moved in the opposite direction of Franklin, toward the front of the stable, Seth rolled in on his gas-powered chair. Without hesitation, Wyatt sprinted to him, blowing by the other men who looked on with a mix of surprise and confusion.

Wyatt threw his arms around his brother, not caring that the other men reacted to this with wolf-whistles and catcalls.

"Shit, Wyatt. Go a little easy, would you?" Seth asked, gasping in pain.

Wyatt hurriedly backed off and examined his brother. Seth's face was half again its usual size and had gone plum purple with bruising. One arm was in a rugged cast and makeshift sling. The opposite shoulder was covered with Frankenstein-esque stitches.

But he was going to live.

"Are you okay?" Wyatt asked.

"Fucking fantastic, thanks for asking."

"No, I mean, I can see you're not. But, are you hurting much."

"Doc gave me something when he was done. A couple red pills. Don't know what they were and didn't ask, but I feel a hell of a lot better than I did before taking them."

"Good," Wyatt said. He wanted to hug him again but stopped himself. He was just so damned happy to see Seth upright and alert.

"Hey, the crip is back!" Pino shouted.

Wyatt turned and saw the man and a few others had come to check out their battered teammate.

"We thought you were worm food," Chester added.

"Thanks for your concern," Seth said.

Pino leaned in for a good look at Seth's swollen face. "I tell you something, amigo, you can take a beating. Maybe Uno, he use you for a punching bag when you can't fight no more."

That drew raucous laughter from the fighters.

"Let's go outside," Seth said, already arcing his chair around to face the exit. Wyatt followed.

"Oh, the boyfriends need some time alone," Chester crowed. "Be gentle, Wyatt. Your little brother already sore. Don't pound him too hard."

More laughter followed them as they headed into the milky dusk.

"Assholes," Wyatt said.

"Yeah. But I guess they mean well."

Wyatt wasn't so sure. He enjoyed being away from them, enjoyed the relative privacy of the training field after everyone else had cleared off it. The stars had begun to emerge in the sky above and they made him think about better places, better worlds.

"I know how we can get out of here," Seth said, snapping Wyatt out of his daze.

"What? How?"

Seth shook his head. "I can't give you the details yet, but it might be soon. Before the next battles."

Wyatt nodded, his hopes high. Were they really going to be done with this place finally? He knew Seth couldn't win another fight in his current condition. If there was some sort of plan to get them out, that would also spare him from giving in to Rainha's demands. And what a relief that would be.

He knew it was foolish and woefully naive, but he wanted to honor Allie's memory, and what they had together, in whatever way he could. Screwing Rainha, even if it was to keep Seth and himself safe, would sully that.

"I heard you got into a fight with some new slave," Seth said. "What the fuck were you thinking? You're lucky Uno didn't massacre you."

"Don't judge me until I tell you who it was. You're never going to believe--"

"Well, well, well. The prodigal son returns," Franklin said from the edge of the stables.

"Franklin." That was all Seth said.

Wyatt watched Seth's expression go from excitement at surviving, at escaping, to pure hatred and fury.

"I tried to kill him. Twice. They pulled me off before I could," Wyatt said.

Seth swallowed hard and turned away from him. "It doesn't matter. It's either him, or it's us."

Wyatt knew exactly what Seth meant. They needed to keep a low profile until whatever plan Seth was hatching came together. "I know."

"I need some grub," Seth announced, turning back to the stables and driving by Franklin without so much as a cursory glance.

Franklin raised a fat eyebrow at Wyatt. "He didn't even say, hello. I don't think he likes me."

Wyatt pushed past him, into the stables where some leftover food sat atop a table. He began loading up two plates, one for him, one for his brother. But Franklin just couldn't help playing the heel.

"Fix me one too, Wyatt. An extra helping of everything. After all,

I'm a much bigger man than you and need to keep the engine fueled."

"Are you looking for another beat down gringo?" Pinocchio called out from the table toward Franklin

Wyatt glanced over and realized the man's wooden nose had been repaired, albeit poorly. Now it was one narrow sliver of wood that stuck out three inches from his face and making him look more than ever like his namesake.

"Just chatting with some old friends, Pendejo," Franklin said.

Seth grabbed his plate from Wyatt and began gingerly pushing food into his mouth.

"I never knew you to be so quiet, Seth. You sure had plenty to say when you were kissing Papa's ass, pretending to be the son he never had. Up until you gutted him like a fish, anyway."

Wyatt couldn't understand why Franklin was trying so hard to provoke another fight. Mabe Pino was right. Maybe he was looking for a beating. But they weren't going to give it to him.

"Fuck off, Franklin," Wyatt said.

Franklin grinned and instead sat on the nearest bench "Not gonna use any of those crazy gadgets on me, are you Seth?"

"They disable them in between battles. But I wouldn't need anything special to kill you anyway," Seth said. Wyatt felt the chill of his words. He knew Seth wasn't lying.

"And here I thought it was your brother that held a grudge," Franklin said.

"I thought you were dead already. Facedown in a ditch somewhere. Did you follow us?" Seth asked.

Franklin shook his head. "It's a long story, and I'm sure you don't really care about the details."

"Try me," Seth said. "I'm bored."

Franklin shrugged. "Why not? I have always enjoyed the sound of my own voice."

34

"We had you pinned down, I know it," Franklin began. His eyes were drifting up, recalling the events that Wyatt had already lived through.

"Most of the folks from the casino were at the wall. The people you betrayed. We tracked you. Both of you, and your mother and that fucking mongrel dog." Franklin looked back to them. "Hey, where is battle-scarred Barb anyway? She get sold off to a brothel? Little long in the tooth, but I suppose if she can still spread her legs…"

Wyatt and his brother looked to their feet, not caring to voice what happened.

It was a shock when Franklin tendered empathy. "Oh. I'm sorry about that. Of the three of you, she was the one who least deserved to die."

Wyatt balled his fist but kept them at his sides. "I don't give a shit what you think. You can keep your sympathies to yourself."

Franklin held up his hands in a *no mas* gesture. "Hey, I'm just trying—"

"Tell us your story, how you ended up here. Leave out the bullshit," Seth said.

Franklin smiled and Wyatt thought that Franklin was incapable of such a thing. Bullshit was his specialty.

"Alright then," Franklin said. "It was the cannibals. They showed up out of nowhere. In the darkness. Those fuckers got the jump on us. They were so damn quick. And absolutely brutal. Most of the others were dead before I even saw what happened to them. We forgot about you and turned all our fire toward the attack. At first, I thought we might could take them. We killed a passel of them. When you have bullets but the other side doesn't, it makes things a lot easier. But they must have outnumbered us ten to one and before long we were out of ammo. They charged all at once. That's when I got this."

Franklin lifted his chin and stroked his throat. A large scar ran from one side to the other, a purple smiley-face. And the sight of it did make Wyatt smirk.

"Three of 'em grabbed me from behind while another came up front. Had some bone sharpened into a knife maybe? I don't know. It happened so fast. Lucky for me, it was shallow. Just hurt like hell and made me think I was going to die. So I dropped to the ground."

"You didn't even fight back. Or try to save some of the others?" Wyatt asked.

"It's called self-preservation. If they'd known I was still alive... well, I wouldn't have been for long." He broke eye contact. "I heard them die. So much misery. Our people."

Then he looked back to Wyatt, eyes narrowed, nostrils reared back. "My people, I mean. You, neither of you, were ever truly a part of us."

Wyatt had a few words in mind but didn't want to provoke a fight and only shook his head.

"Once the cannibals thought they were done, that we were all dead, they took off. Scattered back into the desert like the vermin they are."

"So you what? Just abandoned the people at the casino to come down here and hunt us?" Seth asked.

Franklin continued. "No, I went back. I needed to be patched up, then I planned to get whoever was left armed and prepared to go find you. But when I got back, they were dead."

"Who?" Seth asked.

"All of them," Franklin said. "Every single person at the casino was slaughtered. We'd taken anyone who could fight worth shit out on that first run after you. That left behind all the old folks and fatties. No one capable of defending themselves."

"*Everyone?*" Seth whispered.

Franklin nodded. "It was awful. I made three rounds, just in case I'd missed someone. But I hadn't. They were all dead and more than a few partially eaten."

Seth wiped his face. Wyatt wasn't sure if he was crying, or just shocked. Either way, he wasn't going to bring attention to it.

"You know," Franklin began, "I understand why you betrayed us, Wyatt. Hell, we may have even deserved it after Allie." Franklin looked from Wyatt to Seth. "But you. Why did you kill Papa? He did nothing against you. He loved you. He told me that every single day, to the point I was sick of fucking listening to it. You were supposed to be the next leader. Even over me. He told me he saw greatness in you." Franklin shook his head, disgusted. "And you thanked him by murdering him in his own bed."

To Wyatt, Seth looked half-distraught. He'd never understood the depths of Seth and Papa's relationship, nor the level of betrayal Seth took on his shoulders to turn on Papa and save his family.

When Seth didn't answer Franklin, the man went on. "I made it to the supply room and patched myself up. Have you ever had to suture your own throat? Let me tell you, it is not the most pleasant thing to do."

"If I had a violin, I'd play it for you," Wyatt found himself saying. Although, he was grudgingly impressed. It reminded him of his mother sewing her eye shut what felt like eons ago.

"Everyone was dead and I didn't know what to do. Where to go. So I packed a bag and left, heading back to the wall. You guys seemed so intent on making it through, I figured, what's the worst that could happen? Everything I had helped to build was gone."

"You tried hunting us down?" Seth asked.

Franklin shrugged. "I don't know. Maybe. Part of me thought I could find you and make you pay."

"A real John Wayne move," Wyatt said. He would have laughed if he wasn't so pissed off by the man's presence.

"I know. But what can I say? Sometimes the thoughts aren't the most clear. I knew I probably wouldn't find you. You had way too much of a head start for me to catch up, and that was *if* I chose the right way to go. I'm no tracker and Mexico's a big place. I just headed south."

"Not the best decision of your life," Wyatt said.

"Maybe, but it looks like we ended up in the same place anyway."

Wyatt closed his mouth. That was easier than admitting Franklin was right.

"I kept walking. I saw the pikes. The heads. The warning signs. But for the longest time, I didn't see a single, living soul. It was actually kind of peaceful. It gave me time to reflect on things. My decisions. Not to give you guys any misconceptions, but I do know that not everything I've done is something to be proud of."

Wyatt rolled his eyes. If Franklin was about to apologize or go into some sort of speech about forgiveness and not deserving their ire, he'd be tempted to throw it all away and kill him right there on the spot.

"But none of it really set in. Not until I actually did find other people. And then…"

Wyatt watched Franklin drift in his words. He was looking up at the ceiling again, remembering things and Wyatt caught a glimpse of water in his eyes. Was this man, the asshole of all assholes, really going to force a tear?

Wyatt wasn't buying it. Franklin was a smooth talker and was more than capable of manipulation. After all, he had been taught by the best.

But then, he looked back at them and Wyatt reconsidered. Franklin was full on sobbing. And unless he'd sent time studying method acting, it was real.

"It was hell down there. I don't know what you went through to get to the casino, and I don't know what you went through to get here, but what I had to see, what I had to do... nobody should have to endure that."

Wyatt and Seth exchanged glances. They had been through a metric ton of shit to get to the casino. But, surprisingly, they hadn't had much difficulty once south of the border. They had Roo and Ernesto to thank for that.

Ernesto... God rest his soul. Small favors were so hard to come by these days.

"The things I was forced to do to survive make what I did to Allie, to Rosario, pale."

Wyatt tensed up at the mention of Allie's name. Just hearing it come out of that man's mouth brought back a slew of memories. Of that day. That moment. Watching her die. Listening to her suffer. He had to squeeze his eyes closed to make it through any more of Franklin's story.

"Kids, parents in front of kids, it didn't matter. If someone is trying to kill you, you have to survive no matter what. And I did what needed doing. Maybe this..." He gestured to everything around them. "Is my penance."

Wyatt didn't know what he was rambling about. Kids? Parents? He was content leaving the finer details as a mystery. He wasn't sure he could stomach them if he had to hear it. At least he knew that Franklin had suffered. But no matter how much he went through, it still wasn't enough.

"Eventually, I made it to the docks in Zihuatanejo. Beautiful beaches, even now, if you can believe that. I met some men that said they would take me with them. I didn't trust them, not really. But with everything I had been through, with the rumors about Central America, I had to do something.

"So I got on a boat with them. But that didn't last. They turned on me. Beat me. Raped me. Then threw me in a cage. I suppose what they said was true. A stupid gringo that didn't know any better. We passed through the Panama Canal, back into the Atlantic. I don't know how long went by, but eventually, we ended up here.

"They sold me to some guy called the Drip, who I believe you caught a glimpse of just before that greeting you gave me," Franklin said to Wyatt. "But that didn't work out and..." He shrugged. "Here I am."

35

THE ONLY TIME THE STABLES WERE QUIET WAS NIGHT, AND EVEN then quiet was a relative storm. Several of the men snored. A few cried and moaned in their sleep. And Pino had a habit of unleashing a shotgun fart every fifteen minutes. Wyatt sometimes thought that, if he had a watch, he could set it by those gaseous outbursts.

He was awake when Seth rolled to the entrance of his stall and he was on his feet before his brother came to a complete stop.

They didn't risk a spoken word, instead signaling to one another with their eyes. After days of waiting, it was time.

Wyatt and Seth were getting out of there. Leaving slavery, fighting, and everything else behind. They were going to find their promised land. Their reason for leaving Maine. Their haven in a world that needed one more than ever.

Wyatt grabbed the back of Seth's chair, opting to push him instead of his brother revving the engine on the chair. It was far from whisper quiet and they needed to be as stealthy as possible. Even the slightest noise could wake someone. The moment that happened was either when the clock started ticking, or when the plan fell apart altogether.

As they passed the other stalls, Wyatt stole glances at the sleeping men, ensuring no one was alert and watching. When they came to Franklin's stall, Wyatt paused, Seth's chair nearing a complete stop.

"What are you doing?" Seth hissed.

Wyatt stared at the bastard, sleeping so peacefully. No one deserved a good night's sleep less than Franklin.

With the others dead to the world, he could slip into that stall, wrap his hands around the man's scarred throat, and choke the life out of him without anyone realizing it was happening. Then, with Franklin's life ended, he and Seth could disappear into the night.

It would be so simple. So easy. So deserved.

"Leave him," Seth whispered through gritted teeth. "He's not worth it."

He was, but this was Seth's plan and Wyatt wasn't going to risk ruining it. He resumed pushing, leaving behind the man he loathed more than any other.

After making it past all of them without incident, they emerged into the open air where a cool evening breeze kissed Wyatt's sweat-slicked skin. It wasn't hot enough to perspire but nerves had caused the eruption.

They made it twenty more yards before hearing his voice.

"What are you two plotting now?" Franklin asked, his voice carrying across the night.

Both Wyatt and Seth turned and found him standing on the precipice of the field.

"What are you doing up?" Wyatt asked.

"I could ask the same thing. Matter of fact, I just did," Franklin said, a little louder.

"Fuck off," Wyatt whispered.

"Oh really? That's how you're going to talk to me right now?" Franklin said, approaching a volume that would surely wake everyone.

"Alright, alright. Keep your voice down," Seth said. "We're getting out of here."

"Then I'm coming along," Franklin whispered grinning.

"Sorry, but we've hit our asshole quota," Wyatt said.

"I know you hate me," Franklin said. "But use your head. You either take me with you, or I shout, *'Swarm'*, and bring every man in the compound down on your heads."

"Or I could just kill you instead," Wyatt said, his blood pumping hard.

"Think you can manage that before I alert this whole camp?"

"Alright," Seth whispered. "You're in."

"The hell he i—"

"Wyatt, we don't have a choice. We either bring him, or we don't get out of here. Besides, he can be an extra pair of eyes to make sure we haven't been spotted. Will you do that?" Seth asked Franklin.

Franklin smiled and lifted his hands, submissive. "Hey, I'm all about the team. Hoora and all that shit."

Wyatt steamed in front of them. He knew that Seth was right, but all the joy he'd felt over escaping had been halved.

"Fine. But remember, this is Seth's show. We do what he tells us, no questions asked," Wyatt said.

"Works for me. At least the brains are in charge and not the ass," Franklin commented.

Wyatt ignored the jab, even though he would have preferred to smack the smile off his face.

Seth pointed to the west side of the field where the electrified fence hummed. "We need you positioned at the spot near the alley. If the guards come around, you have to distract them while we take down the electricity. When you hear it go out, join us over there." Seth pointed to a spot fifty yards away. "We'll cut the wire and push through. Got it?"

Franklin nodded. "Sure. If I see any guards, I'll tell them I couldn't sleep and decided to squeeze one out."

"Fine. Just make sure they don't see us," Seth said.

"Will do, boss," Franklin said. "See, it's not hard to be a team player. You should keep up, Wyatt." Franklin tapped Wyatt on the shoulder and began to swiftly make his way across the long training field. Eventually, he reached his lookout point and waited there.

"I don't like this at all," Wyatt said.

"And I don't care," Seth said. "Follow me."

Wyatt did as Seth manually pumped the wheels on his chair. They made their way to the door leading to Doc Eunuch's medical room.

"Are we breaking in?" Wyatt asked.

"Just wait," Seth said. His face was pinched, nervous, but soon the door opened, and his expression switched to relief.

Doc hobbled out of the doorway. "You're confident this scheme will succeed?"

"Absolutely," Seth said. "You have the key, right?"

"Right here," Doc said, opening his hand. "Molded it while checking Huberto for glaucoma. He didn't suspect a thing."

"Secret Agent Doc, right here," Seth said, cocking his thumb at the man.

Doc beamed with a prideful smile.

"Let's go," Seth said, pushing back to the stables and toward the gate.

"What's going on?" Wyatt asked. "The electrical box is back there."

Seth smiled. "We don't need to cut the power. We're unlocking the gate and getting the fuck out of Dodge."

"So, Franklin..."

"Just bought the biggest river of shit this side of the Amazon. We don't need to kill him. In this place, he'll be dead within a week."

Wyatt grinned, impressed with his brother's quick wits and powers of deception. The kid was so damn good it was scary. Thank God they were on the same side.

At the gate, Doc deftly popped the lock with his makeshift key and eased it open, the hinges giving a protesting whine that put all three men on edge. But, upon looking around, it seemed no one else had heard the sound.

As they slipped out of the compound, closing and relocking the gate behind them, Wyatt couldn't help but think about Franklin standing by the fence, waiting for the power to go out so he could escape with them.

Waiting for freedom that would never come.

It was delicious.

36

They moved swiftly and silently, but the further they went the less they felt caution was needed. They were half a mile from the compound and entering the city.

Random street lamps threw long shadows and they tried to move within them. Wyatt had expected the roads and alleys to be teeming with addicts and sex workers, but they hadn't seen a person. He wondered if there was a curfew, or if people were so unconcerned with their sins that they were comfortable fulfilling them in the light of day and had no need to hide them in the dark.

None of them spoke as they made their way through the maze of streets. Wyatt and Seth had only been through them once, but Doc navigated them with ease. Twisting and turning his way through the grid, taking them closer to what passed for civilization here.

Finally, they turned down a street that seemed familiar from their walk in. And it was filled with people.

Prostitutes and their customers. There was a nightlife after all.

They all looked at the newcomers the same way. With silent, suspect eyes. As if to say, *You don't belong here.*

But the workers who weren't already occupied still tried making a buck.

One woman who was missing her two front teeth slithered up next to Wyatt. She smelled like potpourri and feces and he struggled not to gag.

"I got a three for one special," she cooed, pushing her tongue through the gap in her teeth. "I'll blow your minds and won't stop there."

"We're not interested. Get off." Wyatt pulled his arm free.

She huffed as the three continued past her. "Don't know where you're from, but the city at night ain't no place you want to be."

Wyatt ignored her as Doc led the other two down the alley. She may have been right, but there was no other choice. And the more familiar the streets looked, the more anxious Wyatt was to get to the water. To get off this island. The closer he came to freedom, the more he craved it. The more he knew he'd die without it.

Doc turned left at the next intersection, but Wyatt knew that wasn't the route they'd taken upon arriving on the island. They should be going straight ahead, down the alley where he'd seen all the drugs addicts.

"No. It's this way," Wyatt said.

Doc looked into the black abyss and shook his head. "I don't think so. That doesn't look safe to me."

"Nowhere here is safe," Wyatt said heading into the stygian route.

"Come on, Doc. We'll be okay," Seth promised.

Doc's throat clicked as he swallowed hard, but he relented and followed.

Which was good as the last thing he wanted was to waste time arguing. The longer they were in the open, exposed, the greater the chance something could go wrong.

But as he ran further into the alley, he started to wonder if Doc was right. Because instead of addicts getting their fix, the backstreet was filled with corpses.

Some were recent and still looked fresh, but most had been there for days, maybe a week or more. A few had burst, spilling internal organs infested with maggots. The smell made him think of Akeldama and the pile of defeated fighters. It made him even more determined never to go back.

They turned another corner, and what Wyatt found sickened him. Fifteen, maybe twenty people sat on the pavement, each one chained to the next. Their faces were battered and swollen. They moaned constantly in pain. But, worst of all were their mouths which were crudely sewn closed with nylon fishing line.

What the hell had they stumbled upon?

As if to answer his question, a gang of men carrying melee weapons emerged from a nearby loading dock. There was no chance to hide before Wyatt and his party were spotted.

"Who the hell are you?" asked a hulking man carrying a sickle.

"No one. We're just trying to find the docks," Wyatt said. "We'll turn around if this isn't the way."

He was worried this would take a bad turn and if it did, they were outnumbered four to one, and he didn't imagine either Seth or Doc were up for a fight.

"No, no. It's fine. You're going the right way," the man said, his voice surprisingly cordial.

The bound and mutilated men and women nearby belied his geniality, but whatever their business was, Wyatt wasn't going to get involved. He just wanted out of there. He moved forward a yard, two, then his progress was stopped by the gang blocking his way and they made no sign they were moving.

"Can we go on?" Wyatt asked.

"*You* can, but let us have those two weirdos. They look like fun toys." The man twisted his wrist side to side, side to side, the moonlight reflecting off the sickle's blade.

"We'll find another way," Seth said. "Sorry for bothering you."

But they couldn't. Ten more men stepped behind them, surrounding them.

The people chained up in the alley tried to scream, tried to beg, but their attempts barely escaped their sutured lips.

"I bet their holes look just as pretty as their mouths do," the leader commented to his crew.

Wyatt's eyes widened as he realized what the people chained to the walls in the alley were used for. No way that was happening to him. He wished he had something, anything he could use for a weapon, but all he had were his fists. He clenched them, then whispered to his allies. "You ready for this Seth?"

Seth was facing the opposite direction, looking at the other ten men behind them. "There's way too many," Seth said.

"What other choice do we have?" he asked.

Doc had pressed himself into the brick wall, trying to melt into it. He'd be no help with their upcoming fight and, even though Wyatt knew it would end badly, he planned to make a stand regardless.

And it was time to prove it.

37

The gang charged Wyatt's trio from both sides.

They were trapped. Outnumbered.

We die tonight, Wyatt realized. And, in a way, it was almost a relief. The road had been so long. The journey, so hard.

Just as the thought hit him, so did a fist. Hard knuckles connected with his cheek, splaying open the skin with a splatter of blood. Another hand flew at him, but he ducked just in time and threw his own punch, connecting with the large gang leader's jaw. The man stumbled backward and spit blood.

All things considered, it wasn't a bad start.

Then, the attack came from all fronts. He felt a fist connect with his jaw and he went down. Then the kicking started. Dozens of booted feet pummeled him. One blow broke a rib, another stomped his hand.

He looked for Seth, for Doc, to see how they were faring. The answer was, not well. Three men dragged Seth from his chair. Doc was on his knees, arms covering his head as he trembled in submission.

Wyatt tried to fight his way back to his feet, but he couldn't even see where the attacks were coming from. It was anywhere and everywhere all at once.

Then the hands started grabbing at him and pulled him up, lifting him off his feet.

The gang leader, blood trickling from the corner of his mouth, got in Wyatt's face and exhaled rank breath into his nostrils. "Don't fight so hard. We don't want to kill you. There are better ways to use a pretty boy like you."

Wyatt struggled, but they held him tight.

A loud whistle came from the far end of the alley Wyatt, echoing down the street and bouncing off the walls. Everyone, Seth, Doc, Wyatt, and all the members of the gang turned their attention toward the sound.

And what they found was Rainha, silhouetted by the moonlight. She wore a leopard-skin coat which flapped in the gentle, night breeze. Uno stood next to her, dwarfing her, even though she was larger than most men.

Wyatt didn't know whether to be terrified or relieved. So he tried both. He was glad for the interruption, to know he wouldn't end up being used for his holes, but whatever happened after this wasn't going to be good for him.

"Let them go, Hector," Rainha commanded.

"Why should we? Finders keepers, isn't that what they say?" Hector, the gang leader, said cockily.

Rainha shook her head. "They belong to me. I own them."

Hector smirked. "They're fighters? Could've fooled me. You must really be scraping the barrel if you're putting up men like this."

"My business is none of your concern."

"If you value your toys, you should keep a better eye on them. These men came to us. Seems to me, that makes them our property now."

Rainha stepped out of the shadows and into the light, fearless as she approached the large group of thugs and savages. "What you say is true. You haven't stolen from me. Yet. That's why I'm going to let you live, doing this disgusting thing you do." She glanced at Hector's captives, judgment clouding her eyes. "But only if you obey."

"Fuck you," Hector said. "You don't own me, punta!"

"Hector!" one of the men holding Wyatt said, his voice full of fear. "What are you thinking?" He let go of Wyatt, backed away from Rainha, made it five steps, then turned and ran.

A half dozen of the others made similar, swift retreats. No one was left holding Seth or Doc and only Hector and another still clung to Wyatt, but a few other lackeys lurked about, trying to decide whether they were stupid enough to remain loyal to their boss.

"That's a good start," Rainha said.

"This is bullshit," Hector said. He reminded Wyatt of a little kid having a tantrum. "You can't do this. You fucking bitch. You came into my territory. You know the rules."

Don't be an idiot," Rainha said.

"Fuck you. They're mine," Hector said. This time, he meant it. He grabbed a fistful of Wyatt's hair, snapping his head back, and held the sickle against his neck. The blade felt ice cold on his skin..

"Wrong choice, Hector," Rainha said.

She and Uno charged into the remaining gang. The men dumb enough to stay and fight did their best, but it didn't matter.

Wyatt had seen Rainha fight once before against the loudmouth she had bought in the auction. This time it was different.

She was even quicker than Wyatt remembered. She dodged fists, bats, and knives. Not a single hand had been laid upon her as she raced toward Wyatt and the others, ducking and gracefully slipping past would be attackers along the way.

And Rainha had her own weapons. In each hand she held a double-bladed knife and she used it mercilessly. Bodies fell in her wake and those who still had life in them when they hit the ground were finished off by Uno who followed behind, a sledgehammer in his hands.

Panicked, Hector released Wyatt and turned his attention to

Rainha. He swung his sickle, but got only air. His second attempt nicked her coat, slicing an inch long gash through a leopard spot.

That infuriated her.

She slashed with her right hand and cut his throat. As he tried to cover the wound she sent the knife in her left hand across his belly. Intestines poked out of the wound and began to push their way through like rope sausage trying to escape a sack.

Then Uno had ahold of him, one huge hand on each side of Hector's head. He lifted the dying man off the ground with ease, then smashed his face into the brick wall. The sound of every bone in his face breaking sounded like a gunshot in the otherwise quiet night.

Then Uno did it again.

Hector went limp and Uno let his body drop to the macadam.

The few gang members who'd lasted that long spun and fled. Uno looked to Rainha, to see if he should chase them down and end them, but she shook her head.

"Leave them. They can tell their friends what happens to those who disrespected us."

Doc was still cowering between Seth and Wyatt. Seth had managed to climb back into his chair. All three had stood by, helpless, useless, as Rainha and Uno saved their lives. Some fighters.

Uno moved to Rainha's side, awaiting his next order.

And Wyatt fully expected the order to be simple.

Kill the escaped slaves.

38

"If you wanted a night on the town, you should have asked," Rainha said, putting her two knives in the sheaths on her hips. She looked like some sort of apocalyptic warrior, which Wyatt found ironic since he supposed, they were living through the apocalypse.

Uno paced around the three of them, stepping over the dead bodies. The captives on the walls continued to mumble and moan, but it was just background noise at that point. Wyatt was too busy fearing for his own life to worry about their plight.

"Nothing to say for yourselves?" Rainha asked.

"Rainha, I'm sor—" Doc began.

"Shut up!" Rainha screamed. "You know the rules. There's only one way out. If you want it, then you challenge me or Uno. If that's what you want, then we'll throw down right here and now. You win, you keep going on your way. We won't stop you. We won't come to your rescue either."

Wyatt stepped forward. If a fight was inevitable, then he might as well start.

But Seth grabbed his arm, dragging him back. That shocked

Wyatt as his little brother was always eager to brawl no matter how bad the odds. But Seth was also smart enough to know a certain loss when he saw one and, after Rainha's show, there was no doubt she could slaughter all three of them without breaking a nail.

Rainha smiled at the submission. She looked Wyatt over, up, and down, like he was a piece of meat. "I saw blood on Hector's face. Was that you?"

Wyatt nodded.

"I assumed as much. But then you were overwhelmed and needed me to save your asses, am I right?"

None of the trio answered.

"Even after that, still defiant?" Rainha licked her lips, rubbed her crotch, and gave a low groan. Wyatt could tell she was playing with him. Toying with him. "Nothing like a good fight to get the juices flowing," she said.

Then her demeanor flipped. She stood straighter, back to her threatening, cold stance as she eyed Doc. "But you, Eunuch. I'm very disappointed," she said.

The small man kept his head tucked, his back stooped. He looked like a frightened puppy being scolded for peeing on the floor. "I'm sorry, Rainha."

"These two, they're new. They're young. But you, you knew better," she said.

Doc's eyes went wide, even more fear flooding into them. "No, please. I'll be good. Please Rainha. Give me a chance."

She smiled joylessly. "Fine. I accept your challenge," she said.

She spun away and retreated up the alley, back where she came from.

Wyatt watched as Doc ran, as best as he could with the mechanical leg. He grabbed one of the dead men's bats and hobbled toward Rainha. She was so unthreatened that she never even looked back as the sound of his movement.

Doc raised the bat, swung, and Rainha danced to the side. Off-balance from his attempted homerun, Doc stumbled sideways, tried to get his balance, and failed.

He dropped to the ground in an awkward heap, a cry escaping his lips.

Only then did Rainha acknowledge his presence. She turned to the man on the ground, then stepped over him.

Doc didn't even fight back as Rainha placed a foot against his neck, then applied pressure. His frail arms flailed like he was conducting to an invisible orchestra. Then he coughed a mouthful of blood onto her shoe.

"Bastard!" she muttered, backing away from him and crouching down to examine her stained footwear. "This will never come out."

Her head snapped to Uno. "Finish him off."

Uno trudged toward the Doc, choking and gasping, already most of the way dead. He gave the man a long look, then turned his face away as he brought an oversized boot down on the Doc's face, crushing his head.

With a weak gurgle, Doc died.

Wyatt stared at the body of the man that had gotten them out of the compound. He knew the message that was being sent. Doc had been a loyal servant who made one mistake and, as a result, died like a dog in the street. There would be no more second chances for him or Seth, no matter how much Rainha valued them.

She was in charge. And they were hers to do with as she pleased.

"Let's go," she said.

"What about them?" Seth asked, gesturing to the people chained up and helpless. They continued to scream through their sewn shut lips.

"Not our concern," was all that Rainha said.

They left their friend dead in the alley. They left the captives chained and helpless.

This was Rainha's world. And they were only spectators.

39

To Wyatt's surprise, he and Seth faced no punishment for their escape attempt, at least not from Rainha. Uno rode them but hard in training, but even that was barely above the usual. It was almost like it hadn't happened.

Training had ended for the day and Wyatt was heading back to the stables when he heard his name being called.

"Wyatt!" Seth half-whispered, half-shouted.

Wyatt looked and found his brother at the gates, and he was not alone. Abuelita was there too. Seth waved him over and, after a quick look around to make sure none of the others were watching, Wyatt jogged to them.

"It's so nice to see you again, Wyatt," Abuelita said, a warm smile crossing her withered face.

"It's good to see you too," he said.

"I was just telling her how we're on the shit list," Seth said.

"That I already knew," Abuelita said.

"Word gets around, I guess." Wyatt sighed.

"It does." Abuelita looked on the verge of passing out. She held onto the gate with both hands to keep herself upright.

"Are you okay?" Wyatt asked.

She nodded. "Just old. It sneaks up on you." She reached through the gate, running her hand across Wyatt's sweat-slicked arm. "I'm so relieved you're okay. When I heard what happened…"

Wyatt wasn't sure how to respond. Was she sincere or spying on them? Seth ended up breaking the awkward silence.

"We're tough," he said. "We've been through worse."

Abuelita looked at them with possibly the saddest look in the history of the world. "You have?" she asked. "That's awful. Two young men, already experiencing such hardship. So unfair."

Wyatt thought she might cry and couldn't understand why she was so emotional, then he remembered the son she lost, and any distrust he had over her motives faded.

"We'll be okay," he said. "One way or another."

That brightened the woman's expression. "I do hope so. You're both such good boys. You deserve a better life than this."

Abuelita looked past them, to the training field, to the stables.

"Maybe you should tell Rainha that," Wyatt said, drawing a *what the fuck* stare from his brother. He knew the comment was out of line, but if the woman was truly sympathetic to their station, maybe she'd be willing to help.

"I have. More times than I can remember."

"You could try again," Wyatt said and that time Seth threw an elbow into his ribs.

"My daughter listens to no one but herself. The rest of us…" She waved her hand around her head. "Are just gnats buzzing in her ear."

"We know, Abuelita," Seth said, trying to play peacemaker. "We know you'd help if you could."

That wasn't good enough for Wyatt though. "Help us escape. You must know all the ins and outs of this place. There has to be a way."

"Wyatt!" Seth hissed.

Abuelita patted Seth's leg. "It's alright. Your brother is trying to protect you. I could never find offense in that." She looked up to

Wyatt. "Your cohort, Doc Eunuch tried to get you out. He didn't fare very well, did he?"

"You're her mother," Wyatt said, but even as the word came out of his mouth he wasn't sure it made a difference.

"I am. And that matters not at all. A betrayal from me would enrage her. She'd show no mercy. In fact, she'd punish me even worse, out of principle."

Wyatt wasn't sure he believed that, but he knew pushing the matter in this moment would only alienate her. "Okay. I apologize for asking."

Abuelita shook her head. "Never apologize for doing what's right for yourself, Wyatt. Never apologize."

She picked up a wicker basket that sat beside her feet and pulled a plaid cloth off the top. Inside were muffins, freshly baked. The smell was intoxicating. "I made these for you both. But only you. Don't share with the others. They don't deserve it."

Wyatt and Seth each reached through the bars and grabbed three muffins apiece. Wyatt had no intention of sharing and as Seth bit one in half, he appeared to be of the same mindset.

"Sweet baby Elvis," Seth moaned through a mouthful of muffin. "It's like eating a slice of Heaven."

Wyatt decided he couldn't wait and chomped in. His brother was right. They were amazing. He shoved the rest of the muffin into his mouth, almost choking on it, but there couldn't be a better way to go out.

Abuelita beamed. "Enjoy them, boys. And I'll see you around, I hope."

She left them to eat and they did.

40

They were back at Akeldama, sitting in the dugout in preparation for the day's battles, but Wyatt struggled to stay invested in the goings-on. All he could think about was how he'd blown his chance - maybe his only chance - of getting out of this world, this life.

Guards had been positioned in the stables, keeping watch at night. And still more of them stalked the perimeter ceaselessly. He couldn't imagine another chance would arise that would allow both him and Seth to break free of the compound.

And that realization was worse than any punishment Rainha could have doled out.

"It's time for the scourge," Rainha announced, stepping into view.

A smattering of nervous, scared chatter passed between the fights, and for the first time of the day, he paid attention. He was shocked to see her there, and it was clear from the reaction of the others that this was unusual.

"Most of you know what that means. Some of you will find out soon. As you know, I usually don't trek down here to field level, but I wanted to remind you of the most important rule you must follow as my slaves." She looked them over, one at a time. "When you betray me, there are consequences."

Wyatt knew that meant he or his brother - or both - were going to be forced into a battle even though they weren't on the day's schedule.

He heard snickers from the other fighters, catcalls. And all their eyes were on him and Seth. They too knew what was happening. The Morrill brothers were getting punished for their escape attempt.

"I'm a very fair owner. If you haven't realized that already, you should learn it now." She stared at Wyatt. "There are far worse owners out there. Men and women who would let you get fat and lazy, then toss you into the ring unfit for fighting. A death sentence. With me, you have every opportunity to better yourselves. All you need to do is keep me happy." Her mouth turned up in a smirk. "That's not so bad, is it?"

Some of the men mumbled responses. Wyatt remained silent.

"Tell us, Rainha," Chester said. "Who's fighting?" He stared at Wyatt as he asked.

"You can't guess?" Rainha asked.

Laughter filled the dugout.

Then her response silenced them all. "Franklin, come to me."

Franklin looked around at the other fighters. Everyone had the same look on their faces.

Confusion.

"You're going to fight for the first time at Akeldama," she said. "Consider it an honor."

"Him?" Pino asked, his voice annoyed, maybe even pissed off.

Rainha quickly turned to him. "Is there a problem with that?" she asked.

Pino knew enough to stay silent.

"Any man who questions my selection, please make yourself known. You can join Franklin on the field."

The silence continued.

"Good." Rainha glanced at her trainer. "Uno, get him ready."

Uno pulled Franklin out of the dugout, to a small patch of grass where he pumped up the men before sending them out to their possible deaths.

Rainha walked in front of Wyatt and crouched down in front of him, so close that only he could hear her words. "This is for you," she said. "I'm not so bad."

Wyatt watched her walk away, her statuesque figure on perfect display in a white leather catsuit. Then he glanced at Franklin, standing before Uno, trying to work himself into a frenzy for the coming battle.

All things considered, she was right. This wasn't bad at all.

41

Franklin's legs shook as his feet sunk into the blood-soaked grass. He looked ready to jump out of his skin at the first loud noise and Wyatt couldn't help but be excited. He'd have preferred to kill the man on his own, to avenge Allie's murder, but there was an old saying about beggars and choosers, and Wyatt fell fully into the former camp.

"This is bullshit," a voice muttered from beside Wyatt.

Wyatt looked, only to have a shoulder shoved into his side as the man passed by him.

"What's your problem?" He was past the point of avoiding confrontation.

"You," the man everyone called Worm said. He had a large scar on the side of his cheek, one that cut through a dense, dark beard. looked like a narrow atoll in the center of a black sea.

Wyatt never socialized with the other fighters and rarely spoke to them. Not because he thought he was better, but because he was different. These men had all accepted, and sometimes embraced, their station. He worried that if he became their friend, he might do the same. They took that as him being a snob.

"Sounds like a personal problem," Wyatt said.

The man's face went red. He took two charging steps at Wyatt before Pinocchio stepped between them, placing a hand on the man's chest.

"It's not worth it, Worm," Pinocchio said, steering him in the opposite direction.

Worm grumbled but left the altercation before it could get going.

"What crawled up his ass?" Wyatt asked Pino.

Pinocchio scowled at Wyatt. "Nobody is happy about your boy being out there."

"He's not my boy. I hate his fucking guts."

"Doesn't matter. You and your brother, you broke the rules and Rainha did nothing. You even got second helpings of dessert. We're sick of the special treatment you two get."

Wyatt shook his head, audibly. "I can't help that. She does what she wants. I have no say in it."

"We all know what she wants." Pino sneered.

Wyatt narrowed his eyes. "What do you mean?"

"As if you don't know. You got eyes and ears, don't you? She wants your cock, boy. And you'll give it to her if you're half as smart as you think you are."

"Bullshit," Wyatt said. "We getting out of here and--"

Pino made a quacking duck motion with his hand, rolling his eyes. "You already tried that. How far did it get you?" Pino leaned in close. "Tell me about the world outside of the compound. Does it look like a place fit for civilized men?"

Wyatt looked down and didn't answer.

"I keep telling you, Wyatt, all the planet has turned to shit. This," he motioned to their surroundings, "Is the best you're gonna find. So go ahead and fuck Rainha, take whatever pleasures you can get from life." Pino leaned in so close their faces were mere inches apart. "Stop hoping for more, boy. It'll only break your heart."

Wyatt didn't have a comeback for that. It was too raw and honest and - as much as he hated to admit it - probably true.

"Fans," a voice boomed over speakers. "Are you ready for the scourge?"

The crowd erupted.

Wyatt, eager to change the subject, used that toward his advantage. "What is the scourge anyway?" he asked Pino.

"A way to get rid of dead weight." Pinocchio blew a raspberry as he exhaled. "It pits fighters against the worst of the worst. Feral cannibals. They got some psycho bounty hunter who steals them from the north. Then they're starved, to make men into animals. When they're good and ready, they're brought here to battle. It's like nothing you've ever seen."

He saw Wyatt's expression of disgust and nodded.

"It's worse than you're imagining."

Wyatt swallowed hard. He'd seen depravity on the road. Lived through a different kind of madness at the casino. And what he'd found in the alley a few nights ago was awful. Could this really be worse than all of that?

As he pondered that thought, he watched Franklin prepare for the fight that would end his time on earth.

42

In a way, Wyatt pitied Franklin. To be out on the field alone, never having done it before, not knowing what he was in store for. Plus, to be told that he was fighting something called *the scourge*. Franklin's heart was probably beating out of his chest.

Then, Wyatt thought of his sweet, innocent Allie, slaughtered for no reason, and what little pity he felt for the man quickly rushed out of his body.

The gates opened across from Franklin, and immediately the bell sounded over the loudspeaker. There was no introduction, no allowing the other fighters to come out and get settled. Then Wyatt realized why.

Out of the gate at the other end of the field burst five men. Except, when Wyatt took a good look, they barely seemed human.

They bounded out like animals, running on all fours. They kept low to the ground, snarling and sniffing. They were so lean Wyatt could count their rubs, but their flesh was also stretched taut over ropey muscle. They looked built for carnage.

All of them were constrained by leashes that lead back to their handler. He looked more human, and walked upright, but was every bit as wild. His matted hair was in knots on top of his head, as if he hadn't washed it ten years. His face was marred with scars and festering sores. He had no upper lip, keeping his teeth permanently bared.

Wyatt wasn't sure who was more disgusting. The feral cannibals, or the man that made them.

As Wyatt watched, as the entire arena watched, the handler dropped the leashes and the cannibals took off running. Occasionally they stood completely upright and took some steps, but they continued to fall back down to their hands. Something about them not wanting to stay standing gave Wyatt the shivers.

Franklin backed away as fast as his feet could slog through the muck. He wasn't calculated. He was frantic. His eyes searched for something, anything, that could help him stay alive.

Then Franklin set his gaze on a pile of weapons against the wall. He sprinted to them, much quicker than the cannibals that gave chase, and grabbed the first thing his hands laid upon. A wooden spear.

Franklin spun around and looked at the oncoming threat. He held his hand back, concealing his weapon, waiting for them to come to him.

It was a smart move. They were still twenty yards away and hadn't seen him take up arms, but Wyatt would have found a better position, and maybe have grabbed a different weapon. Something steel, Something unbreakable.

When the cannibals were in range, Franklin launched the spear at the pack's front runner. The spear soared through the air, straight and true--

And went five feet over the cannibal's head. It landed in the muddy field, sticking up from the ground. Not a bad toss if Franklin was trying to win the javelin throw in the Olympics. Terrible if he was trying to kill one of the creatures bearing down on him.

Despite the horror of the situation, Wyatt laughed out loud. He wasn't the only one. The crowd burst into guffaws and catcalls. As much as he hated to admit it, Wyatt was beginning to understand why the crowd loved the battles. At least he had a good reason to root for the man to die.

The lead cannibal caught up to Franklin, tackling him to the ground. They splashed into the field together, covering them both with a sour, rotting blood and mud. Wyatt could barely tell them apart as they thrashed about in the muck and, within seconds, were drenched in the gore.

Any mystery as to who was who vanished when the biting started. Franklin bellowed as a mouthful of flesh was ripped from his bicep.

It made Wyatt think back to his first run-in with the cannibals - Red's motley crew. That man's circular logic had insisted they were still people because they cooked their prey and didn't eat them raw. They weren't monsters, they said.

Then he thought of the cannibal they captured at the casino. How thin he looked. How he had been pushed to the way he was. For his family.

While there may have been some truth to all of it, these cannibals in the arena were different. They had been pushed even further. To the point where anything inside them that had once been human was long gone. These were monsters.

The first cannibal was too busy chomping down his mouthful of Franklin tartar to keep fighting, but the man's reprieve was short-lived as the next two were on him. They hit him at the same time, all three tumbling down in a flailing melee.

But instead of joining together to attack Franklin, the two cannibals began fighting each other. One of them, Wyatt thought she was a woman but couldn't be sure, grabbed the hair of the other twisting and ripping. The man being attacked howled, then kicked her in the midsection, trying to break her grip to no avail.

With their attention diverted, Franklin took the opportunity to get the upper hand. He swung, landing a haymaker on the male cannibal, catching him square in the jaw.

The cannibal fell backward, shaking his head, stunned. Franklin then threw his weight on top of the female cannibal, knocking her to the ground and landing atop her.

Franklin screamed as he slammed his face into hers in a crushing headbutt that shattered her cheekbone. Then, as she tried to recuperate from the blow, he bit into her throat and reared back, ripping out a huge chunk of meat. Blood spurted like water from a fountain and within seconds she was on the ground, dying.

It was like a switch had gone off inside of Franklin. Gone was the scared, unsure man who'd shook when he stepped onto the field of blood. In its place was a warrior.

Wyatt remembered him saying that he'd done things a man should never have to do. Now he was seeing the results of being forced to do those things.

Franklin was the wild animal. His eyes so full of ferocious fury it seemed like even the cannibals were afraid.

He screamed as the man he'd punched began to come for him, rushing the cannibal and snatching its rat's nest of hair. Using that hair, he spun, hurling the man into the barriers at the side of the field. When the man hit, bones broke and although he wasn't dead, he wasn't springing to his feet to rejoin the fight either.

The cannibal who'd bit Franklin only then realized what was happening. It swallowed its partially chewed chow and galloped toward Franklin, but the fighter was ready. He caught the cannibal in a headlock, then dragged him to the side, where the other man still laid dazed and broken in the dirt.

He rammed the cannibal's head into the wall, again and again and again, until it was a broken, seeping sack of broken skull. Then, to continue the show, Franklin stepped to the dazed cannibal, raised his booted foot, and brought it down on the man's neck. The sound of his spine snapping carried across the field.

The crowd roared with cheers. They were loving every minute of it even if it was far from the outcome anyone had expected. Wyatt was sure they were used to seeing the lone fighter be massacred, eaten, devoured in front of their eyes. This time, Franklin had turned feral.

The last two cannibals charged Franklin, but he was prepared, calm, and quick. He grabbed another of the carved spears, this time, not holding it over his shoulder. This time, holding like it was a club.

Just as the first cannibal came within reach, Franklin stepped to the side and swung. His aim was dead on and he connected with the cannibal's throat. It dropped to the ground, gasping for breath, its windpipe crushed. His face went red and then he was gone.

Franklin looked at the last cannibal and quickly spun the spear around. Its momentum was too great to stop and the thing impaled itself through the abdomen.

Franklin pushed hard, running the spear through until he was face to face with the attacker. Then, Franklin spat in its face and ripped the weapon to the side. The cannibal's stomach tore open, spilling intestines onto the ground before falling and dying in its own steaming guts.

With the crowd screaming with bloodlust, Franklin growled low, but loud. Then he turned to the handler - the filthy, lipless man who'd created these creatures. Franklin howled like he was an animal. Like he had swallowed the souls of the cannibals and had become them.

The handler never stood a chance. Franklin charged and Wyatt could have sworn that he saw Franklin take to running on all fours for a quick gallop. Like a flash of light, gone in a blink. As soon as he caught up to the handler, he stood tall.

The man brought up a club, ready to strike, but Franklin was too fast. He grabbed the man's wrist and twisted his arm, wrenching it backward, popping his shoulder out of its socket. Then, Franklin kicked the man in his kneecap, folding the joint backward. With a scream, the handler fell to the field, writing in pain, dropping his club.

Franklin picked it up, rose it high above, then brought it down with every bit of strength he possessed. It smashed into and through the handler's face, knocking a baseball-sized hole where the man's nose and upper teeth had once been.

Franklin kept pummeling him with the club until there was nothing left. Just skull fragments inside a loose sack of bleeding skin. Franklin's chest heaved up and down as he stared at the mess he created. He dropped the club into the pile of flesh and looked to the crowd.

They went wild. One man had taken down a pack of feral cannibals and their handler. It was unbelievable. They were cheering him on as if he was the heavyweight champion of the world.

And Wyatt supposed he was.

He couldn't believe it himself.

43

Rainha stood, hands on the railing of the owner's box, just like she always did. Let the others drink and gossip. She'd keep her attention on the battle, even if it was expected to be short.

Although she didn't know why Wyatt hated Franklin so much, so knew one thing. Wyatt wanted him dead. And she believed that granting that wish would make him trust her. And what worse way to die than at the hands of feral cannibals? Wyatt would love her for this. She was certain.

But then the unexpected happened.

Franklin didn't lose the battle.

Not only did he not lose, but he owned that fight like it was his bitch. He slaughtered every last one of the freaks and then took out the handler like it was a day at the office for him.

She was surprised.

And nothing had surprised her in years.

Wyatt wasn't going to be happy. But did that really matter to her? In the end, she knew she would get what she wanted from him. She always did. She had more pressing matters at hand anyway.

The results of the battle weren't sitting well with the other owners. They'd paid good money to the handler and financed his trips to the north to capture the cannibals. It was an expensive endeavor, but worthwhile because the crowd lived for the scourge. Now the cannibals were all dead and their money had been wasted.

Via their grumbles, she knew they blamed her. It was always Rainha's fighters who won when they weren't supposed to. But, fuck them.

Let them bitch. Let them moan. Let them complain about her fighters being too strong. It only meant she was the best and they all knew it. She wasn't there to make friends. She wasn't there to socialize and party. She was there to be in charge. To be in control. To have the money, to have the power.

She licked her lips and already could hear their voices growing louder, their words angrier.

"This is a travesty!" exclaimed one of the other slavers. She couldn't tell who it was, but it didn't matter as most agreed with him.

"Listen," the Drip said, "I understand this wasn't what we hoped for, but I don't blame Rainha." He was always the diplomatic one. Never one to throw shade, at least, not in her presence. He was a good kiss ass. And she knew he hated her.

The whiners lowered their voices, but she could still hear them,

"These fights are fixed."

"She drugs her men so they're almost indestructible!"

"We need to do something about her..."

"You do not want to cross this line," Drip said to whoever was the most heated.

Rainha finally turned around and went to the group. She could feel the tension in the air. She could feel the hatred. But most of all, she could feel the fear. She fed off of it.

She looked at every single one of their faces. Some were tense, worried at what she would do. Others were angry. And most of them just looked stupid.

Rainha laughed at them.

It was funny to her that they thought their opinions mattered. It was like believing a spider loses sleep over the plots of the flies.

"I'm glad you find this funny," a man, Needle, with a pinched, pointed face said as he jabbed a stubby finger at her. Of course, he would have the biggest mouth. He was the primary owner of the scourge.

She didn't admire what Needle did, but she used it to her benefit. A small piece of cash instead of feeding and housing a loser was usually a better solution. Plus, she still profited from it when she could.

"I do find it funny, Needle," she said. "I can see that you don't agree, but listen to that." She put a hand to her ear, hearing the cheers from the people in the stands. "They seem to have got what they wanted. Blood. Or, more specifically, a *slaughter*."

Needle's ratty face was beaming red now, but she knew he would never make a move against her. If he did, it would mean his ultimate end. "She put in a good fighter! We all agreed the scourge was only for the dregs. Cheating whore!"

Everyone looked to Rainha as if expecting her to fly into a rage and kill the man on the spot. Instead, she only crossed her arms.

"It's okay," the Drip said. "We all know that nothing is guaranteed."

"I can't help it if my worst fighters are better than your best," Rainha said.

"Rainha is right. The crowd is happy, we all make money. A surprise result like that is good now and again. Keeps people on their toes," Drip said, putting his hand on Needle's shoulder. Needle shook him off, but he backed down.

The Drip acted like he was on her side, but she knew what he was doing. Rainha could kill them all right then and there, but what end would that be? She needed them to continue providing their services to the island. Food, animals, the sex trade. Remove any of those things from the island, and it would be chaos.

Besides, without competition from their fighters, she would just be pitting her men against each other. While that was not unheard of, she liked to reserve that for special occasions.

She knew she needed to make an offering to Drip. To reward him for his servility. And she had the perfect plan in mind.

44

"After today's events, you are due a celebration," Rainha said to the men grouped outside of Akeldama.

Seth noticed how often her eyes fell on Wyatt and the way she looked at him. He said a thanks to the big guy upstairs because her infatuation was keeping them alive.

If Rainha had pitted him against the scourge, in his current condition... it wouldn't have been comely. And as much as Seth loathed the woman and her condescending attitude, a part of him was grateful. A very begrudging part.

The fighters speculated amongst themselves, trading theories on what the reward might entail. All except himself, Wyatt, and Franklin. The latter of that trio was still covered head to toe in mud, blood, and who the fuck knew what else. He smelled like a combination of a slaughterhouse and outhouse and Seth smiled to himself as he thought that fragrance wouldn't exactly fly off the shelves in Macy's.

"Enough chatter!" Rainha bellowed and the group turned quiet. "Any man who thinks it more important to hear the sound of his own voice rather than mine should know that Needle is looking for new members of the scourge. I'd be happy to volunteer you."

Not a single word was uttered from any of the men and Rainha flashed her bitchy smirk.

"Now, as I was saying. We have had a string of great battles. And your efforts have not gone unnoticed. Those who make me money get rewarded. That's what I always say, and I am a woman of my word. But today, Franklin really added the cherry on top of this sundae."

Seth thought about that metaphor. He couldn't recall the last time he actually had a sundae or a cherry for that matter. Did ice cream even exist anymore? If it did, he bet Rainha had some hidden away in her mansion.

Rainha continued. "After all the excitement, I'm sure you have some extra pent up energy."

She was right, of course. The men were practically electrified after Franklin's show. As Seth despised the man, he had to admit it was one hell of an impressive feat. He would have been on his feet if he had two, and the ability to stand.

"You'll be taken to the Drip's brothel. There, you will have your choice of any of his women - or men - to do what you please," she said.

The older fighters exploded in cheers. And even Seth, with his broken arm and wrecked shoulder, couldn't keep the smile off his face. He needed a way to blow off some steam after Doc's death, after the failed escape attempt. And, if all went as planned, he'd have more than his steam blown.

LED BY RAINHA, the men filtered into the brothel where the walls were painted deep, almost blood, red, and the floor was covered with cream-colored shag carpet deep enough to lose your feet in. The only light came from ornate chandeliers, as the building itself had no windows.

At the front of the lobby stood a plus-sized man who looked like the world's largest Maître D'. The man stared straight ahead not making eye contact with any of them.

Rainha breezed past them, skipping a lounge and disappearing up a flight of stairs. Seth glanced up at Wyatt, uncertain what to do next, but the other fighter streamed into the lounge, making a beeline to the prostitutes who feigned excitement at seeing them.

"This is our reward?" Wyatt asked. "We risk our lives and in return, we're supposed to have sex with some random stranger while Rainha picks up the tab?"

Seth shrugged his shoulders. His brother really was a prude. "You know what they say. 'When in Rome...'" Seth wheeled himself into the lounge and didn't check to see if his brother followed.

As he took in the prostitutes, Seth was shocked at how clean they all looked. The streetwalkers he'd seen when entering the town and again on his futile escape attempt seemed to have crawled straight from a gutter.

The women he saw in the brothel, much to his surprise and delight, were lovely and, at a glance anyway, seemed healthy. They weren't up to the standard of Papa's wives, or his own Rosario, but these women would have turned heads while strolling down any sidewalk in America, back when people still strolled down sidewalks.

They wore fine silk lingerie, teddies, and nightgowns. They had full breasts and round asses. Plump lips and juicy thighs. And not a festering sore to be seen.

Seth was already squirming in his chair, trying to hide the growing bulge in his pants, when the Drip stepped into the room, drawing everyone's attention.

"My friends," he said. "At Akeldama, we are enemies, but here in my home, we are all friends. Please, browse my roster of beauties and choose whoever you would like to get to know better. I offer the finest men and women on the island and you are guaranteed a good time."

He gave a little bow, then vanished behind heavy velvet curtains.

Now, Seth did look for Wyatt and found him lurking at the

passthrough, still not in the lounge. And from the look on his face, Seth knew he was going to be a pain in the ass about this.

He sighed, really not wanting to deal with Wyatt's holier than thou act when he had a raging hard-on in his jeans, but Wyatt was always there to talk him through tough times, and he knew he should do that same.

He started to turn his chair in Wyatt's direction, when Uno sidled up next to his brother and settled his big hand on Wyatt's shoulder.

"Rainha wants you upstairs," Uno said and, without waiting for Wyatt to move on his own, began steering him toward the staircase.

As he passed by, Seth thought he looked... relieved. Alone time with Rainha would have scared the piss out of Seth, but he assumed that his brother wasn't interested in what the brothel had to offer anyway.

They were brothers, but they definitely had different views on the world.

As Seth turned back to the bevy of beauties, he spotted Franklin leaning against a wall, his face still a mask of vacant shock, like a man who'd just survived a nuclear explosion. It annoyed Seth that the asshole was still alive, but they were here because of him, so he supposed he had to give the bastard a smidge of credit. At least he was good for something.

"Rainha should come down here and let us each have a turn," Worm announced loud enough for everyone in the room to hear.

The men laughed, boisterous, eager, and Seth found himself chuckling along.

As soon as Uno returned from the stairs, they stopped laughing. Seth was sure their afternoon of fun would come to a fast end if that man heard them joking about their owner.

"Like you'd know what to do with her," Seth said once Uno was out of range. "She'd look at you once and your cock would shrivel up and look just like your name. A little worm."

"Fuck you, Seth. Big talk from a boy who needs a pimped out chair to keep him alive."

Their trash-talking carried no weight, no animosity, and for the first time since arriving at Rainha's compound, Seth began to feel like he fit in.

Seth looked to Franklin again. "Let's hope that asshole doesn't ruin it all for us. If one of the women goes in to kiss his neck, he might lose his mind and bite her face off."

That got a rise out of Pinocchio. He guffawed. "Seth, you're a special kind of asshole, aren't you?"

Seth shrugged with a grin. It quickly dropped when Uno came back around.

"He certainly is," Uno said. "Stuck in that chair and can't get his pecker up, so he must get men to invade his special asshole to achieve pleasure!"

Seth's eyes went wide. Uno rarely said a word to them outside of screaming at them for doing something wrong and now, there he was, talking shit about him and, what, accusing him of being gay? The man might be able to fight, but he sucked at trash talking.

If those were the best insults the big man could come up with, Seth wasn't impressed, but the other men, maybe giddy over where they were and what they were about to do, or maybe because they were afraid of Uno and wanted to please him no matter how terrible his jokes, burst into laughter.

"Ha," Chester shouted, pointing at Seth. "He got you good boy!"

Seth looked at Chester who had his arm around a girl who looked no more than twelve. "Says the man who has to bang children because his cock's too small to please a grown woman."

The room went dead silent and Seth was certain he'd gone too far. That they'd be back to hating him and maybe, to top it off, Uno would throw him into the street before he could even dip his wick.

Instead, Uno was the first to laugh. He clapped Seth on the back almost hard enough to knock him out of the chair. The others joined in until everyone in the lounge was laughing like an idiot. Then Uno grabbed a blonde woman who triple D tits and dragged her into a side room without another word.

Relieved, Seth decided he should focus on finding a woman he wanted to spend the afternoon with rather than pithy one-liners. Instead she found him.

A girl his own age, or maybe a year or two older, came up beside him. She was full-figured, had a mane of fire-red hair, and wore a corset that drew his eyes straight to her cleavage.

She hopped into his lap, wrapping an arm around his neck. "You're funny," she said.

Seth swallowed hard. "I try."

She kissed him so quick he didn't have a chance to kiss back. "Does it work?" she asked.

"Does what--"

Instead of letting him ask the question, she grabbed his dick which was a throbbing hunk of iron in his pants. Her eyes lit up and she slid off him, grabbing his hands instead, pulling him away from the crowd and toward a private room.

And Seth was more than eager to follow.

45

As Wyatt stepped into the only room, he wasn't expecting what he found. In retrospect, that was naivety on his part.

Rainha sat atop the largest bed he'd ever seen, and she was completely nude. Her hand worked between her legs and, as soon as he saw her, he spun away.

"Oh, I-- I didn't--," Wyatt stammered.

He heard the bedsprings groan as she moved. "Look at me."

Wyatt took a quick peek through squinted eyes, like a man stealing glances at an eclipse.

Now, Rainha was on all fours, crawling toward him, her muscles and curves rolling and flexing as she moved, catlike.

"I said look, not peek. You're a man. I'm sure I don't have anything you haven't seen before."

He turned to face her and didn't look away that time. She was right, it wasn't anything he hadn't seen before. Although, maybe not in such a powerful, exquisite package. And not from a woman who owned him and controlled every aspect of his life.

"Do you like what you see?" She rocked back, unto her knees, sitting up straight so he had a good look at her.

At *all* of her.

"You're beautiful," he said, and he meant it.

"I know. Now get over here and fuck me."

He could feel his pants getting tighter, but it was all physical, instinctual, his body reacting to the sight, not his mind. Because when his mind took over, all he could think about was the only woman he'd ever been with - Allie - and how much he longed for her.

"No," Wyatt said. His big head winning over rather than the smaller one.

Rainha lost the seductive, confident smile she'd been wearing. The only thing she'd been wearing. "What do you mean *no?*" she hissed.

"I mean no. I can't"

"After all I've done for you?"

"You mean buying me like a was the best apple in the cart? Am I supposed to be flattered by that?"

"I saved you. I saved your brother. I sent Franklin out there today to fight the scourge." She threw her hands in the air, animated. "What more do you expect?"

"Franklin?" he asked. "You put him in there for me, right?"

She nodded.

"Well here's some news for you. He didn't die. In fact, he came out a damned legend! You woke up something in him and now I don't know if he even can be killed."

She smirked, some of the annoyance leaving her face. "I find it funny," she said. "That you think you can talk to me like this. That you think you can deny me and go on as if you have some power."

She stood and walked across the bed, to him. She looked like a supermodel strutting down a runway, completely nude, and had the face and attitude to go with it.

He had to fight back his own body's response to the show. But it was easy when he thought of what she was to him.

She effortlessly stepped off the bed, to the floor, and didn't stop until her body was pressed against his own. She smelled like sweat and lavender, her musk filling his nose and turning him on even more.

He looked away from her, searching for something to distract him from her beauty, and settled on a water spot on the wall.

She grabbed hold of his crotch, caressed expertly. "I can make you." Rainha's lips parted and her tongue danced across them when she felt him grow in her hand. "See, you want this as much as I do. Why fight what comes so naturally?"

Wyatt looked away from the water stain and met her hot gaze. "I don't want to sleep with you. Not with you treating us the way you do. Not with you *owning* us."

She laughed, planting her hands on his shoulders, her grip so strong he knew he'd never break it. "I'm tired of your chaste boy act. Be a man, Wyatt." She ran her tongue along his face, twirled it around his ear. "You'll enjoy it. I promise."

He knew she wasn't going to let him go without getting what she wanted. "Go ahead, Rainha. Use me. Take what you want like you always do, but remember that I wasn't a willing partner."

Her brow furrowed, then shoved him hard. He stumbled, colliding with the wall.

"Leave me, you petulant child. This was your last chance," she said.

She climbed back on the bed and propped her legs open, pleasuring herself since he wasn't interested. If Wyatt had it in him, he would have blushed.

"Close the door on the way out," she said.

Wyatt did as she asked and leaned against the hallway wall, hoping he hadn't just signed death sentences for him and his brother.

46

Early the next morning they were back to training.

It was all they did on days that didn't include a trip to the arena.

Wake up, eat breakfast, start training, eat lunch, continue training, eat dinner, train until dark, and then they'd have the night to recuperate and relax.

Their life was killing and training to kill on an endless, soul-crushing loop.

Seth was out in the field, punching at one of the wooden sparring dummies. Wyatt was surprised at how Seth's injured shoulder had come around. His other arm was still in a cast, but he even used that to his advantage, using it to block blows, using it to bludgeon. He'd be back in the battles soon. Not that that was a reason to celebrate.

Wyatt worked the chains, building his strength up. He had seen a noticeable difference since he started training. Much of it was due to the regular, filling meals, something he'd been lacking for years. Between the food and work, he was putting on some muscle. He's always been quick, but now with his strength building, he would be an even harder opponent to fight.

If it wasn't for the killing they were forced to do, part of him might have been able to enjoy it. It felt like a prison, but he was getting accustomed to the routine. Or brainwashed by it. But with each passing day, he felt it harder and harder to imagine a life after this place.

Uno stomped to where Seth was training. A man who always seemed on the verge of flying into a rage, today his temper was even hotter than usual.

"You're not hitting hard enough," he barked at Seth.

Seth nodded and started throwing more ferocious punches. Uno stood over him, making sure he was doing as told. Wyatt could see his brother tiring, but he still gave it his all. The wooden dummy shook with each punch without complaint.

"Too slow," Uno said next. "You'll never win a fight moving like a turtle. First too weak, then too slow. You'll be crushed by an experienced man."

Seth's frustration was obvious. He started to hit harder and faster, trying to keep up with what Uno was saying. His face burned red from exhaustion and anger.

Uno stepped to the side, grabbed something off the ground, then moved back to Seth.

"Here, use this," Uno said, launching a weight in the air at Seth.

Seth's eyes went wide as the forty pound dumbbell tumbled end over end on a collision course with his face. Uno had made it look feather-light when he threw it, but it was far too heavy for Seth to handle and all he could do was get his cast up at the last second, blocking it.

Wincing, Seth rubbed the cast where it hit, all while Uno chuckled.

"What the fuck was that?" Seth demanded.

"You're weak like a girl! Your little prick doesn't work. You have to use gadgets to win fights. You do not belong with the rest of us. We are champions and you're..." Uno paused, choosing his next words carefully. "A gimmick."

Wyatt wasn't sure where this new hatred for Seth came from, but

Uno was not someone he wanted to get into a fight with at any cost. But when Seth was angry, he made poor decisions.

And right then, Wyatt witnessed it happen.

Seth clenched his teeth, spittle frothing from his mouth. He balled his good hand into a fist and, when Uno was close enough, he swung.

Seth connected with Uno's crotch, causing the beast of a man to buckle at the waist.

"Did a girl ever hit you like that?" Seth asked, his face full of frenzied satisfaction, still oblivious to what a stupid move he'd just made.

Not a single soul in the training ground made a noise. Everyone stopped what they were doing. All eyes were on Seth and Uno. Wyatt was sure that nobody was breathing because he sure as hell wasn't.

Wyatt took a step toward them. As much as he didn't want to, he had to get involved. He didn't plan to throw a punch but thought he might be able to defuse the situation with words. It was worth a try because, if Uno and Seth ended up fighting, his brother was a dead man.

Before he could take another step, someone grabbed Wyatt and pushed him against the side of the fence, holding him tight against it, keeping him away from his brother and Uno.

It was Franklin.

His face was so close Wyatt smelled the breakfast on his breath. Breakfast, and a rotting tooth.

"This isn't your fight, Wyatt," Franklin said.

"Get the fuck off me," Wyatt said. He pushed Franklin, but Franklin held firm.

"Seth made his choice when he threw that punch."

"Let me go, asshole," Wyatt said.

"I'm trying to save your life right now. Uno will kill you."

Wyatt twisted, squirmed, and broke free. "What the hell do you care if I'm dead?"

Franklin grabbed Wyatt again and Wyatt was more than ready to get into a brawl of his own. But when Franklin grabbed Wyatt's face and turned his attention to the corners of the field, he realized Franklin was right.

"The guards are watching, just waiting for an excuse to unload," Franklin said.

The guards had their weapons drawn. They were ready to take someone down, but who?

"And look," Franklin said, tilting his head to the gate.

In the distance, Wyatt saw Rainha. She watched everything through the other side of the fence. Wyatt swallowed hard and nodded to Franklin. Peace, at least for now. For whatever reason, Franklin had just saved Wyatt's life. But it didn't mean that he owed him anything in return.

Uno charged Seth, but the boy was ready. The training had prepared him for this.

He ducked underneath the brute's swing and grabbed onto his large bicep. It was good that Seth was quick because he didn't have his chair at full capacity. No weapons, only a motor to move it.

Uno yelped as Seth climbed onto his back and started punching the huge man's neck. Seth looked like a fly buzzing around the head of an elephant, being as annoying as possible.

Uno swung his weight around and Seth's leg flung back and forth as he did, but his arms hung tight. Seth finally brought his mouth down onto Uno's shoulder and bit as hard as he could.

Uno grunted as the blood ran.

"You fucking mosquito," Uno yelled. "You fight like a dirty fucker!"

Wyatt was certain Seth took that as a compliment and his brother dug deeper with his teeth. But Uno was a machine. He could take the pain. And even worse, he could use it to his advantage.

Uno swung his torso forward, almost as if he was going to roll into a somersault. Seth's leg went over Uno's head and he lost his grip on the brute's shoulders. He landed with a hard thud on the ground that the entire camp felt.

"What's your fucking problem," Seth spat from the ground.

Uno punched Seth in the mouth, bloodying both lips. But he wasn't dead. Uno had either pulled his punch, or Seth had gotten very lucky.

"I liked Doc Eunuch," Uno spat. "It's your fault he's dead. You used him for your own agenda."

"You fucking killed him!" Seth screamed. "He was my friend and you killed him!"

"I had no choice."

Seth tried to get up, but Uno kicked him down. Uno grabbed the weight from the ground and held it over his head.

Fuck the guards. Wyatt couldn't suit by and watch his brother die. He steeled himself to join the fray, to sprint into the fight--

But he didn't have to.

"Enough," Rainha yelled.

The instant her voice called out, Uno dropped the weight next to Seth. Everyone parted as Rainha walked onto the training grounds.

"Uno. You are my trusted trainer. If you feel it's necessary for you to finish off this boy, I permit it."

Uno looked to Rainha, then to Seth, his chest heaving with anger as he surveyed the small gnat on the ground, his face covered in blood.

Finally, Uno shook his head. He turned and walked away.

Rainha looked to Wyatt, a devious glint sparkling in her eyes. Wyatt knew whatever she was thinking wasn't good.

47

Wyatt waited until the others were asleep before going to Seth's stall. He had a feeling his brother would still be awake, and he was right.

"Can't sleep either, brother?" Seth asked as he arrived.

Wyatt nodded. He'd tried to be quiet, to sneak in unheard. Fat chance of that. "You have ears like a hawk."

"That's funny to picture," Seth said. "Ears on a hawk."

Wyatt chuckled. It was. But the humor faded in shot order as he took in Seth's swollen and bruised face.

"What was that about today?" Wyatt asked him.

"He hates me," Seth said, his voice matter of fact. "Doubt I'll ever be able to change his mind."

"No. I don't mean that. I mean, what were you thinking in fighting him, Seth? He could have destroyed you. He would have smashed your head like a watermelon if Rainha hadn't shown up."

Seth pushed himself into a sitting position. "I don't know about that. I was doing pretty good for a while there."

Wyatt sighed. Getting his brother to be serious about anything was always so damned hard. "You need to be more careful and keep your temper in check."

"And what else? Sit back and let Uno shit on me nonstop? Let all these fuckers make fun of me for being a cripple and a pussy? I'm tired of being the butt of everyone's jokes, brother. I'm not going to take it."

"You'd rather die?"

Seth paused, thinking. "Wouldn't you?" he finally asked.

Wyatt considered it. He thought about how hard it must be for Seth to be surrounded by able-bodied men, forced into a life where what you could do physically defined you. To see men who were barely smart enough to breathe without being reminded get treated better than you solely because they had two working legs. And knowing you would never be able to change that.

Yeah, he wouldn't sit back and take that either.

But he wasn't going to tell Seth that. He wasn't going to encourage him to keep acting foolish. Instead, he decided to change the subject.

"I've been thinking more about escaping," Wyatt said.

It was Seth's turn to sigh. "We tried that, remember?"

"So, what? We never try again? We just live as slaves for the rest of our lives?"

"It could be worse," Seth said, sounding all too much like the world-weary fighters who told Wyatt the same thing. "The food's good. The pussy was great. Of course, you wouldn't know about that." He flashed a Cheshire cat grin.

Wyatt just shook his head. "Seriously though. After the next battles, when we're moving from the dugout to the exit, I think that's when we make our move. Everyone's tired, distracted. I think we'd have a good chance, Seth. I really do. We just need to get the timing per--"

"Go to bed," Seth said. "We'll talk about this some other time, but for now, just go to bed."

Seth flopped onto his side, turned away from him and disconnected from the conversation.

Without an audience to hear his plans, Wyatt left.

48

As was typical of the weekend, they were taken to Akeldama for the day's battles, but unlike most trips, they weren't told who would be fighting ahead of time. But the gnawing worry in Wyatt's gut assured him he would be in the ring, killing or being killed.

He was ready for it though. And he was even ready to escape after winning his match. Seth still hadn't shown much interest in the plan, but Wyatt didn't care. He'd drag his brother out of there kicking and screaming if it came down to it.

He knew, deep inside where you try to hide from your truth but can't, that the plan wasn't even half-assed. That he'd likely get killed before he made it ten yards from Akeldama. An escape in broad daylight was near impossible, but he was going to try it anyway.

What did he really have to lose? Rainha had made it clear she was finished with him. He'd likely be put in battle after battle until he finally lost and died. Why keep making her more money? Why keep killing other men solely to save his own ass?

His decision was made. Today was the day he was leaving

Akeldama either on his feet and free, or dead and dragged into the gutter.

As they waited in the locker room to get word on who was fighting, Rainha came to them. On this day she sported a firetruck red catsuit and boots so high they added another five inches to her already towering frame.

Even Uno seemed confused with the goings-on. He raised an eyebrow as he watched her. "Ma'am?"

"I came to tell the men who will battle," Rainha said as she strolled back and forth in front of the men, taking in each of them, barely looking at Wyatt.

Did she feel guilty? He doubted it. She was just annoyed that he wouldn't screw her and didn't want to give him the satisfaction of seeing her face.

A full minute passed as she dragged out the suspense.

"Who?" Pino finally shouted.

"Such little patience," she said. Then she went to Uno, leaned into him, and whispered in his ear.

For the first time ever, Wyatt saw Uno look surprised. Then, the man nodded and Rainha backed away from him.

"Seth will be fighting in today's battle," she announced.

Wyatt's stomach sank. She had finally come through with her plan to get back at Wyatt. And she was trying to kill his brother in order to punish him.

The cold-hearted bitch.

He turned to Seth and saw a look of determination on his face. Wyatt knew he was going to give it his everything, but his brother was still injured. His cast was still in place and his shoulder wound had become infected, seeping watery pus, limiting his movement. Anyone could tell he wasn't ready to fight yet.

But Rainha didn't care.

The woman glowed with self-satisfaction. "Today's battle is special. A treat for our fans who I'm sure are going to love it," Rainha continued. The words dripped from her mouth.

Wyatt's mind began to crank, trying to figure out what was going down. Then he remembered the shocked look on Uno's face and he put the pieces together. Rainha was bringing Uno, the undefeated fighter, out of retirement to fight Seth.

To kill Seth.

He wanted to jump over the rail and strangle her.

"I can do it," Seth promised. "I'll fucking massacre whoever I'm against."

Wyatt wasn't sure if he was pumping himself up, or throwing it back in Rainha's face.

"I'm glad you think so because it's not going to be easy," Rainha said.

"Don't do this, please." Wyatt found himself pleading to the woman that owned them.

She turned to Wyatt, her face mock confused. "You want something from me? After denying me what I wanted? Such a fool you are."

"It'll be okay, Wyatt. I'm ready to get back in there," Seth said.

Seth was a scrapper. And with his loaded chair, he might be able to drag out the inevitable. But how was his injured brother supposed to beat the man who'd taught him how to compete in the arena? How was he supposed to topple the man who'd never lost a fight? It was impossible.

"You can't do this," Wyatt said to Rainha. "You can't make him fight Uno."

"Seth isn't fighting Uno," Rainha said with a smile. "He's fighting you."

49

Seth sat in the locker room, rocking his chair back and forth on two wheels as he prepared for the fight that was minutes away.

Was he really going to fight his brother to the death?

He couldn't do that. And he knew that Wyatt couldn't either.

What would they do if the brothers stepped on the field, sat in the grass, and didn't lay a hand on the other?

"They'll kill you both," a voice said from the doorway.

Seth spun around and saw Uno standing there.

Great, now this asshole had shown up to browbeat and humiliate him before what was shaping up to be the worst moment of his life. Just what he needed.

Uno stepped into the hollow locker room. "If you don't fight, if you don't take up arms, they'll kill you both. I know. I've seen it before."

"So, what? I'm supposed to kill my brother? Or let him kill me?" Seth asked, suddenly unconcerned with the man's opinion.

Uno shrugged and straddled one of the benches. "That's your choice. I know what I'd do if I were you."

"What's that? Roll over and die? Because a cripple like me could never beat someone like Wyatt?"

Uno shook his head. "You can win if you use your brains. It won't be easy. Your brother is strong and fast, but he's also not as smart as you. I've seen it in the way you both fight."

Seth exhaled a disgusted huff. He didn't want a pep talk. He didn't want anything except out of this arena and off this hellhole of an island.

"I don't like pitting blood against blood," Uno said. "It's perverse. But it's not my decision."

He stood and strode toward the exit. "Someone is dying today. Don't let it be both of you."

Seth grabbed a towel from the bench and wiped away the sweat that was seeping through his pores. "Why are you being nice to me? I thought you hated me. I don't get it."

Uno half-turned to face him. "I've been here a long time. I've been in your shoes."

"You had to fight your brother?" Seth asked, shocked.

"Not my blood brother. But one of my brothers in here. The only person I could trust, really." His face darkened. "Rainha did it to make me a better fighter."

"And?"

"It worked. I won that battle like all the others. Maybe it worked too good." He shrugged. "Nobody wants to fight me anymore. Do you know what it's like to be trained to do nothing but fight, and then be denied doing it? I never have the honor of stepping onto the field. I must sit back and watch."

To Seth, Uno's words sounded crazy, but then again, he had never been trained for one thing and had it taken away from him. Maybe all those years had screwed with Uno's head. But it still didn't answer his question.

"So why help me?"

"Because you're the first person that has thrown a punch at me, knowing exactly who I am, and what I can do, in over a year. And I respect that."

Seth laughed. Who knew that getting into a losing battle would have created an ally?

"Now, you get out there and fight. Do you understand me?"

Seth swallowed hard. He did understand.

50

Wyatt stood on the field, facing Seth.

What a sick joke this was. Did Rainha really think that they were going to fight? That they were going to try to kill each other?

The crowd was stomping, chanting, excited to see brother against brother, but they were going to be very disappointed.

Wyatt looked at his feet sunk into the blood-drenched field and wanted this to be over. He was certain that repercussions would await them for refusing to fight, but he'd take them. Even if it meant going to the slaughter and having to fight a pack of hyenas or a jaguar or even a damned elephant. He'd take his chances.

Seth didn't say a word, but neither did Wyatt. It was like they had a silent agreement. They were brothers. They didn't need to express words between the two to know what the other was thinking. No fighting.

Then the bell rang out over the loudspeaker.

The crowd cheered.

Wyatt looked around, taking in the screaming bastards and almost smiled as he thought about how pissed off they'd all be when nothing happened to satiate their bloodlust.

"They're going to be awfully disappointed when—"

Seth swung a haymakerWyatt, nailing him in the jaw. Wyatt spun around, gripping his face where the pain surged, feeling blood boil from his gums and something clattering around inside his mouth. He spat and out came a wad of blood, and a tooth.

He stared at it for a long, disbelieving moment, then looked to his brother.

"What the fuck, Seth?" Wyatt asked.

Seth pulled back and swung again, but this time Wyatt stepped out of the way.

"Seth, stop it. We don't have to do this," Wyatt said.

Seth shook his head. "You know that's not true, Wyatt. Someone has to die or we both get executed."

"So you're going to kill me?" Wyatt asked, backing away as Seth slammed his joystick forward, coming at him.

"Maybe. Maybe not. But we at least have to give them a show. Look up there," Seth motioned with his head. Wyatt looked and saw the guards perched on watchtowers above the crowd. "They're going to gun us both down if we don't fight."

Maybe Seth was right. Maybe they would murder them if they didn't fight. But he wasn't going to kill his brother.

As his tongue went to the hole where his tooth had been, he realized he wasn't wholly against giving them a little entertainment, though.

"Alright, Seth. If that's how you want it, get ready to get your ass kicked," Wyatt said with a smile.

As Seth rolled toward him, Wyatt made a last-second sidestep, then swung, landing his fist across his brother's cheek. But he didn't put his shoulder into it. He wasn't trying to hurt him.

Seth shook it off and they went toe to toe, exchanging jabs and taps. It was like watching grade-schoolers fight and the crowd quickly became restless.

The *boos* started to roll in. Some fans hurled trash onto the field.

Wyatt looked up and saw the guards getting restless as well. All guns were trained on them.

This faux fight wasn't working out as he'd hoped.

"Come at me, brother," Seth said, his face too serious for Wyatt's liking. "Show me what you've really got."

Wyatt stared with bewildered eyes. Was he serious about this? "Seth, I'm not gonna hurt you."

"As if you could," he said, then swung with all his strength, landing a fist right in Wyatt's gut.

Wyatt fell backward into the mud, holding his stomach. The wind had been knocked out of him and he couldn't catch his breath.

That little prick hit hard.

Once he was able to suck in air, Wyatt shouted, "That fuckin' hurt, Seth."

"It was supposed to. Now come on."

Wyatt climbed to his feet but made no move to retaliate. "Fuck you." He turned to the crowd, to the luxury box, to Rainha. "Fuck all of you!" he screamed.

This was insane. Let them shoot him. He was done.

Then, as he watched his brother, Seth pulled a machete from the pouch at the side of his chair and raised it in the air.

"Seth, you ca—"

Before he could finish, Seth swung the machete, but the arc was too wide and Wyatt dove out of harm's way.

Wyatt crab crawled away, hand and feet sloshing through the saturated soil "What do you think you're doing?"

"Fighting. That's what we do, right?" With that, Seth pushed the button on his chair.

Wyatt rolled and hit the ground, his face splashing into a puddle of rancid blood. It filled his mouth, his nostrils. Flames roared above him and would have roasted him like a pig on a spit if he'd been half a second slower.

His mind was racing at what was happening and he couldn't

grasp what Seth had just done. He crawled to his feet, the blood soaking the front of his body. "Seth—"

"Shut up, Wyatt. You think you're so much better than me that you need to half-ass it? You think it's impossible for me to hold my own against you if you actually tried?"

"That's not what this is about. I know you can fight." Wyatt looked around at his surroundings. There wasn't much to hide behind, just a lot of space to retreat. He could make that work while he talked his brother down.

At the very least, Seth's turn seemed to have pleased the guards and the crowd. They had squealed as soon as the flame shot out from his death chair.

"Then what is it? Protecting me is one thing, but it's more than that, isn't it? You pity me. You look down on me. You always have."

"Seth, what are you even—"

"I should never have left the casino," Seth said, squaring up to Wyatt. "Papa believed in me. He loved me. He treated me like an equal."

Wyatt could feel the anger brewing inside him. "Papa was a maniac. You know that."

"Do I?"

"He killed Allie!"

"Did you ever stop and think that maybe she deserved it?" Seth asked as he hit the button again, shooting more flames out.

Wyatt was way ahead of him. He stepped to the side, avoiding the fire. But this time he didn't dive away. He lunged at his brother and got on top of his chair. He punched him in the face, once, twice, a third time.

Seth's face was bloody, but he glared at Wyatt and the cold, steely look in his eyes sent Wyatt over the edge.

"You're fucking hero is the reason my girlfriend is dead. The reason our mother is dead. If you would have just listened to me, we could have all got away. Instead, you fell for Papa's bullshit. He played you like a fucking violin!"

Wyatt wailed again and again. The crowd loved it. But Wyatt wasn't doing it for the crowd anymore.

Seth pushed against him, but Wyatt had the better angle. He wasn't going to stop.

Out of the corner of his eye, Wyatt saw Seth press a button with his left hand. He had almost forgotten all about it.

Wyatt quickly fell backward, off of Seth's chair as the buzzing saw came around.

He just barely missed having his head lopped off.

Wyatt jumped up, just in time to grab Seth's hand that was trying to hit the button for round two of the saw. He kept him from making the connection, then threw his head downward onto Seth's face which hadn't yet healed from his scuffle with Uno.

Seth yelped as Wyatt broke his nose again.

Wyatt grabbed the machete from the mud and raised it over his head, ready to slam it down on his brother and end this.

Then Seth opened his eyes and stared back at Wyatt. "Do it. Everything you said is true. So do it."

Wyatt's heart was pumping hard and fast. He wanted nothing more than to drive the blade down and let it all out. For Allie, for his mother, for himself.

Two deep breaths.

That's all it took. He threw the machete back into the mud. "I won't."

Seth looked at his brother, tears rolling down his face. "I deserve it, Wyatt!"

"No." Wyatt grabbed his brother and Seth tensed up. But instead of fighting, Wyatt wrapped his arms around him and hugged him as tight as he could. "I'm not going to kill my brother. Not for any mistakes you've made. Not for vengeance. Not for anything. Do you hear me?"

Wyatt was crying now, too.

Seth nodded, his chest hitching with sobs. "I'm sorry."

"I am too. I'm so sorry, Seth."

It felt right. It felt good. It felt like all the pain of the past months was finally over.

Yet the crowd hated it.

They wanted blood.

They wanted carnage.

They wanted death.

"What happens now?" Seth asked, still locked in his brother's arms.

"I can answer that," Rainha said as she stomped toward them, leather boots sinking into the bloody field.

Wyatt and Seth cut their embrace and turned to face her. Akeldama had gone quiet as a library.

"We fought," Wyatt said to her. "We did what you wanted and I learned my lesson."

Rainha nodded. "Yes, you did. And maybe you have."

"I'll do whatever you want from now on," Wyatt said.

"I know you will." She flashed a smile that didn't come within a mile of reaching her eyes.

"Good," Wyatt said. "So tell everyone this is over."

Rainha folded her arms. "Your charm has worn off, Wyatt. There is one rule on this field and one rule only. Someone has to die."

Seth and Wyatt exchanged glances, but neither one of them moved.

"Then let it be me," Wyatt said, stepping within arm's reach of the woman who owned him.

"No!" Seth yelled.

Rainha looked Wyatt up and down, inspecting him, trying to determine whether he was preening or truly meant it. "You are willing to die for your brother?"

"If that's what it takes," he said. He held his chin high, ready for anything.

She looked Wyatt in the eyes and shook her head. "You were the winner, Wyatt. That's not how it works."

In a flash, Rainha flung her arm out. So fast Wyatt barely saw it happen. She threw one of her blades, the same weapon she'd used to annihilate the men in the alley the night she saved them. The knife zipped through the air, flew past Wyatt--

And hit with a thud behind him.

"Wy—"

Wyatt spun around and saw the knife buried to the hilt in Seth's chest. He dashed to his brother, grabbing the handle of the knife as blood raged from the wound. It was in tight, had penetrated the bone, and was unmoving.

He stared into Seth's eyes as he tried to remove the blade. They were full of fright and he was still crying.

"Seth, it's gonna be okay. It's gonna be. I'm sorry, okay. I'm sorry," Wyatt said to his brother.

But it wasn't okay. Seth slumped sideways in his chair. His eyes fell shut. His breathing stopped.

He was dead.

The crowd cheered as Rainha exited the field, leaving Wyatt kneeling next to his brother's lifeless body.

51

Seth is dead.

The thought ran over and over in his head. Wyatt stared up at the ceiling, focusing on the small imperfections in the wood. Each knot and splinter, his mind chanting the same thing again and again.

Seth is dead.
Seth is dead.
And he was.

The night chill hit his skin. He could feel the goosebumps run along his arm and down his back, but he didn't care.

He didn't care about anything.

He didn't care what happened to Rainha. He didn't care what happened to Franklin. And he sure as hell didn't care what happened to himself.

Nothing mattered anymore.

Everything he had done. Leaving his home, leaving the casino, getting to this point, it was all a giant waste.

He wondered what would have happened if they never left Maine. Maybe they would have starved. Maybe they would have been attacked and killed. Maybe they would have frozen to death during a Nor'Easter.

But they would have died together.

And now here he was.

In hell.

Alone.

He was the reason everyone he cared about died. Trooper died saving him. Allie died because she loved him. His mother died because she believed in him.

And now Seth was dead because Wyatt had angered Rainha.

Everything was his fault, yet he was the one still drawing in breaths.

It was so unfair.

Nothing mattered anymore. Maybe he could escape. Maybe he could get to the city. Maybe he would be gunned down. Or maybe he would be caught by someone else. He didn't care.

He just wanted to die.

"Wyatt?" The voice came in from the stables. Wyatt didn't look to know it was Franklin.

Maybe Franklin could put him out of his misery. Maybe he should get up, punch Franklin in the face and let the man go wild on him, and rip out his throat.

He deserved it. That and so much more.

Wyatt climbed to his feet and stepped to Franklin. "You wanna fight me? Maybe punish me for what happened to everyone at the casino? Do it." There was no emotion in his voice, other than the wall of tears he held back. But he didn't think that counted.

"What? No, I—"

Wyatt punched Franklin in the face. "Come on, let's go," Wyatt said. He knew his punch didn't have much heft to it. But he just needed it to be enough to trigger the man.

He swung again, but this time Franklin grabbed Wyatt's wrist and held it tight.

Good, now Franklin would fight back, and Wyatt would let him do it.

But Franklin didn't throw any punches. And when Wyatt tried to swing his other arm, Franklin grabbed that one, too. He twisted him around, pulling him close, and got into his ear.

"I don't want to fight you," Franklin said and shoved him into the hay.

This time the tears couldn't be held back. "Just kill me!" Wyatt exclaimed.

"No," Franklin said. "I won't do that."

"Why not? You killed Allie. I loved her more than I knew was possible. My mom is dead. My brother is dead. My father and my friends are dead. What else is there? Just fucking kill me," Wyatt said. He took steps forward as he spoke and opened his arms up to Franklin, submissive, welcoming death.

Franklin swallowed hard and met Wyatt's eyes. "I wish I could take back what happened to Allie. I really do. I won't insult you with an apology, though. I did it, and I can't take it back. I'm sorry about Seth. I'm sorry about everyone else, but we've all lost people." He flashed a rueful smile. "Hell, we've all lost everyone."

Franklin backed away from him. "Take tonight to get it all out. Mourn. Cry. Whatever you have to do. But in the morning, you need to be Wyatt again. The man that walked from Maine all the way to fucking Texas. The one who survived thieves and cannibals. The man that took down Papa. The one that bested me. That bested every last person up until now."

Wyatt could hardly believe the words or the sincerity in his voice.

"That is who you are. That is who I need you to be."

Wyatt shook his head and wiped his tears. "Why does it matter to you?"

"Because we need each other."

"To fight?"

"To escape," Franklin said. "I'm getting out of here, but I need your help."

52

Franklin led Wyatt to the gate where Abuelita paced. She was clad in a black dress that dragged on the ground as she walked. An ebony shawl covered her hair and most of her face. She trembled, perhaps in fear, perhaps because the night was cold, as she approached the pair.

"What are you doing in here?" Wyatt asked. "You could get hurt."

When she got close enough that he could see her face clearly he realized there was no fear inside the small woman.

"Take this," she said, shoving something metal into Wyatt's hand.

"What is it?" he asked, holding it up. His eyes were adjusted to the darkness and he could tell immediately what it was.

A key.

The key.

"Why?" he asked.

Franklin eyed the two of them warily. Wyatt could tell that he didn't trust the woman. But Wyatt knew she could be trusted. She was the only person he could trust.

"I saw what happened on the field today," she said.

"I thought you didn't watch the fights," Wyatt said.

She shook her head. "I don't make a habit of it. But something felt different today. Rainha was different. So I went to see what was brewing. And I saw what she did."

"So you're helping us get out of here?" Franklin asked.

Abuelita turned to him, nodded, then back to Wyatt. "I will get the guards to leave. Nobody will be around for the next ten minutes. It'll be enough time to get away."

"But what about—"

"I left a boat in the harbor. It's under a tarp. It'll be the only one there. The pirates aren't in tonight and won't be for a couple of days. Nobody will steal the boat because it belongs to Rainha. And nobody dares steal from Rainha."

"Except you. And now us," Franklin said.

Abuelita shrugged.

"But why?" Wyatt asked.

"Because of what she did today. I saw the love between you and your brother." She crossed her heart with her hand. "You risked everything. Stepped in front of your brother. Offered yourself instead. Out of love."

Abuelita was crying now. "So many of these men, they are slaves here." She tapped her head. "And here." She tapped her heart. "If they got away, they wouldn't know how to live because they're dead inside. You still have hope, Wyatt. You still believe people can be good. You don't belong in this place."

The three of them stood a moment before Franklin spoke up. "You don't care if I scoot out of here with him though, right?"

She shook her head. "Go with him. Protect him."

Wyatt put his hands on her shoulders, looking her straight in the eyes. "Are you sure about this? If Rainha finds out what you did she might--"

Abuelita shook her head. "Just go. Straight to the harbor, no side routes this time. You'll be safe."

"And what about you?" Wyatt asked. "What happens to you?"

"Do not waste your worries on me." With that, she turned and left them, her black ensemble vanishing into the night.

53

"Let's go," Wyatt said, already moving toward the gate.

"Wait," Franklin said, grabbing Wyatt's arm, stopping him.

"What? Why?"

Franklin shook his head. "You got out of here once before."

Wyatt nodded, his patience growing thin.

"And you didn't make it."

"That's because we were outnumbered on the alleys. That won't happen this time."

"What if it does? Or what if Uno and Rainha catch us. Ten minutes isn't a ton of time and they know their way around better than we do. Do you seriously think we can take them both out?"

Wyatt took a deep breath. Franklin was right, once again. The asshole. "What else are we supposed to do?"

Franklin thought for a moment then smiled. "We need to try something else."

Before Wyatt could say anything, Franklin was inside the stables, shaking one man awake, then moving on to the next, and the next.

Wyatt rushed to Franklin and grabbed him. "What the hell are you doing?" he asked.

"We need them," Franklin said.

"I'm going to kill whoever just woke me up," Pinocchio said groggily. "I had a dream I was in bed with Eva Longoria."

"Like you'd know what to do with her," Chester cackled and, with that, all the fighters were awake.

Wyatt had no idea how they were getting out now. Franklin might be right that he and Wyatt needed help from the other slaves, but the other men didn't need them. It had been made clear many times over that they weren't interested in escaping.

"We are getting out of here," Franklin said, matter of fact. "Who wants to come with?"

"Oh, fuck off with that," Worm said.

"You're going to get yourself killed, and the rest of us with you. No thanks," Pino said.

As expected, Wyatt was right. Nobody was interested and now a stable full of men knew their supposedly secret escape plan. So much for sneaking away undiscovered. Hell, someone would probably alert the guards before Wyatt could even get the key in the lock.

"Are you all really so dim that you can't see your futures?" Franklin asked loudly.

All attention was on him again, and from an audience that was anything but receptive.

"In here, all that awaits you is death. If we pull this off, you can all be free men."

Franklin leaped onto the table as everyone watched. "I know it's a rough world out there. Believe me, I've been through it. So has Wyatt."

Wyatt shrunk back at the mention of his name, but he had to admit, Franklin was doing pretty well. All those years with Papa had probably given him a metric ton of experience bullshitting people.

And the men were listening.

"Fuck risking your life for someone else and getting what, food, and a stable bay in reward? If we pull this off you could run this entire island. Why be slaves when you can be kings?"

Everyone nodded, but nobody seemed completely on board. Not until Pinocchio stepped forward.

"I am getting a little bored with the routine," he said. "Maybe we go out there and die, but we take the same risk every weekend in the arena. I say, we follow the pretty man!"

Wyatt couldn't believe his ears. Franklin had actually done it. He'd convinced them that they could escape.

Hopefully, there was a big enough boat. But he suspected the man was only using the others to further his own cause.

As long as Wyatt got to the boat, too. But he wasn't worried as Franklin was many things, but not a sailor. He needed Wyatt for that part.

In a single file line, the men streamed out of the stables, to the gate. Wyatt checked and saw no guards in sight. Abuelita had lived up to her promise.

He unlocked the gate and ushered the men through it. Franklin was second to last with Wyatt bringing up the rear. With that, they were out. And free. At least, for the moment.

54

Rainha sat up in bed, alert after being awakened from a restless sleep. She was always on guard, even when sleeping.

Better to be prepared than dead.

A rustling sound alerted Rainha that her nerves weren't wrong. She sprung out of bed, grabbing the knife from the nightstand. Most people of her station would have slept with a gun nearby, but she was much more comfortable with a blade. A gun was too impersonal. A knife, though, in close quarters was the best weapon. Quiet, quick, and unassuming.

She crept barefoot to the door across, tiptoes stealthily across the cold tile. With no time to dress, she had to do this in nothing but small sleep shorts. But that would make her movements less restricted, so it was for the better. Without knowing where the intruder was located, she would need every advantage she could get.

She peered into the hallway and saw nobody, waited, listened.

A door closed on the third floor above her. The floor of the mansion no one ever used. It was eased shut with care, but the click of the latch gave them away.

Rainha danced down the hall and to the stairs, not making a

sound as her feet padded against the floor. She held the knife at the ready as she hit the top.

The intruder had given up on discretion. Lights flicked on in a closed room. The room that, years earlier, had been her brother's bedroom.

She heard glass clink against glass, shuffling feat, then a loud sigh.

Instead of being alarmed at the intruder, Rainha's mind quickly switched to what they could be pouring. Her eyes went wide and her heart rate picked up.

It couldn't be...

Her mind shot straight to it.

Her Balvenie 46-year-old bottle of scotch.

Rainha quickly shot into the room, knife raised, ready to slice into the jugular of whoever was drinking her whisky.

Her eyes fixed on the intruder who sat on the couch, back turned away from her, facing the sliding glass doors that looked out onto the city. A vague hint of pink lingered in the sky signaling that sunrise was less than an hour away.

Without making a sound, she slithered behind the intruder, grabbed the hood covering their head--

And immediately dropped the knife.

It was her mother.

"I thought you were an assassin," Rainha said. Then she looked back down to the bottle that sat on the table.

It *was* her Balvenie.

Annoyance flared inside of her, but her mother didn't seem to care.

"Always so paranoid." Abuelita pushed a glass of the scotch across the table to Rainha.

She was mad but, at the same time, it was open. What else was there to do but drink it?

Rainha rose the glass to her lips and inhaled it deeply, breathing in the malt and oak. She took a sip and let the velvety flavor coat her tongue and then her throat. She sighed as the vanilla and spice lingered in her mouth.

Her mother sipped from her own glass. "Now this is what they call, *good shit*," Abuelita said.

Her mother always knew how to relate to the commoners.

"Why did you open this?" Rainha finally asked. "This was for a special occasion." Rainha grabbed the knife from the floor, then dropped into a leather chair that hadn't had an ass on its cushion since her brother died. A small puff of dust exploded into the air.

"I wanted to feel close to see Manuel." Abuelita finished her drink in a long swallow.

"Are you going senile? My brother is dead."

"Not his body," Abuelita said. "His spirit!" She gestured around the room as if pointing at ghosts only she could see. "It's still here, you know. You keep this all hidden away like a filthy secret, but my son is still here!"

Rainha could only shake her head. She didn't have time for this nonsense. "You're drunk."

"I might be."

Rainha stood, moving to the door, tired of this inane chatter. "Be more discreet when you leave. I could use some rest." She made it to the doorway before her mother spoke again.

"I set Wyatt free."

Rainha spun back to her, not believing her own ears. "You what?"

"The other one too. Franklin, I think is his name."

She charged her mother, fury boiling over inside her. "How dare you? They belong to me!"

Abuelita poured another snifter of whisky but, in her rage, Rainha backhanded the bottle out of her old fingers hitting it with such force that it shattered against the wall. Both women were bathed in scotch and shards of glass.

One of them sliced into Abuelita's face, just to the left of her eye. Blood trickled down her cheek like a fat, crimson tear. "I put up with you too long. I tolerated your behavior when I should have known better. The slaves, the fighting, that's bad enough. But what you did today..." The tear of blood slipped into her mouth, coated her teeth. "What you did to the brothers was evil."

"Again with the sanctimonious nonsense! You didn't complain when you lived like a queen in my mansion. Nor when you partook in the riches I earned." Rainha pounded her bare chest. "I treat them the way I do because they must respect me! Do you know how hard it is being in this position, especially—"

"As a woman, right?" her mother asked.

Rainha held her tongue, her eyes glaring at her mother.

"Is that what happened to your brother? Did he not show you enough respect?"

Rainha seethed, gritting her teeth. "No more of this drama! I've heard it too many times."

Abuelita stood, moving so close they were almost touching and, even though her mother was nearly a foot and a half shorter, Rainha could feel the old woman's anger. "Then tell me the truth for once! What happened to Manuel? Why did you let him die?"

Rainha shook her head. It had been a very long time since she'd allowed herself to think about that night. So long that she started believing the lie that she had told her mother all those years ago. She had it down so well. So rehearsed. She began to tell it again.

"I told you, Manuel and I were making a deal when it took a bad turn. We had to fight back, but they caught him and--"

"I don't believe you, Rainha. He was my son! He was your brother. Those boys today showed me how real siblings should behave."

Rainha raised the knife. Abuelita was her mother, but she wasn't going to listen to anyone disrespect her. "And what was I supposed to do? Be like Wyatt and let them kill me instead of him? I suppose that's what you wish happened, right? Because you always favored him. He was always your golden child, so perfect, while I was never the person you wanted me to be. So you tell me the truth. Do you wish I would have died so that he lived?" Rainha's chest heaved up and down as she screamed. "Tell me!"

Abuelita now had real tears mixed in with the blood, but she didn't back away despite Rainha's fury. Instead, she nodded.

"Yes. I do wish you had died. But you didn't." She stared with unblinking, unafraid resolve. "You lived and became a monster. And now I have no children anymore!"

Rainha swatted her like a fly, her hand connecting with her mother's jaw. Abuelita fell backward, stumbling over the couch, before hitting the floor in a heap.

Once Rainha was certain she was alive and conscious, she stood over her. "Clean up this mess before you go to bed. I have to go fetch my slaves."

Rainha rushed out of the room and down the stairs. After grabbing a leather trench coat and slipping it on, she stepped outside and breathed in the fresh air, forcing herself to calm down. Not even bothering to close the door behind her.

Dashing into town without her head on straight wouldn't catch Wyatt who doubtlessly would be more careful about his escape route this time around.

She needed to focus. She needed to--

A figure plummeted through the air, crashing into the ground at her feet with a crushing, wet *thud*.

Rainha stepped back and felt warm, dampness on her cheek. She wiped at it and looked at her hand in the moonlight. It was blood.

She peered down to the figure that lay on the ground in front of her, then looked up to the open sliding glass doors. And then back to the twisted, broken body on the concrete.

Abuelita had leaped from the third floor to her death. Her neck and torso were twisted in ways that a daughter should never have to see her mother.

But, then again, Abuelita had no children anymore.

55

As they ran through the streets, predawn continued to gradually brighten the sky. Orange had intermixed with the red, painting a kaleidoscope of colors above them.

The all-nighters were finally down for the count while the early risers were just beginning to come awake, but the few who saw Wyatt and his brethren watched with suspicious eyes. It was only a matter of time before everyone on the island knew what was happening. They had to be faster.

Ahead of him, several of the men broke to the right.

"No!" Wyatt screamed. "Over here." He pointed down the street where vendors' food carts hadn't yet been uncovered for the day's business.

"I think you're wrong, amigo," Pino said.

"I'm not. The harbor's--"

"That way," Rainha said.

All the men turned and found her and Uno watching them. Rainha's hair was wild, as were her eyes which were bloodshot.

Has she been crying? Wyatt wondered, but couldn't believe it. She probably just looked that way from being awoken so suddenly.

"Wyatt's right," Rainha said. "The harbor is to the east. Not that any of you will be seeing it today. Or ever again."

The men grumbled in annoyance and Wyatt knew he was losing them. That in seconds, they'd cow to Rainha and march their way straight back to the stables, which might as well be their cells. He had to find a way to stop that. He had to win them back.

All he had was bravado.

"Do you really think the two of you can defeat all of us?" Wyatt asked Rainha.

She cocked her head, confused or amused, he wasn't sure which. "You expect these men, my men, to have your back, Wyatt? I thought you were smarter than that."

Wyatt glanced back at their untrusting eyes. He could see Rainha was right, but he had to continue on with the act if he was to have any chance.

"I do. Because you might own them, but they're *my* brothers!" He turned, speaking to the men. "She murdered my real brother. She didn't even give him a chance to fight back. And she'd do the same to each and every one of you because all we are to her are commodities. Property."

Chester, of all people, nodded in agreement. A few others joined him. That gave Wyatt the energy to go on.

"Only we know what it's like to go into Akeldama and put our lives on the line week in and week out. While we do that, she sits with her rich friends, eating shrimp and drinking champagne as they place bets on which of us are going to die. As soon as we stop making her money..." Wyatt made a cutting motion across his throat.

He turned back to Rainha. "Yes, Rainha, I do think my brothers have my back. I know they do. And I know every last one of us will fight you right now rather than go back to your prison."

"That's quite the speech, Wyatt." She stared past him, to the others. "Is he right? Do you choose him over me? His promises of freedom?" She spat out the last word.

"Aye," Pino said.

And the others all joined in, a chorus of ayes, yeses, and fuck yeahs.

"Fine," Rainha said. She turned to Uno. "Kill them all."

56

Before Uno could do just that, Wyatt screamed. "Stop!"

Everyone stared at him. Not only Rainha, Uno, and his fellow slaves, but a bustling crowd which was forming around them and taking all of this in.

Wyatt felt like a rock star center stage just before the concert kicked off. The people wanted a show and he'd rather give them one than be part of a massacre.

"Rainha, I challenge you."

She barked a laugh. "You? Challenge me? To What? A crying contest?"

Many in the crowd - many who had seen his emotional outburst at Seth's death - bellowed laughter. He suddenly felt much less like a rock star.

"To a battle," he said.

"I'll destroy you," Rainha said. "Everyone knows that."

"Maybe," Wyatt said. "But if I win, then all of these men, including Uno, including me, are free. All of your slaves at the mansion and training ground, everyone who follows your commands at the compound too." He stepped toward her, fearless. "If I beat you, all of your slaves win their freedom."

"It won't even be a contest," Rainha said, but Wyatt thought he saw a glimmer of doubt in her eyes.

"Let's do it and find out."

With the crowd watching, he had the upper hand. If she declined, she'd look weak and weakness meant she lost her control over these people, this island. She had to fight him.

And Wyatt knew he would likely die, but he didn't fear death. He welcomed it. But having the chance to bring down Rainha in the process would at least bring some joy to the last few miserable months of his life.

He refused to break eye contact with her until she answered.

"Fine," Rainha said. "If it's a fight you want, it's a fight you'll get."

She shrugged off her trench coat, revealing that she was nude aside from the shorts. The crowd gasped and some fool even dared to whistle in admiration.

Wyatt didn't care about her body. He just wanted to end this, one way or another.

57

"Give me your swords," Rainha said to Uno who passed her two short-bladed weapons and then she spun back to Wyatt.

"Don't think you can beat me on the level?" Wyatt asked.

She tossed one of the swords toward him. He caught it by the blade, slicing open his palm, but refused to show pain.

"Feel better?" she asked.

Truthfully, he did not feel better. He had seen Rainha in action and she scared the hell out of him.

And like that, she was rushing Wyatt. Her feet were fast and light, almost like she was floating instead of running. When in arm's reach, she lunged with her blade.

Wyatt spun and just barely dodged the sword from piercing his chest. Instead, it grazed his arm, drawing a trickle of blood. He rushed to where she was standing before, the two of them switching places.

"First blood already?" she asked with a smile.

This time, Wyatt rushed her, swinging the blade. As he did, he followed her with his eyes. He wasn't focused on his swings. He was studying where she went, how she moved. At first, she ducked and rolled to the side. Then, when he swiped again, she sidestepped and hurdled forward, making her own attack.

Wyatt dove a half-second too late and the sword sliced into his side, metal scraping across his ribs. It hurt like hell but he didn't let on.

Again and again, they repeated the same routine. He was fast on his feet, but she was faster. He was quick with his blade, but she was quicker. She was like a figure skater, this city street her ice rink. Meanwhile, he was shooting pucks at a hockey goal.

And he wasn't doing a good job.

She was too good, too strong, too experienced. With each attack, he came away with a new wound. And they seemed to be getting deeper and deeper.

She was toying with him.

That had to be it. There was no way he should still be alive. He had seen her kill that first man in the training field in under thirty seconds. Then all the men in the alley. Wyatt could fight, but he couldn't fight that well. Not against someone like her. She was like a cat torturing a mouse, giving it just enough hope that it continued to try.

"You're letting your brothers down, Wyatt," she taunted.

"Stop fucking with me and fight," he growled.

She laughed. "Are you sure that's what you want? Because I could do this for hours," she said.

They danced some more on the pavement. He swung his blade and threw a punch. Nothing landed. Instead, she avoided any damage, slicing with her sword as she did. This time it went across Wyatt's chest, shredding his shirt and spilling blood.

It burned like fire.

His breathing was labored, tired. And she was as calm as ever.

There was no way he was going to win. There was no way he could even touch her.

Just as Wyatt realized it was a completely hopeless battle, a scream shot out over the entire crowd and echoed through the streets.

58

Wyatt looked into the crowd and saw the Drip kneeling on the ground, holding a hand across his throat as blood gushed out. The young woman who'd bedded Seth in the brothel stood over him a dagger in her hand.

Another yelp of pain echoed from a new direction. There, two men were beating Monger to death with clubs.

A man screamed, "This is what you get for turning men into animals!" and Wyatt saw him with a rope around Needle's throat as he dragged him into the open while other slaves stomped him to death.

"What is this?" Rainha asked, whipping her head to Wyatt.

He shrugged as if answering a friend when asked for directions. He really had no idea. He was trying to work it out for himself.

Then the yelling filled the streets. Men and women, scores of them, hundreds, flooded out of buildings and dwellings. Slaves revolting against those who had owned them.

It was a slaughter.

Rainha raised her sword, ready to defend herself. She spat on the ground as they came. "You fucking ungrateful swine," she said.

Three men charged her. Wyatt didn't recognize them, but it didn't matter. Their would-be attack on her was short-lived.

She stepped to the side, slicing and dicing each of them as they arrived. Wyatt watched as one man's face slid off his face, her blade chopping from under his chin, up out of the top of his head.

"Who's next?" Rainha shouted.

She was grinning, wild, and enjoying it. Wyatt wasn't sure if it was the fight, watching the other slavers die, or if the bloodlust had taken her over too.

"Come on!" she shouted as more men ran at her. She was ready again, but Wyatt saw that it was Franklin coming, along with two other fighters.

Rainha killed the first one, then impaled the second through the belly, jerking her sword and spilling his guts in a steaming pile. Then she was ready for Franklin, but he stopped in his tracks. Instead of charging, attacking with a sword or spear or his hands like all the others who'd tried and failed, he raised a rifle, leveling it at her.

"What's that old joke about bringing a knife to a gunfight?" he asked, pulling the trigger.

The gun fired and Rainha went down in a tumble. She cried out in pain as she landed face down in the street.

Wyatt looked to Franklin, still holding the rifle, smoke wafting from the barrel. He clenched his fists, expecting the worst, expecting Franklin to finally take his revenge. But Franklin dropped the rifle to his side.

"Let's go," Franklin said, waving him in.

"Where'd you get a rifle?"

Franklin grinned. "We took out some of the guards. Really makes you wonder why people fucked around with swords all the time when you have these babies." He patted the stock of the gun.

"You could have left me," Wyatt said.

"I need someone to drive the boat, remember."

Wyatt did remember. Franklin was smart, he had to give him that.

"Come on, things are going to get a lot worse if we sti—"

An explosion from a nearby building shook the street and cut off Franklin's words. Smoke and fire filled the air. Everywhere people were yelling, screaming, fighting, dying. There were thousands, as many as packed Akeldama every weekend. Maybe more.

What had begun as a revolt was turning into a bloodbath and there were no longer clear lines. Humanity and reason had vanished and now all people wanted to do was kill, not caring who or how that happened.

Wyatt scanned the area, trying to find a path out of the madness. Franklin was doing the same when--

A blade embedded itself in his hand. The rifle clattered to the pavement and Franklin let out a pained gasp.

They both looked and saw Rainha alive and on her knees. A bullet hole on her left shoulder seeped blood, but she was still more than capable of fighting back.

Wyatt dove for the rifle grabbed it, but a nearby scuffle knocked him off his feet. He hit the ground hard but held onto the gun.

Laying on his belly, he swung the barrel to where she'd been, but she was gone.

Then a foot slammed into his jaw.

Rainha kicked him again, that time snapping his nose.

He saw Franklin charge her, tackle her. The duo bounced off a wall, but Rainha, even wounded, quickly regained the upper hand and overpowered him. She had a fistful of the man's salt and pepper hair, jerked his head back, then brought a knee into his belly, doubling him over.

She slammed her elbow into his back, dropping him to his knees.

Wyatt knew she'd kill him in short order and tried to aim the gun through the crowd. He lined up a shot, squeezed the trigger, and--

The rifle clicked. Empty.

Wyatt shoved his way through the melee, somehow reaching the two of them. He raised the gun, slamming the stock into the back of

Rainha's skull. Blood splattered and she immediately spun to face him, her face a mask of wild fury.

"Two against one, eh?" she asked. Then she looked into the mass of madness. "Uno!" she screamed. "Uno, come!"

Wyatt swung the gun again, but she caught it in both hands, tearing it from his grip. She used the butt end to hammer Franklin in the face, then stabbed at Wyatt with the barrel. It hit him in the throat, leaving him gasping for air.

Then Rainha threw the gun to the side, instead wielding her sword. "I never liked firearms," she said. "Nothing romantic about them."

Still struggling to breathe, Wyatt was an easy target. She swung the sword embedding it in his collar bone. A geyser of blood erupted from the wound, then more shot out when she jerked the blade free.

She swung again, that time chopping into Wyatt's forearm, the blade digging in deep. His hand hung limp, useless, and nearly severed.

He scrambled backward, trying to get away from her, but she kept coming, Kept swinging.

One blow connected with his thigh, taking out a fist-sized hunk of flesh in the process. The next hit his shin, reverberating as it bounced off the bone.

Even now, she was playing with him, dragging it out, making him suffer when she could have killed him with any of the cuts.

But she was close now, he could see it. As the blood ran from a myriad of wounds, she realized he was going to bleed out. And she didn't want to let him die that easily.

Rainha reared back, brought the sword down, aiming at his face when--

Supper leaped through the air and sunk his teeth into her wrist. He latched onto the hand holding the sword, his teeth burrowing into her skin until she dropped the blade.

With her other hand, Rainha punched the dog once, twice. On the third blow, Supper let out a miserable yelp and released her.

Then she kicked him, sending him skittering a yard away. She was moving on him, going to finish him off.

Wyatt tried to stand but couldn't, so he crawled. He wanted to save Supper even more than he wanted Rainha dead. But he was so weak, so tired, he moved in super slow motion.

Rainha stood over his dog and raised her foot in preparation to crush Supper's skull--

Only to fly backward.

Wyatt couldn't grasp what had just happened. Until he saw Uno.

The man had flung Raina like a rag doll. Then, he moved to where she'd landed on her back and straddled her.

"You don't hurt the dog!" he said.

Uno grabbed her by the neck with both hands. He hoisted her off the ground and into the air, fingers tightening over her throat. She flailed with her arms. Kicked with her legs. Every blow landed, but Uno - the undefeated - was the one man for which she was no match.

Her face went red, then maroon, then deep blue as she was starved of air. Her coloring, Wyatt thought, matched the sky which had transitioned from night to dawn while everything was going down around them.

Uno jerked his hands to the side, snapping Rainha's neck, and she went limp.

It was going to be a beautiful day.

Franklin grabbed both of Wyatt's hands and lifted him to his feet. The pain in his nearly severed arm was exquisite, but being upright helped clear his head.

Uno dropped Rainha's lifeless body into the gutter, then turned to them. He stared with confused anger in his eyes. "What now?" he asked.

59

In under an hour, the city had descended into chaos.

Rainha and the other slavers had been running the show for so long, held so much power, that everyone had become acclimated to living under their thumbs. Now, with the power brokers dead, there was no one capable of regaining control.

This wasn't the inmates running the asylum. It wasn't unrestrained vengeance. They were letting out every ounce of hatred they'd bottled up for so long out all at once. And they unleashed it on each other.

Weak from blood loss, Wyatt couldn't run on his own but his new allies came to his aid, Franklin and Uno each wrapping an arm around his back so he could be dragged through the streets. Supper, still limping from Rainha's attack, loped along.

Men sprinted at the three of them as they fled. They were covered in blood as rags hung from their bodies. Hatred and anger filled their eyes. Lust for blood.

Franklin swung the rifle like a baseball bat, the stock colliding with the nearest man's mouth and shattering his teeth. He dropped to the ground in a heap as the other two continued to close in.

One clutched a tire iron. The other a metal rod. They charged, but they never had a chance. Uno grabbed their arms, one in each hand, and squeezed with bone-crushing force until they dropped their weapons. Then he flung them like they were toys into the nearest building. They were dazed, but still alive.

Uno moved on them, ready to finish the fight, but Wyatt grabbed the tree trunks he had for arms. "No time. It's either kill them and die here or run and maybe live."

Uno stared at him, the same lust for blood in his eyes that he had seen in the attackers. He breathed heavily. Wyatt knew he longed for a good fight.

"Uno, please. We need your help," Wyatt pleaded.

Uno blinked and glanced back to the fallen men. He nodded, then grabbed Wyatt, lifting him with one arm as he charged like a bull through the wild brawls.

Nobody was off-limits. Vendors died trying to protect their wares. Slaves killed fellow slaves. One of the prostitutes from the Drip's brother scalped a man who was on his knees, pleading for his life.

In thousands of miles on the road, through runs in with cannibals and madmen, Wyatt had never witnessed anything like it. It was hell on Earth and he began to doubt their chance of making it through the chaos and reaching the harbor.

What a sick twist of fate that was. Bring down Rainha, destroy the whole twisted system of slavery that ruled the island, then get trampled under the feet of the newly freed.

They pushed on, continuing up a street--

Only to find it blocked by a box truck that had been rolled onto its side, blocking their escape route. They turned around, to find another out, but there was none. A sea of violent, crazed men and women filled the area to its brim.

"We have to go over!" Franklin shouted as he headed to the truck, using a wheel as a foothold as he climbed onto it.

Wyatt tried to grab on with his hands, but the arm that was

barely attached gave free and he stumbled backward. He'd never be able to climb on his own and, in the condition he was in, he was only slowing the others down.

He took a look back and saw the mob of madness getting closer. In seconds they'd be upon them dragging them into the wanton destruction.

"Please leave me," he ordered Franklin and Uno.

"Fuck that," Franklin said and grabbed his good arm.

Uno picked him up by the waist and, between the two of them, they got him atop the truck.

Supper jumped, trying to make it on his own, but with his missing leg and the damage from Rainha's assault, he didn't make it, crashing back to the ground with a pained yip.

As Wyatt looked down at his hurt dog, then beyond, he realized it was all coming to a fast end. The horde was on them, already flailing away at Uno with bats and swords, pipes and knives.

The big man took one blow after another, but he wasn't going down easy. He fought back, kicking in faces, bashing in skulls He dropped over a dozen men in under a minute. A pile of bodies was growing around him.

But this wasn't twelve against one. It was twelve hundred against one.

Uno caught a bat to the skull, flaying open his skin to the bone. Then someone rammed a metal spear into his back and out his stomach. Uno grabbed the man who'd impaled him and pulled him into a bear hug, skewing the man on his own weapon. Then he shoved him away and the man landed in the mound of corpses.

A man slammed a sledge hammer into Uno's knee with a sickening crunch. Then a woman with a blue mohawk sliced into his throat with a blade. Blood spurted with each beat of his heart.

It was over. The man who'd never been defeated was. He dropped to his knees as the crowd pummeled him, battered him, stabbed him.

Yet somehow, he found the strength to grab Supper, and he lifted the dog above his head.

The feral crowd went for him, ready to rip the dog to pieces, but Franklin grabbed onto Supper's fur and dragged him onto the truck with them. To safety.

But that wouldn't last long.

The crazed crowd was already scaling the truck coming after them, desperate to kill them.

As Wyatt took one more look at Uno, dying on the ground under the feet of the city, he knew there was no time to mourn.

There was only time to run.

60

Franklin half-carried, half-dragged Wyatt to the harbor. On this side of the city, there were random fights but the great majority of people were behind them, not ahead, and they covered ground as quickly as possible.

"Over there," Wyatt said, pointing to the small boat underneath a tarp. Abuelita had come through for them, just as she'd promised.

"Oh shit," Franklin muttered, glancing behind them.

Wyatt looked back and saw the mob rushing their way. It was a sea of chaos rolling at them, unstoppable.

"Motherfuck," Franklin grumbled again.

That time, Wyatt followed his eyes and saw a group of forty men racing down the docks. It was impossible to know whether they were coming after Wyatt, Franklin, and Supper, or the vicious mob, but either way, Wyatt's small group was in the middle of hell that would be upon them in seconds.

"We need to go, now," Wyatt said, stating the obvious. This was their only chance. They had to get to the boat and onto the water before they became numbers in the massacre.

So, they turned toward the boat, moving to it as fast as their wounded tired bodies could go. Franklin was exhausted from helping him and Wyatt tried to force himself to run, to find strength somewhere inside him.

It half-worked. He managed to take a few clumsy steps on his own, then got into something of a rhythm. His feet echoed against the wooden dock.

The boat was twenty yards away.

Fifteen.

Ten.

Five.

Then, they were there.

They were going to make it. They were going to live.

He could scarcely believe it. It seemed impossible. It felt too good to be true.

And it was.

"Untie the rope," Wyatt told Franklin who dropped to his knees and began freeing the rope from the cleat.

Wyatt grabbed the tarp from the boat, dragging it off and letting it fall into the water.

He stared at the motorized dinghy, still unable to believe that he'd finally found his freedom.

And then pain filled his mind and forced out all other thoughts.

Everything surged black. He shook his head to clear it, then felt sweaty hands on his torso. His vision came back and he saw Franklin, holding him, cradling him.

"What happened?" Wyatt asked.

Franklin shook his head, "Nothing."

But Wyatt felt hot wetness running down his legs. He thought he'd pissed himself and looked down, embarrassed.

That was when he saw the spear. It had entered on his left side, just above his hip, and exited on his right, jutting through his ribs which were shattered and poking through his flesh in ragged chunks.

"Oh my God," Wyatt said. His breathing picked up as he

realized where the pain was coming from. "You have to get on the boat."

Franklin nodded. "Take a breath and let it out," he said.

Wyatt took a gasping mouthful of air in and as soon as he pushed it out, Franklin ripped the spear out of him. The pain was excruciating and Wyatt screamed so loud he thought his vocal cords might rupture.

Franklin carried Wyatt to the boat, half-dropping, half-throwing him into the hull. Supper jumped in beside him.

"Get the boat ready, I'll hold them off," Franklin said, holding the spear up as his new weapon.

As Wyatt crawled toward the motor, his blood spilled into the hull, painting everything red. The motor was electric and took him a few seconds to figure out how to start, but then it kicked to life, the propeller spinning in the air, just waiting to be lowered into the water for their getaway.

But where was Franklin?

He turned back to the dock, the motion making his head swim, and through heavy eyes saw the horde on top of Franklin. He was doing his best to put up a fight, but he was already on his knees and fading fast.

Wyatt tried to stand, to go and help, but between the boat rocking in the water and his blood loss, he didn't make it a full step before he was down in a heap of pain and misery.

"Go!" he heard Franklin shout.

He pushed himself up and saw the man he'd hated, the man he wanted to kill, staring at him.

"Get the fuck out of here, Wyatt!" Franklin shouted, just as a club came down on his head and split open his skull. His body toppled into the water, turning it red.

Men reached for the boat, grabbed onto it, ready to board and kill him too.

Wyatt dropped the propeller. The spinning blades chopped off the hand of the nearest man who hooted in surprise. Then Wyatt put the propellor in the water and the dinghy lurched forward, almost hopping. A man who'd been holding on was dragged off the dock and Wyatt heard him scream as he was ripped to shreds by the blades.

The boat raced into the harbor, the screams of madness fading, then disappearing completely.

He was free.

61

Sunlight faded to black, which faded to sunlight, then back to black.

Wyatt opened his eyes for what seemed like the hundredth time since boarding the boat. He was so tired and cold even though the day was hot.

Nobody was near him. Nobody was coming for him. For all he knew, everyone on the island was dead at their own hands.

All that was left was Wyatt and Supper.

That was all that mattered.

His eyes went shut. The world went black.

Then Supper barked.

Wyatt's eyes popped open. He grabbed hold of the gunwale and used his last bit of strength to pull himself up far enough to see out of the dinghy.

He stared and saw it in the distance. It looked like...

Land.

So far away.

Maybe he would reach it. But it would be a while.

The motor had died and the waves seemed to be pushing him that way.

That was good, he supposed. A chance.

Wyatt tried to sit up, but the pain was too great and he was too weak, so he laid on his back and stared up at the sky.

He'd waited years to see a sky this blue. He'd dreamed of this.

Well, not exactly this.

It was so beautiful he felt tears leak from the corners of his eyes. Supper, glued to his side, licked them away. He reached out and buried his hand in the dog's fur, petting and scratching him.

"You're the best dog," Wyatt whispered because that was all he could do. "The best dog and my best friend."

Supper kept licking his face with his sandpaper tongue.

"I never deserved a dog as good as you."

But Supper seemed to think otherwise. He snuggled tight against him, his fur saturated with Wyatt's spilled blood. Pints of it Much more out than in.

His warmth felt good and Wyatt shifted from petting him to holding him.

The waves sloshed back and forth, rocking him like a baby. Urging him to close his eyes and sleep.

Just a little longer.

A little more time.

A few more minutes to hold his dog and see the sky.

So gorgeous it hurt.

But his eyelids were so heavy. Too heavy.

They drifted, fluttered.

Closed.

He heard his mother's voice. Singing. It was a tune she'd serenaded him with when he was a boy, back when the world was still a good place.

Blue days, all of them gone.

Her voice sounded so pure, so close he was certain she must be in the boat with him.

Nothing but blue skies, from now on.
His eyes opened. He took one more look.

The End...
For now.

AFTERWORD

We hope you enjoyed "Valley of Dying Stars." It was a wild ride! We have a few ideas for future books in the series, but for the time being, this is "the end." Will Wyatt and Supper reach the island? Will they find a place where they can live in peace and prosperity. Well, we'll leave that up to your imagination for now.

Please take a moment to sign up for our mailing lists where you'll get free stories and novellas and stay on top of all future releases.

Tony Urban's list - http://tonyurbanauthor.com/signup

Drew Strickland's list - https://www.subscribepage.com/cc3

Happy reading!

MORE FROM TONY & DREW

Her Deadly Homecoming

Hell on Earth

Within the Woods

Soulless Wanderers

Buried in the Backwater

Made in the USA
Monee, IL
06 August 2024